The Best Friend Experiment

Susannah Nix is an award-winning and *USA Today* bestselling author of rom-coms and contemporary romances who lives in Texas with her husband. On the rare occasions she's not writing, she can be found reading, knitting, lifting weights, drinking wine, or obsessively watching *Ted Lasso* on repeat to stave off existential angst.

Chemistry Lessons Series

SUSANNAH NIX

The Best Friend Experiment

PAN BOOKS

First published by the author 2020 as *Experimental Marine Biology*

First published in the UK 2024 by Pan Books

This paperback edition first published 2025 by Pan Books
an imprint of Pan Macmillan
The Smithson, 6 Briset Street, London EC1M 5NR
EU representative: Macmillan Publishers Ireland Ltd, 1st Floor,
The Liffey Trust Centre, 117–126 Sheriff Street Upper,
Dublin 1, D01 YC43
Associated companies throughout the world
www.panmacmillan.com

ISBN 978-1-0350-2601-2

1 3 5 7 9 8 6 4 2

A CIP catalogue record for this book is available from the British Library.

Typeset in Sabon by Jouve (UK), Milton Keynes
Printed and bound by CPI Group (UK) Ltd, Croydon, CR0 4YY

For my family

Chapter One

When Brooke Hilliard had decided to become a marine biologist, she'd never imagined it would involve so much earwax.

That's right. Earwax.

Whale earwax, specifically.

Most people didn't know that baleen whales produced earwax like humans did. The oily gunk built up in their ear canals over time, hardening into giant, tapered plugs. Their earwax plugs looked kind of like super-gross candles, but in cross section they revealed layers that corresponded to the years of the whale's life, and could be studied like tree rings or the ice cores that climate scientists used to look into the past.

You could learn all kinds of things about the places a whale had been and the things it had done, just by analyzing its earwax. Information about their migration, diet, stress levels, reproduction, sexual maturity, and pollutants in their habitats—it was all there. If you knew what year the animal died, you could not only determine how old they were, but basically piece together their entire life history, year by year, like a biography.

Just from their earwax. Imagine.

Everyone carried memories of their past selves within them, but whales quite literally carried around a biological record of their own lives. In the same way the rings of a tree trunk could be carefully carved away to reveal an image of the young sapling it used to be, the layers of earwax that built up in a whale's ear canal preserved snapshots of its younger self.

It was really pretty cool, once you got past the ick factor of working with nasty old globs of earwax that had been building up inside a whale for decades. Fortunately for Brooke, she'd left all her ick factor behind in seventh grade, the first time she'd cut into a squid while her lab partner stood uselessly off to the side making retching sounds.

Lots of kids said they wanted to be a marine biologist when they grew up. But by the time most of them reached high school biology and realized it wasn't all cavorting with dolphins, they set their sights on another dream.

Not Brooke. She didn't mind the dissections or the rote memorization of biochemical processes and Latin terminology. In fact, she thrived on it. And now here she was, at the age of almost twenty-six: a marine biologist in the fourth year of her PhD program, analyzing earwax.

"What the poxy hell are you doing here so early?"

Brooke smiled at the sound of her lab mate's voice and threw a glance over her shoulder. "I'm always here early. The question is, what are *you* doing here so early?"

Tara Phillips sauntered into the lab and snatched something off one of the tables. "Forgot my earbuds last night. Going for a run." She was dressed in colorful, mismatched spandex and bright orange running shoes.

"Masochist." Brooke turned her attention back to the enzyme-linked immunosorbent assay in front of her, otherwise known as an ELISA. She didn't mind waking up early—in fact, she enjoyed being the first one in the lab every morning, so she could work without any distractions—but she despised exercise of any sort.

Tara grinned, showing off the gap in her front teeth. "Says the person who's in the lab working before eight a.m." She wandered closer and peered over Brooke's shoulder. "Whale, whale, whale, what do we have here? Are you doing another ELISA? I thought you'd finished all the data collection for the cortisol abstract."

"This is something else." Brooke bit down on her lip as she concentrated on the multichannel pipette she was using to measure liquid into the wells of a microtiter plate.

She was testing progesterone levels in the fat extracted from the different earwax layers of a single female whale, which would give her information about the animal's reproductive history, such as when it became sexually mature and how many pregnancies it had had. She'd already done the work of cutting the earwax layers apart and mixing them with solvent to extract the lipids. The hormone assay she was doing involved a lot of pipetting and a lot of steps, and required concentration because if you messed any of them up, the samples were ruined.

"What's that, then?" Tara asked.

"It's for the graduate student award at NAMMC." Brooke had just found out about it. The deadline was less than a month away, which was a bit of a tight turnaround. But she was ahead of the game on her dissertation research, and confident she could put something together in time.

"Bit ambitious, don't you think?"

That was almost exactly what her advisor had said when Brooke had asked if she'd give her a recommendation for it. She'd seemed surprised Brooke had decided to go for it, but she'd wished her luck and agreed to write the recommendation.

"Monica Speight is submitting for it too," Brooke told Tara.

Monica was a year ahead of Brooke in the program and everything Brooke aspired to be. Top of her cohort, top of their research team, top of the department. She was every professor's favorite grad student, and every undergrad's favorite teaching assistant. She'd been picked for the top fellowship two years in a row and had more papers accepted to conferences than any other grad student in the entire college of life sciences. While everyone else was scrambling to find a postdoc position, Monica Speight would probably have programs lining up to court her.

Brooke didn't just want to *be* Monica, she wanted to *beat* her.

Ever since she'd entered the program, Brooke had been stuck in Monica's shadow. No one cared that Brooke was top of her own cohort, or that she came in a close second to Monica in almost everything. There was never a chance to stand out and be recognized for her own achievements with Monica hogging all the glory.

Just once before Monica graduated, Brooke was determined to beat her at something.

Tara snickered. "Yeah, of course she is. That one's never seen an award she couldn't win. I suppose that's why you're

4

going for it too? The next step in your plan to Single White Female our Monica."

"I'm not trying to Single White Female anyone."

"Come on, you two are like peas in a pod. You even look alike."

Brooke supposed they sort of did, if you didn't look too closely. Brown hair, brown eyes, medium heights and builds. But where Monica's complexion had a uniform golden glow, Brooke's went to paleness and freckles. Lots of freckles.

"I just want to prove I can beat her at something. It's not a weird love–hate obsession, like with you and Mathias."

"Bite your tongue!" Tara shot back. "Mathias is my nemesis. It's not a love–hate obsession, it's hate–hate."

Tara and Mathias were both third years, and they'd been feuding since the moment they first laid eyes on one another.

"Because of that one time he accidentally upset your experiment two years ago."

"That was no accident. He totally did it on purpose!"

"I seriously doubt that. You should let it go." Brooke actually thought Mathias was pretty nice. And his Norwegian accent was kind of sexy.

"It's not just that. He doesn't follow the cleaning schedule unless you nag him about it, and he's always using my pipette tips instead of refilling his own tip boxes. Plus he leaves crumbs all over the desk in the office."

"Why don't you talk to him about it? Maybe if he knew it bothered you, he'd try to improve."

"Screw that. I'd much rather wage a silent war of passive aggression. Like with you and your bestie Monica."

"Fair enough," Brooke said, knowing there was no point

trying to reason with Tara. She was completely unreasonable on the subject of Mathias. There was actually a pool going among the grad students about when Tara and Mathias were finally going to bang it out. Brooke had twenty bucks on the week of October 4–10, which was coming up fast.

"That reminds me: What's a mansplainer's favorite animal?"

"A whale, actually," Brooke answered automatically. "You told me that one last month."

"Dammit! I'll have to up my game. Right! Good luck with your ELISA. I'm off on my run. Back in an hour." Tara gave a salute on her way out the door.

Brooke went back to working on her hormone assay. Twenty minutes later, as she was putting her samples on the plate shaker where they'd spend the next two hours, she felt her phone vibrate in the pocket of her lab coat. After disposing of her gloves, she went into the shared office next to the lab and checked her messages.

She grinned as she saw the text from her childhood friend Dylan.

Hey! What are you doing week after next?

Brooke hadn't heard from Dylan in months and hadn't seen him in years, but it didn't matter. They were the sort of old friends who could pick back up at a moment's notice. Every so often, one of them would randomly reach out to the other, and they'd fall right back into talking like no time had passed at all.

They'd always been like that: drifting in and out of each

6

other's orbits, but always coming back around again eventually. As reliable as the sun and the moon.

> **Brooke:** *Nothing much. Why?*
> **Dylan:** *I'm coming to LA for a shoot! Wanna hang while I'm there?*

Dylan was an underwear model in New York City. Honest to god. It made Brooke giggle every time she thought about the fact that she was friends with a real live underwear model.

Technically, he didn't *just* model underwear, but it was more fun to think of him as an underwear model than a shaving cream model, cologne model, wristwatch model, or any of the other myriad products he'd pimped.

> **Brooke:** *Yes! I'd love to see you!*
> **Dylan:** *Any chance I could crash on your couch?*
> **Brooke:** *Of course! Mi casa es tu casa.*

Brooke's phone rang a moment later. *Call from Dylan Price* it said on the screen, above an old prom selfie of the two of them all dressed up in formalwear and making silly faces for the camera. She'd forgotten that was the photo she'd assigned to him and smiled at the memory, feeling a rush of fondness for her oldest friend.

She'd met Dylan when she was seven, the day her family had moved into the house across the street from his in Baton Rouge. On her first day of second grade at her new school he'd been the only kid she knew, and he'd made a point of introducing her to everyone as "my new friend Brooke." His

7

status as her favorite person in the world had been pretty much cemented from that moment forward, and the two of them had been inseparable through elementary school.

Once they got to middle school, Brooke had tested into the accelerated classes, while Dylan struggled to maintain passing grades. Still, they'd managed to stay friends, even into high school, as she juggled honors classes while he got involved in track and band.

Dylan had been a gangly nerd with glasses, braces, and acne—until the summer before their junior year, when he experienced a huge growth spurt, got his braces off, and his mom got him Proactiv and contact lenses. Almost overnight, Brooke's sweet, dorky friend transformed into a total hottie. Girls started taking an interest in him for the first time, and he made the most of his newfound popularity, dating his way through most of the marching band's woodwind section.

And now he was a model whose glistening bare abs had once adorned a billboard in Times Square. Go figure. But in her head, Brooke still thought of Dylan as the kid who lived across the street and had always looked out for her.

"You're really coming to visit?" she said excitedly, answering his call as she sank onto a desk chair.

"Yeah! If you're sure you don't mind me staying with you." His voice was warm and resonant, and it instantly took her back to all those nights they'd spent on the phone, baring their adolescent souls to one another. It felt like a lifetime ago and also somehow only yesterday. "I'm also totally fine getting a hotel if that works better for you."

"Perish the thought! I happen to have a five-star couch. I'm pretty sure it's more comfortable than most hotel beds."

8

"Cool. I figured this way we'd get to see more of each other."

"Yeah, it'll be great. How long will you be here for?" She reached up to twirl the thin brown hair she'd pulled back into a ponytail.

"A week, from Sunday to Sunday. Think you can put up with me for that long?"

"A whole week! Wow! That's a long photo shoot."

"The shoot's only one day, but I thought I'd take the whole week, make a vacation of it. I could use a break."

Brooke was honored he'd want to take a whole week of vacation to hang out with her, but also a little mystified. From what she could tell from his social media, Dylan seemed to be doing really well. She would have thought he could afford to go pretty much anywhere he wanted for vacation. So why would he want to spend it crashing on her couch?

"Is everything okay?" she asked, biting her lip.

"Sure. Yeah. Terrific. Just working too much."

She'd always been able to tell when he was lying. "Really? Kinda sounds like it might be more than that."

He let out a soft sigh. "It's nothing special. I'll tell you all about it when I'm there."

"Deal." It would be easier to wheedle the truth out of him in person, and they'd have plenty of time to talk through whatever he needed. Too much time, maybe. She wasn't sure how she was going to entertain him for a whole week.

"How are things with you?" Dylan asked. "How's life treating my favorite marine biologist?"

"Good. Boring. You know." Testing hormone levels in whale earwax couldn't stack up to Dylan's glamorous life in

9

New York. Based on his social media, his life was basically an endless series of cool parties with beautiful people in elegant Manhattan apartments. Not to mention all the traveling he did. Just in the last year, he'd posted photos from Paris, Prague, Phuket, and Tulum. Brooke's poky apartment couldn't possibly compare, even if her complex did have a pool. "I hope I'm exciting enough for you."

"Excitement's the exact opposite of what I'm looking for. All I want is to spend a nice, quiet, relaxing few days hanging out with an old friend."

She grinned as it hit home how much she'd missed him. "I can definitely make that happen."

"And maybe watching some martial arts movies. Assuming you still like martial arts movies?"

"Always." It had been one of their favorite things to do as kids. They'd wasted endless Saturdays watching Jackie Chan and old Bruce Lee movies on the floral couch in Dylan's family room.

"Good. Sounds like heaven."

It was funny how years could pass and their lives could go in two totally opposite directions, and yet they still managed to have a connection.

"I'll see you in a couple weeks, then," Dylan said.

"Can't wait."

After she said goodbye, Brooke pulled up the old prom photo of her and Dylan again. She hadn't thought about that night in a long time, mostly because she'd tried hard to forget about it.

It was supposed to be a friend date. Purely platonic.

They'd made the pact their freshman year. If both of them were single when senior prom rolled around, they'd be each other's safety date. Purely as friends, of course. That had been the intention, anyway.

The night hadn't exactly gone as planned though.

Brooke had been coming off a bad breakup, and she'd always assumed Dylan only asked her to prom because he'd sensed she was having a rough time. He could have had his pick of prom dates but instead he'd invoked their prom pact. It was him looking out for her, like he always had.

"Wouldn't it be more fun if we went with each other?" she remembered him saying. "We always have a great time together, and this way our prom memories will be of each other, instead of some rando date we'll probably never see again after graduation."

Even if it was just a pity date, Brooke jumped at the chance. She'd had a uniformly awful senior year, and the prospect of going to prom with one of her best and oldest friends was so much better than any alternative she'd been able to imagine. She probably wouldn't have gone at all if it hadn't been for Dylan.

Not when Kyle would be there with his new girlfriend. After what he'd done to her, Brooke couldn't bear the thought of facing him alone.

But Dylan had pulled out all the stops to make sure she had a good time: corsage, limo, dinner at a fancy restaurant. With their diverging romantic pursuits, they hadn't hung out just the two of them in a while, and it was nice to have Dylan all to herself again. She'd had so much fun dancing the night away with Dylan, she barely even noticed Kyle and his new girlfriend and all the shitty looks he and his friends shot her way.

For that one magical night, it had felt like no one existed in the world but her and Dylan.

After the last dance, when their feet hurt so much they could barely walk, they piled back into the limo waiting to take them home. Brooke was riding an endorphin high, but also feeling a buzz from the flask of Jack Daniel's that Dylan had smuggled into the dance. They were both a little drunk, to be honest.

That was the only explanation she could think of for the kiss.

Brooke remembered being tired and resting her head on Dylan's shoulder. At some point, he'd turned his head so he was looking down at her, his face only inches from hers. Then his hand had curled around the back of her neck, and the next thing she knew he was kissing her.

Until that moment, she'd never thought about Dylan like that.

Well, maybe she'd thought about it a little.

More than a little.

But she'd never imagined he would ever think about her like that.

It completely blindsided her. But it also felt amazing . . . and *right*, in a way kissing Kyle had never felt. The electric *zing* Brooke felt when Dylan's lips touched hers was unlike anything she'd ever experienced. It opened up a whole world of possibilities.

But just as she was starting to adjust to the idea, he'd stopped and pulled away.

She would never forget the look on his face. Embarrassment and regret and horror all mixed into one. Actual *horror*. Because he'd kissed her.

Stammering an apology, Dylan backed as far away from her as the limo seat would allow.

"Let's forget this ever happened," he said, wiping his hand across his mouth, and Brooke's heart broke in two. Because he hadn't meant it. He hadn't wanted to kiss her. It had just been an accident, a drunken mistake, and now he wanted to take it back.

Just when she was starting to *like* the idea of kissing Dylan. *Really* like it.

They'd never spoken of it again after that night. Both of them had worked hard to pretend it was no big deal. But it had been a big deal to Brooke. Even now, seven years later, she felt her stomach clench at the memory.

That wasn't going to cut it—not *at all*. Not when Dylan was coming here to sleep on her couch for a week to get away from whatever was going on with him in New York.

He was coming to her because he needed a friend, and she intended to be the friend he needed—not some sad, pining girl carrying a torch for him.

Dylan had always, *always* looked out for her, and now, finally, she would get to return the favor.

Which meant not dwelling on the most painful chapter in their history. *Let's forget this ever happened*, he'd said, and that was exactly what she'd do. The memories of that night were going back into the lockbox where Brooke had buried them years ago.

She was *not* going to think about kissing Dylan while he was here.

Not at all.

Not even once.

Chapter Two

"Here's to Cheese and Wine Fest 2020!"

Brooke clinked her glass of Syrah against the wine glasses of the other bachelorette party revelers gathered around the table.

"And to Penny!" Olivia said beside her, raising her glass again. "And her last week of being single!" They all lifted their glasses as they cheered and whooped for the bride-to-be.

Brooke had known Olivia since college and had subsequently become friends with Penny through her. Some of the other women at the table were members of Olivia and Penny's knitting group who Brooke only knew a little—although she'd sublet her apartment from Esther, who was sitting across from her. The remaining three women, who were from Penny's yoga class, Brooke had just met for the first time tonight.

They'd all come together for Penny's bachelorette, which had started off with mani-pedis and champagne at a nearby salon before moving to the wine bar where they were currently situated. On the table in front of them sat a collection of open wine bottles and the biggest cheese board Brooke had ever laid eyes on, hence "Cheese and Wine Fest 2020."

"Woot! Woot!" shouted the yoga friend in glasses, whose name was Melody and whose left hand sported a diamond engagement ring the size of a Fiat. "I'm so sad I'm not going to see you walk down the aisle though."

Penny was getting married in a week, back home in Virginia, so they were having her Los Angeles bachelorette this weekend. Olivia, as Penny's maid of honor, was the only one of them making the trip for the small family wedding. But once they got back from their honeymoon in two weeks, Penny and Caleb were hosting a separate wedding reception here for all their LA friends.

"I know!" Penny said, pursing her lips in a pout. "But the church is tiny and my family is *so big*, and the reception's just going to be at my parents' house. The party here will be much better. Bonus: you won't have to watch my great-aunt Naomi eat cake without her teeth in."

"Ew!" Esther wrinkled her nose as she reached for another piece of Manchego from the cheese plate. They'd all been stuffing their faces with cheese for twenty minutes and barely seemed to have made a dent—that was how massive the cheese board was.

"When are *you* getting married?" Penny asked Melody, brandishing a cheese straw like a lecturer's pointer. "It feels like you've been engaged forever."

"It feels like forever to me too." Melody frowned as she twisted the big-ass ring on her finger. "It's just complicated with his family and everything."

"Families make everything complicated," Olivia said, shooting Brooke a commiserating look.

Brooke reached over and squeezed her friend's arm. She and Olivia were both California transplants who had fled out of state for college because they'd wanted to put some distance between themselves and their complicated familial relationships. As undergraduate roommates at Cal State LA, they'd bonded over the fact that they were both from the Gulf Coast area, as well as the fact that neither of them looked forward to going home over holiday breaks.

"You should do a destination wedding," one of the other yoga friends suggested. All Brooke knew about her was her name was Lacey Lopez, she looked like she could crush a watermelon between her thighs, and she was in a relationship with Tessa, the third yoga friend who was also apparently the yoga instructor. The whole yoga end of the table was intimidatingly fit and beautiful, making Brooke feel self-conscious about her bird legs and flat chest.

They were also all in relationships. As Brooke looked around at their group, she realized everyone else there was either married, engaged, or in a serious, long-term relationship. She was the only single one out of the nine of them.

Cool. Cool cool cool.

Not that she minded being single. On the contrary, she loved it. She wouldn't trade places with the others for anything. Brooke liked being on her own, and had spent enough time on the dating market that she considered herself lucky she didn't currently have to deal with a man in her life.

The only thing she minded about being single was that when she was outnumbered by the happily coupled, the conversation often turned to topics that didn't interest or include her.

"None of my family or friends could afford to go to a destination wedding," Melody said.

Lacey shrugged. "Get Jeremy's mom to pay for everyone. It's not like she can't afford it."

Melody shook her head. "She doesn't approve of destination weddings, so she'd never agree to that. Something about sand and formalwear. She has very particular ideas about what a proper society wedding should be, most of which have to do with impressing her rich friends and business associates."

"This is why Jonathan and I are never getting married," Esther announced as she claimed another piece of Manchego. "Both of our families are nightmares, and the thought of them all together at a wedding gives me anxiety sweats. It's too much trouble. And for what? A meaningless ceremony and a giant cake?"

"Very nice." Esther's best friend Jinny, who'd just gotten married a few months ago, jabbed Esther with her elbow. "We're here to celebrate Penny's wedding, and you're bad-mouthing weddings!"

"Ow!" Esther rubbed her arm where Jinny had assailed it. "I wasn't talking about your wedding or Penny's! Just weddings in general."

"I'd have a wedding for the cake alone," Olivia said with a shrug. "You're doing it right, Penny. Two receptions means getting two cakes."

Penny's face lit up as she turned to Olivia. "Wait! Does that mean you and Adam have started talking about marriage?"

"Noooo." Olivia gave a definitive head shake as she topped up her chardonnay. "Definitely not."

"Why not?" Penny asked. "You've been together long enough."

"Leave her alone." Cynthia, another member of the knitting group, wagged her finger at Penny and pushed her empty wine glass toward Olivia for a fill-up. "Just because you're getting married doesn't mean the whole world has to."

Olivia and her boyfriend Adam were taking it slow. They still maintained separate apartments, and as far as Brooke knew they didn't have any plans to move in together. Not because they weren't happy—in fact, they seemed deliriously happy—but because they liked it that way. Olivia said it was good for them to have their own spaces to retreat to sometimes.

Brooke valued her alone time, so she could definitely relate. Sometimes she'd try to picture herself in a serious, committed relationship, sharing her whole life and her home with someone else, but the prospect actively repelled her.

As far as she was concerned, she'd get better value out of a new vibrator than a new boyfriend.

Lately she'd been thinking what she really wanted was a booty call buddy. Someone she could call when she was in the mood for company and ignore when she wasn't. You wouldn't think it would be hard to find. If books and movies and most of the internet were to be believed, the world was full of emotionally distant men who were only interested in the physical aspects of a relationship. And yet she'd never managed to stumble across one.

Maybe you had to venture into online dating for that. *Ugh.* Brooke couldn't bear the thought of it. She didn't want it bad enough to deal with weeding out all the creeps and jumping through hoops just to find out if someone was attractive or repulsive.

Brooke was convinced she just wasn't cut out for couple-dom. She'd tried dating—again and again and again—but it always felt like more trouble than it was worth. The physical intimacy could be a lot of fun—although too often it was a disappointment—but emotional intimacy never seemed to follow. As soon as a guy tried to get closer to her, she started itching to get away.

She couldn't even put the blame on the men, necessarily. The last few had been perfectly nice, decent guys. It must be her fault.

The closest she'd ever come to cohabitating was when her last boyfriend had a burst pipe in his apartment building and had to stay with her for three weeks until it was fixed. They'd driven each other up the freaking wall. By the time Garrett's apartment had been habitable again, they were both on their last nerve and ready to call it quits. Brooke had never been so happy to see the backside of a relationship, and she hadn't been tempted to date again since.

She was even a little nervous about Dylan staying with her for a whole week. Sure, they'd been friends forever, but they hadn't spent any real time together in years. Even when they used to hang out regularly, they'd never shared a living space. She could always go back to her own home at the end of the day.

What if he drove her bonkers? What if they'd grown apart so much since high school they didn't have anything to talk about? What if he'd turned into a douche in New York? Or a dirtbag? Or a snob?

Which reminded her, she still needed to get some things for her apartment before he arrived next weekend.

The conversation at the table around her had returned

SUSANNAH NIX

to the subject of destination weddings, which Brooke had no opinions about, so she slipped her phone out of her pocket and navigated to the Pottery Barn website as she nibbled on a piece of English cheddar. If she was going to have a houseguest, she should probably upgrade some of her amenities.

"What are you looking at?" Olivia asked, leaning in to peer over Brooke's shoulder.

Brooke looked up guiltily from her phone. "Towels?"

"Are you shopping?" Jinny asked. "Let me see!" She held out her hand and Brooke passed her the phone. "I like those," Jinny declared with an approving nod. "Their towels are really nice and thick."

"I like that they look like fancy hotel towels," Brooke said. They were a lot nicer than her current towels—and a lot more expensive too.

"Didn't you just buy new towels last year?" Olivia asked. "You did! The cute ones with the whales all over them."

Brooke accepted her phone back from Jinny. "Those are Target towels and I got them in the kids' department. I was thinking of investing in something a little more grown-up before Dylan gets here." At the time, she'd thought whale towels would be cute—but now they seemed too juvenile for company.

"Who's Dylan?" Esther asked.

"Just a friend from high school," Brooke answered, putting her phone away. "He's coming to LA next week and he's going to stay with me."

Cynthia made a face. "Why are you buying new towels for a man? He's just going to leave them in a heap on the floor with his dirty gym clothes and socks."

"You'd understand if you'd seen this guy," Olivia told her. "He's next-level gorgeous."

"Oh my gosh, is this Hot Butt we're talking about?" Penny asked, leaning forward. "He's coming here?"

Brooke blinked at her. "Hot *what*?"

Penny reached for her wine glass. "The underwear model, right?"

"How do you know about him?" Brooke was almost positive she'd never mentioned Dylan to Penny. She didn't talk about him *that much*, did she?

"I might have told Penny about him," Olivia admitted with a shrug.

"And we totally stalked his Insta too. Hoo boy!" Penny fanned herself with her hand.

Olivia grinned. "And then Penny started calling him Hot Butt because of that one pic where—"

"Yes, I know the one," Brooke said, cutting her off. She'd tried to block out the memory of that one particular photo of Dylan lying facedown on a bed, completely butt-ass naked. She preferred to maintain a dichotomy between her feelings for her childhood friend Dylan and her feelings about the disturbingly hot man in his Instagram feed.

"Because he's got such a hot butt," Penny explained.

"Yeah, I figured it out," Brooke said, wishing everyone would stop talking about Dylan's butt.

"It's all round and shiny." Penny sighed dreamily. "Like two perfect, ripe apples."

"That's all Photoshop," Brooke felt the need to point out. Dylan didn't actually look like that in real life.

Did he?

He couldn't possibly. She hadn't actually seen him in

21

person since he moved to New York, but *god*, she hoped he didn't look that good in person.

"Oh no, that one was an unretouched outtake," Olivia offered unhelpfully. "It said so in the caption. *Au naturel*."

Esther rested her chin on her hand. "So what are you going to do with your hot underwear model while he's here?" Her mouth twisted into a smirk. "I can think of a few things . . ."

"He's like a brother," Brooke insisted. A brother she used to have a huge crush on, granted, but that was a long time ago.

Esther tilted her head to one side. "Is he really though? *Is* he like a brother?"

Olivia nudged Brooke with her elbow. "Yeah, didn't you go to prom with him?"

"Well, yes," Brooke admitted. "But only as friends." *Mostly. Sort of. But not exactly.* Wow, all this cheese was making her mouth dry. She reached for her wine glass and took a drink.

"Didn't you *kiss him* on prom night?" Olivia persisted.

Brooke gulped down more wine and wiped her mouth before answering. "That was just a fluke. A one-time thing. We both regretted it instantly." One of them did, anyway.

Esther grinned across the table at her. "Okay, so what I hear you saying is he's less like a brother and more like a hot guy friend you've totally macked on at least once."

Brooke turned a glare on Olivia. "I'm regretting ever telling you anything about him."

"So you do like him!" Penny accused, pointing a cheese straw at Brooke. "I knew it!"

22

"No, definitely not. Not like that." Brooke reached for the bottle of Syrah and poured herself another glass.

"Then why are you buying new towels for him?" Lacey asked from the other end of the table. "Who gives a shit about towels?"

"I happen to love new towels," Tessa said, sticking her tongue out at her girlfriend.

Brooke fidgeted in her seat. "He lives in New York City, and goes to all these swanky parties, and hobnobs with celebrities and New York fashion people, and travels all over the world staying in fancy hotels and resorts. I just don't want him to think I'm lame. Scratch that. I don't want him to know how lame I *am*."

"Sounds to me like you like him," Melody said, and Tessa nodded her agreement.

"I think we should change the subject back to Penny and her upcoming wedding," Brooke announced, turning toward the bride-to-be. "Are you excited?"

Penny's smile faltered a little. "Mostly nervous—not about getting married, but about all the family stuff. We still don't even know if any of Caleb's family are coming, and my mom is freaking out that there won't be anyone sitting in the front pew on Caleb's side of the church."

"Would they really not go to their own son's wedding?" Olivia asked. "I mean I know there's some tensions there, but would they really miss his wedding?"

Brooke thought about her own parents, who hadn't been to visit even once since she'd moved here, not even for her college graduation. Would they show up if she was getting married? Or simply make up another excuse not to come?

She had a feeling she knew the answer.

The irony was, Brooke used to be really close to her parents. Sure they'd been strict, and they'd pushed all three of their kids to be overachievers, but she'd believed they loved her in their own slightly rigid, constrained sort of way. She'd spent most of her childhood vying for their approval and preening when she managed to secure it—which was often, since she was a good student who rarely got herself into any sort of trouble.

Until she'd gotten herself into the worst kind of trouble.

Her parents hadn't been thrilled when she'd first started dating. They held strict views on relations between unmarried men and women, and there had been grave concerns about their daughter having a boyfriend. But Kyle was from a good family who went to their church. Brooke's parents knew his parents. He and Brooke belonged to the same youth ministry and had matching Virginity Pledge Cards, complete with Domino's Pizza coupons on the back. He seemed as safe a choice for their daughter's first boyfriend as they were likely to get. And so, reluctantly, they'd given their blessing to the relationship.

Little did they suspect that, despite the virginity pledge and abstinence education, Kyle was as horny as any red-blooded boy of his age—and Brooke was equally keen to find out what all the fuss was about. The Deed turned out to be somewhat less magical than she'd imagined, but still fun enough for repeat performances whenever they could contrive to be alone. Unfortunately, neither of them had wanted to risk being seen buying condoms, and birth control pills were wholly out of the question, so they'd foolishly relied on the "pull and pray" method of contraception.

Their praying skills, as it turned out, weren't so good.

24

Brooke's relationship with her parents had never recovered after the ignominy she'd brought upon herself and the family. Though whether the greater crime in their eyes was her promiscuity or her choice to terminate the pregnancy was still unclear. Not that she cared what they thought anymore. They'd essentially written her off, so she'd returned the favor.

"I'm just trying to keep Caleb from freaking out," Penny said, and Brooke snapped back to the present conversation.

Cynthia gave Penny's arm a squeeze. "Whether his parents come to the wedding or not, you'll both be just fine. This is your day. Don't let anyone spoil that."

"That's right," Brooke said with feeling. "With or without his parents, at the end of the day you and Caleb will be married, which is all that really matters."

Fuck Caleb's parents, and fuck hers too.

Blood didn't make you family; it was just an accident of nature.

Family were the people who stood by you no matter what, not the ones who were nowhere to be found when you needed them.

Chapter Three

Brooke adjusted the new throw pillows on her couch and stepped back to survey her work. Frowning, she rearranged them so they looked more natural. *Casual.* That was the effect she was going for. Like they'd just been tossed effortlessly onto the couch.

Ugh, no.

Now they looked haphazard. She readjusted them so they weren't quite so messy. Only now they looked too staged, like she was trying too hard. She didn't want Dylan to think she'd spent hours trying to make her apartment look Pinterest-perfect for him—even if that was exactly what she'd done.

She checked the time again and did a brief calculation in her head. According to the airline website, Dylan's plane had landed on schedule. Allowing time for him to deplane, pick up his rental car, and drive from LAX to her apartment, he should be arriving . . . any minute.

Nervously, Brooke prodded the pillows again, resisting the urge to stand out on the balcony and watch for him. She'd offered to pick him up at the airport, but since he'd rented a car to get around while he was in LA, it had made more sense for him to drive himself to her place.

Now that she was really looking at them, she was worried her new pillows might be tacky. They'd seemed clever at the store, but in hindsight she feared they were a little too . . . lame. Or weird. Or something.

She'd intended to get something fashionable and grown-up—two adjectives that would not normally be used to describe her aesthetic—but then they'd had this cute whale pillow, and Lord help her, she was helpless to resist a good whale pun.

Everything Whale Be Okay, it read in curly script alongside a smiling cartoon whale. She'd picked a velvet cushion in a complementary shade of turquoise for a pop of color that she hoped would help disguise how plain and boring her couch was, but now she was wishing she'd gotten the geometric patterned pillows instead.

Welp—or whale-p as she liked to say when she was feeling punny—the damage was done. They were her pillows now.

Should she crease them or something? Was that a thing people did? Or just a thing her mom used to do?

As she was repositioning her new cushions for the umpteenth time, Brooke heard the dreadful sound of her cat hawking up a hairball somewhere in the apartment.

"Come on, Murderface, not now!" she groaned.

The cat's timing was impeccable, you had to give him that. He always managed to perform his hairball expulsions at the worst possible moment. Like when she was about to sit down to eat. Or that time she'd brought a date home and the cat had yacked right in front of the couch just as things were starting to get hot and heavy.

Although in retrospect, she probably should have thanked Murderface for his attempted intervention on that particular occasion, because that guy had turned out to be a dud in the bedroom.

Following the retching sounds into the bathroom, Brooke came upon her big brown tabby, Murderface McGee, just in time to watch him splorch out a giant hairball on her brand-new white bath mat.

"Awesome. Thanks very much for that," she muttered as the cat trotted off proudly, swishing his tail like he'd just left her a gift wrapped up with a bow.

She tore off a handful of toilet paper, picked up the hairball, and flushed it down the toilet. Of course it had left a big, gross stain in the middle of the bath mat, which would have to be washed now. There wasn't time to throw it into the machines downstairs, but hopefully she could hand wash it before Dylan got here and leave it hanging up to dry.

Tossing the bath mat into the tub, she turned on the water and started washing. Miraculously, she managed to get the stain out with a liberal application of elbow grease and Oxi-clean. Unfortunately, she also managed to soak the entire front of her gray T-shirt like she'd been through Splash Mountain at Disneyland.

Also unfortunately, just as she'd finished draping the bath mat over the shower curtain rod to dry and was planning to go grab a clean T-shirt, there was a knock at the apartment door.

Dylan.

He was here, and Brooke looked like the loser in a Super Soaker fight. Cool. Just like old times, then.

Drying her hands on her jeans, she hurried to the front door and pulled it open.

Whoa.

Okay, so, Dylan was unreal levels of hot now.

She'd known he was hot from his photos, obviously, but only in a theoretical sort of way. In her mind he was still the sweet dork she'd been friends with in middle school. The Dylan in all the carefully posed selfies and photo shoot out-takes he posted on Instagram had never seemed real to her. Wasn't everything on Instagram supposed to be fake anyway?

Dylan's hotness was not fake. In fact, he was somehow even hotter in person than he looked in his photos. Much, *much* hotter. Like his hotness emitted a stream of particles that reacted with everything they came in physical contact with.

Brooke had been trying to stay calm and low-key about this whole visit, but when he broke into a grin on her doorstep, she was pretty sure she had a hotness-induced ministroke.

"Hey! Did I catch you in the middle of something?" His eyebrows twitched over his sparkling blue eyes as he gestured at her chest.

"What?" Brooke looked down and remembered her sopping wet T-shirt, which was clinging to her chest like Saran Wrap, and just when her nipples had chosen to protrude through her bra like a pair of nail heads. Horrified, she tugged the wet fabric away from her body. "Oh, sorry. Just cleaning up a last-minute mess."

"I love your place," Dylan said, darting forward to brush a kiss against her cheek. Which was a thing they did now, apparently. Kissed on the cheek like a couple of French socialites.

Before she'd properly recovered from *that*, his arms wrapped her up in a hug.

29

She let out a long breath as her body instinctively relaxed against his. This, at least, felt normal for them and more like the Dylan she remembered. He smelled familiar underneath the fancy cologne he was wearing, and she couldn't help grinning as she squeezed him back. "It's so good to see you."

"I know. It's been too long."

Almost six years. Not since the last time she'd gone home for Christmas.

He let go and stepped back, breaking into another grin. "You look great."

"I look great? *You* look great!" She reached out and punched him in the arm, which was a bit like punching an extremely smooth tree trunk. "Look at you. My god!" He definitely hadn't had so many muscles the last time she'd seen him, and he hadn't been so stylish either.

Those faded-to-perfection jeans he was wearing probably cost several hundred dollars off the rack. And that plain black T-shirt that fit his body like a glove had almost certainly been custom tailored. He'd come a long way from the kid who'd once had a different Star Wars tee for every day of the week.

He ducked his head and made a wry face, which was so much like the old Dylan she remembered, the one who'd always been uncomfortable with compliments, that she relaxed a little more.

"Come in." Brooke grabbed his hand and tugged him the rest of the way into her apartment. "You can drop your bags anywhere."

"I love this building," he said as he propped his backpack and roller bag by the front door. "It's so LA."

"It is pretty great, isn't it?" She loved her old courtyard

building in Palms with its murky swimming pool and eclectic neighbors. "I took over the lease from a friend of a friend. It's hard to find somewhere affordable that allows cats."

Dylan thrust a hand through his dark blond hair as he peered around the small apartment, his eyes sliding right past the new throw cushions on her couch. His hair was just long enough to hint at the curl Brooke remembered from when he used to wear it shaggier, back when his personal grooming routine consisted of a reluctant trip to Fantastic Sam's every six months. Nowadays he probably got a hundred-dollar haircut from a celebrity stylist every two weeks like clockwork.

"Where is the famous Murderface?" he asked. "I'm dying to meet him after seeing all the pics on Facebook."

"I wouldn't get too excited," Brooke said. "He'll probably spend your whole visit hiding under the bed."

"No way. Cats love me. I'm gonna win him over." Dylan wandered into the kitchen and stooped to study the photos on the front of Brooke's fridge. Smiling, he extended a long finger to straighten a group photo of Brooke and the other volunteers from her first field research trip in Alaska.

"I wouldn't bet on it," Brooke countered. "He really doesn't like strangers."

When her now-ex Garrett had done his ill-fated three-week stint at her place, Murderface had only come out of hiding when Garrett left the apartment. She'd actually been a little worried he was going to give himself a urinary tract infection. The cat, that was, not Garrett.

Dylan spun back around and winked. "He's gonna like me. I'm irresistible."

The effortless sexual magnetism emanating from that wink nearly gave her another ministroke, but something about the smile underneath it rang hollow. Brooke recalled his promise to tell her what was going on with him, but decided to hold off pressing him about it until he'd had a chance to settle in.

"Are you hungry? I was thinking I could take you out for dinner." She had the perfect place in mind: a quiet, cozy Mexican restaurant that reminded her of one of their favorite haunts back home. They could settle into a booth and catch up over tortilla chips and margaritas.

His smile deflated a little. "I'd love that . . . but I'm doing a water cut for this shoot tomorrow so I can't."

"A water cut? What's that?"

He rubbed the back of his neck, which caused his incredible biceps to flex and the room to feel suddenly much smaller. "You drink two gallons of water a day for a few days, then decrease your water intake the day before a shoot so your body sheds a bunch of excess water weight. It's how you get that shredded and separated look that makes your muscles really pop, you know?"

Oh, she knew all right. She'd drooled over enough *Men's Health* covers in the grocery store checkout line. She just hadn't realized what kind of effort went into it. "I always thought that was all drawn on in Photoshop."

"They do that too, usually. Anyway, I'm only allowed small sips of water until ten tonight, then no food or water at all twelve hours before the shoot."

"That sounds awful. Is it safe?" She didn't love the idea of Dylan fasting and dehydrating himself on the regular, and it kicked her protective instincts into high alert. Not only did

32

it sound like a recipe for an eating disorder, but dehydration could be really hard on the body.

He shrugged off her concerns. "My trainer knows what he's doing. It's no picnic, but he's got it down to a science. As long as I follow his plan, it's fine." She must have been frowning, because he came closer and took both her hands in his. "I promise I'm not doing anything stupid, okay?" His blue eyes looked into hers, beaming earnest sincerity directly into her soul.

Brooke gazed back at him and nodded, too overwhelmed by the nearness of him to argue. His cologne clouded her senses, and his eyes were hypnotizing as they stared into hers. She was suddenly very aware of her heartbeat, which had begun to pound a little too fast and too loudly.

Dylan squeezed her hands before letting go, and Brooke exhaled when he put distance between them again as he sauntered out of the kitchen. Her fingers were still tingling where he'd touched her.

She clenched her hands into fists and blew out a breath, willing her heart to simmer down. There were a whole seven days of Dylan yet to get through, and she needed to find some kind of equilibrium around him. "We won't go out, then. I guess I shouldn't offer you a beer either."

He let out a wistful sigh as he bent to peruse her bookshelf, which contained mostly biology and oceanography texts. "No, no beer tonight for me. Tomorrow though." Straightening, he patted his insanely flat stomach with both hands. "I'm going to want to consume my weight in carbs, so get ready."

"It's a date." She winced as the words came out of her mouth. Using the word "date" in relation to Dylan brought up old memories and feelings she didn't need to be giving brain space to right now.

"But listen, don't worry about me tonight." He smiled, and a trail of nerves lit up inside her, from her stomach straight to her heart. His face was too perfect. Perfect nose, perfect lips, perfect jaw. Even his damn eyebrows were perfect. "Go ahead and eat or drink whatever you want. We can even go out and I just won't have anything."

"No way." She shook her head, rejecting both his suggestion and her own wayward thoughts. *It's just Dylan*, she reminded herself, superimposing the memory of a ten-year-old boy over his perfect adult visage. *The same old Dylan with the same old face he's always had.* "I'm not dragging you to a restaurant and making you watch me eat. I've got leftovers in the fridge I can eat tonight."

"You sure you don't mind staying in?" He gave her only a one-second look before blinking away, embarrassed again. "I know it's kind of lame."

"It's not lame at all," she rushed to reassure him. "Staying in happens to be my favorite activity."

He rewarded her with another one of his dazzling smiles, and she felt her stomach zip all the way up her spine.

No more of that, she silently scolded her stomach. *That won't do at all.*

Chapter Four

An hour later, they were settled at opposite ends of Brooke's couch. Brooke had finished her leftover Thai food while they talked about her research, Los Angeles, and the photo shoot Dylan was doing the next day for a men's magazine.

"So what's going on with you?" she said when she decided he'd skirted around the subject long enough. "What did you mean about needing a break?"

"Oh, you know. Just the usual." He shrugged, trying to slip off the hook.

She pinned him with a look, refusing to let him off that easy. "No, I don't know. Tell me."

"Work's just been nonstop lately. I haven't had a real vacation in years."

"Weren't you just in Mexico a few months ago? I distinctly remember pictures of you on a beach." She also remembered the Speedo he'd been wearing. She remembered it much better than she remembered the picturesque beach scene behind him.

He leaned back against the corner of the couch, his limbs loose and sprawled like one of his photo spreads. "That was a working trip. I'm always working. If I'm not on a shoot,

I'm in the gym training for one, or I'm networking at parties or going to meetings my agent set up and trying to kiss enough asses to book my next job. When I'm not doing all that, I'm trying to stay on top of my social media, because if you don't keep pushing out content you'll drop off the radar. Or at least that's what everyone says."

"Sounds exhausting."

"It is. I just wanted a few days where I don't have to think about any of that shit." He shook his head like a dog flicking away a pesky fly. "On the bright side, I'm on meds now for ADHD. Imagine if my mom had bothered to get me tested for it twenty years ago. I might have made something of myself."

Brooke stretched her leg across the couch and nudged him with her foot. "I'd say you've made quite a lot of yourself, Mr. Big-Time New York Model."

Dylan looked down at her turquoise-painted toenails and smiled faintly. "Yeah, I guess. Anyway, as a bonus, the meds suppress my appetite, so it's easier to keep my weight down."

"But do they help with the other stuff? Focus and decision-making and all that?" His ADHD diagnosis didn't surprise her at all. Looking back, it seemed obvious now that his problems in school had stemmed from that. It really did suck that none of his teachers or his parents had ever done anything to help him.

He gave a one-shouldered shrug. "Yeah, I think so. It took a while to get the dosage right. But now that we have, I can definitely tell a difference."

"That's great." She gave him another nudge with her toes. "I'm glad you're finally getting treatment that helps."

"Me too." He laid his hand on top of her foot, giving it a

gentle squeeze, and she became suddenly, keenly aware of why the foot was considered an erogenous zone. She'd never really gotten it before, but the warm weight of Dylan's hand on her foot lit her up like a Roman candle. Her skin felt too tight, and she was uncomfortably warm. Her upper lip tingled as if she was about to break out in a sweat.

Sucking in an unsteady breath, Brooke retracted her foot, tucking it safely beneath her. "So that's really all this vacation's about?" she asked, trying to get the conversation back on track. "Overwork?"

One of Dylan's stupidly perfect eyebrows arched. "Yeah. Why?"

"On the phone you sounded . . . I don't know. Unhappy? I thought it might be something more than that."

"Naw. I didn't mean to make you worry or anything."

She smiled at the sound of his Louisiana accent beginning to peek through, as if he was shedding the influence of living in New York as he relaxed.

"I always worry about you," Brooke replied, hearing her own accent come out to match his. It was like they were both reverting to their younger selves, peeling back the layers they'd built up since leaving home.

Dylan's brow furrowed. "Why?"

"I don't know. You're up there in New York by yourself. I wish you were closer."

"I wish that too."

His eyes stayed locked on hers for a long moment, and she struggled not to squirm under the weight of all that male beauty. She wondered if she'd ever get back to the point where she could feel him looking at her without going light-headed and breathless.

She had to. Being attracted to Dylan's body was regrettably unavoidable. Being attracted to *him* was absolutely off-limits.

"So what are we gonna do this week?" he asked, breaking the spell. "I'm completely at your mercy."

Brooke refused to let her mind conjure any dirty images of what she might like to do with him at her mercy. "Unfortunately, I kind of have to work most of the week."

"That's okay. I'm more than capable of entertaining myself."

"I wish I could take more time off while you're here, but I'm TAing two classes this semester, plus I've got office hours, and on top of that there's this award I'm submitting a paper for, and the application deadline is Wednesday."

He grinned. "That's my Brooke. Still an overachiever."

Her heart gave a small trill at the words *my Brooke*, and she warned her heart to simmer the fuck down. "I'm probably wasting my time with the award. There's no way I'm going to get it."

"Stop second-guessing yourself and go for the thing. You have to give people a chance to tell you yes."

It felt like old times, having Dylan here in person boosting her morale. It was so much better than talking on the phone. She felt fifteen again—in a good way, not the pimples and hormones and existential teen angst way.

"I've got a car," he pointed out. "I can entertain myself while you're being smart and awesome."

"Tell you what," Brooke offered. "I don't have class or office hours on Friday. Maybe I can take the whole day off and we'll do something fun together."

"Sounds great. But only if it works out. Don't jeopardize

your shot at this award for me. We'll still get to hang out in the evenings." His expression changed as something occurred to him. "I probably should have asked this before I invited myself to stay at your place, but are you seeing anyone? I'm not stepping on any toes here, am I?"

She snorted. "No. God no."

"Why do you say it like that?"

"Dating and me haven't really been working out." She picked at a hangnail on her thumb. "I think I've gone off the whole concept."

His voice softened with pity. "I'm sorry to hear that."

Brooke shrugged. It was something she'd made her peace with, but she didn't expect anyone else to understand. The whole rest of the world seemed obsessed with finding their one true love.

"What about you?" she asked, looking up. "Anyone special in your life?"

"Hardly."

"What's up with that? You're a total catch."

His mouth flattened. "Everyone I meet is so focused on their careers and getting ahead. I don't want to say they're all shallow and fake, but . . ."

"They're totally all a bunch of shallow fakers?" she guessed.

Dylan smiled and shook his head. "It can sure feel that way sometimes. It's hard to know if people actually like you for you, or if they're using you because of what they think you can do for them."

"That sounds kind of awful."

"It's fine." He ducked his head as he shrugged, so she wouldn't see that it wasn't actually fine at all.

She'd never imagined, looking at his social media, that he might actually be lonely. How could someone as wonderful and gorgeous as Dylan ever be alone? Those posers he knew in New York had no idea what they were missing out on.

"Do you still like it?" she asked. "Modeling, I mean?" It sort of seemed like he didn't. But then how many people actually liked their jobs? Maybe this was just normal career dissatisfaction.

His head tilted to the side as he reached up to rub a hand over his jaw. "I like that I'm good at it. It's pretty much the only thing I've ever been good at."

"That's not true. I seem to recall you making a mean lasagna."

He looked pleased by the compliment. "I am a decent cook. It's one of my few legitimate skills. Although everyone I know is always on a diet—including me—so I don't get to put it to much use."

He'd worked in the kitchen at Carrabba's back home. It was how he'd saved the money for his first trip to New York when his Instagram account started to take off. He'd signed with his first agency on that trip. It had set the ball rolling for all the success that came after: his first catalogue job, his first magazine ad, his first billboard, his first runway show. Dylan had worked his ass off for everything he'd accomplished.

"I also recall you making it to first saxophone at one point," she teased, remembering how excited he'd been at the time.

He laughed, stretching both arms over his head. "I'll be sure to add that to my résumé."

Damn those muscles of his. Brooke looked away so her

eyes wouldn't pop out of her head. "Didn't you also win a couple medals in the hundred-meter hurdles?"

"Yeah, you know, those high school glories don't really translate into practical job skills."

"You were always good at being a friend," she said, darting a look at him.

His eyes flicked over to her and held. "Was I?"

"The best."

"Well, that's something." The way he smiled at her made her feel warm all over. "Kind of hard to make a living at it though."

"I don't know. I'll bet you're good at lots of things you don't even realize you're good at. You never did give yourself enough credit."

"I guess it's lucky I had you around to boost my ego during my formative years." He exhaled a long breath, shaking his head. "Damn, we've known each other for a long time, haven't we?"

"We go back like car seats," she said, smiling as the past enveloped her like a fluffy blanket. Almost all her favorite memories seemed to involve Dylan. She'd spent a lot of time trying not to think about those years, but there'd been a lot of good times amongst the bad. "Where would either of us be if my parents hadn't bought the house across the street from yours?"

"I can't even bear to think about it."

"Me either."

Being with Dylan was so *easy*. She'd forgotten just how comfortable she felt with him. It was amazing how smoothly they dropped right back into their friendship, even after years apart.

SUSANNAH NIX

"Speaking of this week," she said, remembering Penny's party, "a friend of mine is getting married—well, she actually got married yesterday in Virginia, but they're having this sort of wedding reception thing here on Saturday night—and I was wondering—if you were interested—you could come with me. You don't have to though."

Ugh, why was she so nervous to ask him? It wasn't like she cared if he didn't want to go.

"I'd love to," Dylan answered, like he absolutely meant it. Like he couldn't think of anything he'd rather do.

"I know you said you were sick of parties—"

"This is different. I'd love to meet your friends."

His face was too much. She rubbed her hands on her thighs as she felt her cheeks heat.

How was he still single? You'd think the women of New York would be falling all over themselves for a gorgeous, sweetheart of a man like this. Clearly they had no taste.

Brooke blew a breath through her teeth. "Okay. Cool. I don't know what kind of clothes you brought, but it's not super fancy or anything." Her face felt too hot, like she might be coming down with something.

"I'll figure it out," he said as he yawned. He stood up and stretched again. This time his T-shirt rode up, exposing a patch of tanned waist and the waistband of his black underwear.

Brooke's mouth filled with cotton. Yeah, she was coming down with something, all right. She had all the major symptoms: light-headedness, rapid heartbeat, inability to focus, uncontrollable sweating, and dry mouth.

Congratulations, dum-dum, you've got a crush on your oldest friend!

Of all the idea flavors in the world, this one tasted like unmitigated disaster.

"I should probably hit the sack." Dylan threw her an apologetic look as he unzipped his bag. "Sorry I'm so lame tonight."

"No, it's fine! I forgot you're on East Coast time. I'll get you a pillow and some blankets." She jumped up, relieved to have a task to distract herself with.

While Dylan was in the bathroom getting ready for bed, Brooke made up the couch for him and put out some food for Murderface, who was still in hiding.

Dylan emerged a few minutes later in a plain white undershirt, sweatpants, and a pair of glasses. He looked like Clark Kent trying to pretend he wasn't a gorgeous hunk of a man and instead making himself even hotter. Although Dylan had worn glasses every day until the age of sixteen, Brooke had never found them notably sexy on him before. Then again, middle school Dylan had never worn glasses as stylish as the tortoiseshell frames currently making Brooke's ovaries explode.

"Thanks," he said, nodding at the bed she'd made for him on the couch as he crossed to his suitcase.

Eyes up, she reprimanded herself as tantalizing movement under his sweatpants vied for her attention.

Unfortunately, lifting her gaze only left her staring directly into his beautiful face.

She couldn't help staring. It wasn't her fault his lips were so eminently kissable. They were one of the top five beautiful things about him. Sure, his body was nice, but nice bodies were a dime a dozen in the modeling business. His lips, though, were a one of a kind genetic gift. From the artful curve of his upper lip to the slightly sulky plumpness of his lower lip, which stuck out just enough to demand attention. That lower lip was just begging to be kissed—or better yet, nibbled.

Embarrassed, Brooke tore her eyes away from him before he noticed her gawking. She was feeling the loss of their earlier ease, which seemed to have decamped somewhere between her accidentally asking him on a date and that flash of underwear she'd glimpsed.

"Okay, well, if you're set, I'm going to bed," she announced awkwardly.

"I'm all set," he confirmed.

Brooke bid him goodnight and fled the room as fast as her legs would take her.

She dreamed about Dylan that night. It wasn't quite a sex dream, but it was clearly headed in that direction.

In her dream he lay naked on a bed, just like in the infamous Instagram pic. Only instead of the white sheets, king-size bed, and featureless, brightly lit room from Instagram, he was splayed on Brooke's double bed. On her whale comforter from the kids' department. In her bedroom.

Dream Brooke stood in the doorway, openly gawking at him, but Dream Dylan didn't appear to mind her scrutiny. In fact, he seemed to like it. He stared back at her with a hint of a smile on his perfectly shaped lips, his eyebrows slightly raised in expectation. Or was it invitation?

He lay sprawled on his stomach with his arms folded underneath his head and his cheek resting on the back of one hand, just like his pose in the Instagram photo. A lock of thick hair tumbled across his forehead. Brooke's eyes trailed over his naked body, drinking in the muscular curves. Against her will, she registered the lack of any tan lines. He was all flawless, gleaming skin, stretching on forever like a dripping spoonful of honey.

As he gazed back at her, his tongue darted out to lick his lips. He lifted his head, his eyes never leaving hers. "Why don't you come over here?"

Brooke clutched the doorframe, using it both as a support and a tether. She shook her head. "I shouldn't."

Dylan's lips puckered in a sultry pout she'd only ever seen in his modeling work. "You know you want to, Brooke. You've wanted this for years. Ever since prom night."

She shook her head again. He couldn't know that. She'd never let on. She'd worked *so* hard not to let him know.

"Shall I turn over?" he asked with a smirk. "If you want to see everything, you just have to ask."

It felt like her whole body was paralyzed. Even her vocal cords refused to work. She couldn't do anything. Couldn't answer him, couldn't move any closer, couldn't flee.

"All you have to do is say it," Dylan pressed. "Say it, Brooke. Say you want me. Just say the words, Brooke."

She woke to the sound of the shower running. It was right next to her bedroom, and the pipes whistled when you turned the hot water on.

Which meant Dylan was currently naked on the other side of the wall, just like he'd been naked in her dream. Lucky shower tiles, getting a front-row seat to the peep show—

Is exactly the sort of thing you shouldn't be thinking, perv.

Her dream was proof enough of that. Brooke wouldn't survive the next six days if she was going to be having dreams like that every night. Time to nip all those naughty thoughts in the bud.

She rolled over to check her phone: six a.m. Dylan had said he needed to be at his shoot at nine, but with the time difference from the East Coast, he'd probably woken early on his own.

Her class wasn't until ten thirty, but since Dylan was up, she figured she ought to be a good hostess and get up too. She could always go into the lab and get some extra work done. After pulling on a robe over her T-shirt and pajama pants, she wandered out of her bedroom.

The bathroom door was closed, but steam spilled out in the stream of light coming from under the door.

She assumed Dylan couldn't have coffee on his water cut, but hopefully he wouldn't mind if she made some for herself. Rubbing her eyes, Brooke padded past the bathroom and into the living room.

It didn't register at first, in the dim gray light leaking through the blinds, that there was someone in the living room. She was still sleepy, and her vision was blurry from rubbing her eyes. It was only as her sight adjusted that a figure came into focus.

It was Dylan.

He was bent over, digging through his suitcase with his back to her.

Just as naked as he'd been in her dream.

Chapter Five

Dylan was naked.

In her living room.

Right in front of her.

Not in a dream, but in real life.

His ass cheeks flexed as he stooped over his suitcase, and his back muscles rippled like a Michelangelo sculpture come to life. Brooke heard herself gasp, and Dylan spun around, giving her the full-frontal experience.

There wasn't a lot of light in the room, but there was enough.

To see everything.

Everything.

For a second they both stood there frozen in shock. Brooke with her mouth hanging open and Dylan with everything hanging. In all his glory. Completely naked and hot as hell.

"Shit!" he yelped, belatedly trying to cover himself with the pair of underwear in his hand. "I thought you were asleep!"

Brooke covered her eyes and turned her back on him. "I thought you were in the shower!"

"I was letting the room fill up with steam to sweat off a little more water weight, but I forgot to grab clean underwear."

Brooke swallowed, trying to ignore the image of Dylan's penis that was now permanently seared into her brain. "Okay. Cool. Well . . . uh . . . looks like you've got them now."

"Yeah. So. I'm gonna go back into the bathroom."

Keeping her eyes directed at the floor and her hand up to shield Dylan's still incredibly naked body from her view, Brooke moved aside so he could get past her to the bathroom. "Cool. Yep. I'm just gonna go . . ." She waved in the direction of the kitchen with the hand that wasn't covering her eyes. "Make some coffee or whatever."

"Okay. Good."

"Cool." Why was she saying cool so much? Nothing about this was cool! It was the opposite of cool. It was . . .

Hot, actually.

Except no. It was Dylan, and she did *not* want to think about him like that. Okay, she *wanted* to, but she *shouldn't*.

As soon as he'd shuffled past her and shut the bathroom door, Brooke fled to the kitchen and collapsed against the fridge with a groan.

Okay, so she'd seen Dylan's penis. This was fine. Definitely uncharted territory for their friendship, but not really a big deal in the grand scheme of things. It was a perfectly innocent mistake, clearly an accident on both sides.

He was a model, so he was probably used to all sorts of random people looking at his body all the time. For all she knew, he'd even posed for full-frontal nudes. Extremely tasteful ones, she was sure.

It was just a body, right? Bodies were nothing to be

ashamed of. She was a biologist; she knew that better than anyone. If you'd seen one sex organ, you'd seen them all.

Except that wasn't true. Because now she'd seen Dylan's sex organ. And it was Dylan. And he was . . .

Glorious was the word that immediately sprang to mind.

But that was bad. She wasn't supposed to think of him that way. She wasn't supposed to be thinking about his penis at all. But now, god help her, she couldn't *stop* thinking about it, or about him.

It didn't help that he was, at that very moment, naked in her shower. Wetting down his perfect body, lathering the soap over his flawless golden skin, hands sliding over the dripping muscles, gripping his—

Brooke turned on the kitchen faucet and splashed cold water over her face.

Twenty minutes later, she was pouring her second cup of coffee when Dylan emerged from the bathroom—fully clothed in jeans and a T-shirt, thank god, albeit a little damp and sweaty, which did nothing to keep Brooke's lustful thoughts under control.

"Hey," he ventured sheepishly, joining her in the kitchen.

Breathe. You can do this. If she pretended everything was normal, everything would *be* normal.

Brooke forced herself to meet his eye with a broad smile. "Hey! How was your penis—SHOWER, I mean shower. *Oh my god.* How was your *shower?*" Mortified, she covered her face with her hands as her cheeks burned red-hot.

So much for normal.

Dylan snort-laughed. "So I guess we should probably talk about what happened."

"We super don't have to."

49

"I'm really sorry. I didn't mean to flash you."

"No, that's . . . it's fine." She reached for her coffee cup so she wouldn't have to look him in the eye. "Some would even call it a bonus."

"Still." His voice was low and soft, like he genuinely felt terrible, and it tied her stomach into knots.

"Hey, that water cut's definitely working though. Looking good!" She gave him an awkward thumbs-up and immediately regretted it.

Dylan grimaced. "Thanks."

"I guess you can't have coffee?"

He shook his head. "You know what? I'm gonna have a half cup. I can probably get away with that, and I definitely need it this morning."

Brooke got out a mug for him and shifted out of the way as he maneuvered around her in the tiny kitchen to get to the coffeemaker. Her apartment had never felt so small before. Usually it was more than enough space for her and her medium-sized cat. But this morning it felt claustrophobically, suffocatingly small.

"So what do you have going on today?" Dylan asked as he poured himself some coffee.

"Um, you know, the usual. Giving an exam in class this morning, then work on finishing my paper. Maybe get started on grading."

"What's the class?"

"Introductory Bio."

"How big is it?"

"About two hundred students."

"That's a lot of exams to grade."

Brooke made a face. "Yeah. I was actually thinking of

50

going in early to get some work out of the way." She hooked a thumb toward the bathroom. "So I should probably go shower and get dressed."

Dylan nodded as he sipped his coffee. "Sure."

Brooke gave him a weak smile and escaped to her room. Once she'd gathered up her clothes—making sure not to repeat Dylan's underwear miscalculation—she crept into the bathroom, relaxing only when she'd closed and locked the door behind her.

It was as hot and steamy as a sauna in there, and she peeled off her pajamas before brushing her teeth and washing her face. In the shower, she turned the water to cold before stepping under the stream. The frigid temperature shocked her system, raising goose bumps all over her skin, but it didn't do enough to quell the heat suffusing her limbs or the carnal thoughts that had taken up residence in her brain. It didn't keep her from dwelling on the memory of Dylan's naked body.

After standing under the water for as long as she could bear, she got out and pulled on her clothes over her sweaty limbs. Throwing open the bathroom door, she grabbed her hair dryer and retreated to her room again, grateful for the cooler air in the rest of the apartment.

She didn't usually bother with makeup when she went to campus, but today she took the time to apply some foundation, mascara, and tinted lip balm. But only so she'd have more time to pull herself back together after the penis-flashing incident before she had to interact with Dylan again. Definitely not because she was trying to look good for him.

Brooke had no illusions about the chances of him finding her attractive. If that was going to happen, it would have happened years ago. At this point they'd been friends so long he probably didn't even see her anymore, like a comfortable piece of furniture. The guy spent his days surrounded by professionally flawless human specimens. No way could Brooke ever compete with that.

But maybe she wouldn't mind if he at least thought she was cute. That wasn't too much to hope for, was it?

Once she was done drying her hair and getting ready for work, Brooke ventured back out into the apartment. Dylan was sitting on the couch, frowning as he hunched over his phone.

"Everything okay?" she asked.

"Fine." His frown disappeared as he looked up, and once again she had the sense he wasn't telling her the whole truth. "You heading out?"

"Yeah." She went to the bookcase by the door and dug around in the basket of random junk sitting on top. "I'll give you a spare key to the apartment. That way you can come and go as you please."

When she turned around, Dylan was standing beside her, closer than she'd expected him to be. She startled a little, and he took a step back. "Sorry."

"No, you're good." She held out the key, dangling from a Monterey Bay Aquarium keychain. "Here."

"Thanks." He held out his hand, and she dropped the key into it. His long fingers closed around it in a fist. "Have a good day at work."

"You too. I mean, good luck with your shoot." She frowned. "Am I allowed to say good luck, or am I supposed to say break a leg?"

His mouth curved in a smile. "Good luck works great."

"Okay, good luck then."

He stepped forward and pulled her into a full-body hug. "I really appreciate you letting me stay with you." He smelled like her shower gel, and his T-shirt was warm and silky soft against her cheek.

Hugs were a rare commodity in Brooke's life, and her body reacted like a starving kitten, nuzzling into his embrace as she exhaled a long, purring sigh. "It's nothing."

"And again, sorry about the accidental nudity."

She laughed against his shoulder. "Don't worry about it."

It was just an ordinary, innocent hug between old friends. No big deal.

Except it wasn't ordinary or innocent, because she couldn't help thinking about the body that lurked under Dylan's clothes—which she'd now glimpsed in the flesh—as it pressed up against hers.

Even after he let go of her and waved goodbye, the impression of his body lingered on hers, and she couldn't stop thinking about it.

She kept thinking about it all the way into work.

As soon as Brooke parked her car on campus, she pulled out her phone and texted Olivia.

I ACCIDENTALLY SAW DYLAN'S PENIS!!!

Not three seconds later, her phone rang.

"Oh my god!" Olivia screeched as soon as Brooke answered. "Tell me everything!"

"Are you at work already?" Olivia worked in an open-plan office in the renewable energy division of a large

53

aerospace company. The last thing Brooke wanted was all of Olivia's coworkers eavesdropping on this particular conversation.

"Nope, I'm still at home putting on my makeup. You've got five minutes to tell me everything before I have to get in the car."

"It was totally an accident." Brooke felt that it was important to establish that right off the bat.

Olivia made a scoffing noise. "I'm sure. He just accidentally happened to show you his crotch rocket."

Brooke described the incident and the circumstances that had led to it, and Olivia snorted with laughter.

"So he was basically just walking around your apartment fully nude? That doesn't sound like an accident."

"He thought I was asleep. If you'd seen his face—" Brooke squeezed her eyes shut at the memory. "It definitely was not intentional."

"So what's it like?"

"What?" Brooke asked, even though she knew precisely what Olivia was asking.

"His dangling participle."

Impressive was the answer that popped into Brooke's head. But it felt disloyal to tell Olivia that. If their roles were reversed, Brooke wouldn't want Dylan telling any of his friends what her body looked like. "None of your business," she replied primly.

"Come on. Has he got a half-pint wienie or a mighty man-hammer?"

"I hate you."

"Don't leave me hanging here. Get it? I said hanging, like his twig and berries."

Brooke couldn't help laughing. "Stop."

"Seriously though, is it pinkie-sized? Or more like a kielbasa?"

"I'm hanging up on you."

"Come on, you have to give me something. You're the one who texted me to talk about his penis in the first place."

Heat pooled in Brooke's stomach as she replayed the scene from this morning once again, and she bit her lip. "Let's just say he's a very lucky man and leave it at that."

"I knew it! I could tell just by looking at him. Those big hands he's got tell the tale. So how far down his thigh does it dangle? Does it reach his knees? Please tell me it reaches his knees."

Brooke exhaled another laugh. "You're ridiculous and I'm not having this conversation with you. In fact, this conversation never happened. You can never tell anyone what I told you, and when you meet Dylan you absolutely cannot let on that you know. Promise?"

"Of course I promise. Does this mean you're bringing him to Penny and Caleb's reception?"

"I think so. I mentioned it last night and he seemed game." He'd seemed more than game actually. Brooke's chest warmed as she remembered the look on his face when he'd told her he'd love to meet her friends.

"Excellent! I can't wait to see the famous Dylan in person."

"How was the wedding, by the way?" Olivia had texted her a couple photos over the weekend, and it looked like everything had gone off as planned.

"Beautiful. Perfect. Exactly how you'd expect."

"Did you cry?" Brooke asked, reaching across the seat for her laptop bag. "Did Penny cry?"

"I might have teared up a little," Olivia admitted. "Penny managed to look exquisitely misty without messing up her eye makeup. It was Caleb who cried like a baby."

"That's so sweet." Brooke got out of the car and locked it before setting out for the biology building.

"It was adorable. I love that guy."

"Did his parents show up?"

"Yeah. They were kind of weird. Didn't really talk to anyone much. Penny's mom tried to draw them out, but they mostly just kept to themselves."

Brooke nodded at a student she recognized as she walked past the campus coffee shop. "At least they didn't make a scene or ruin the wedding. I know Penny was worried about them upsetting Caleb."

"I don't think anything short of a natural disaster could have ruined that wedding for Caleb. He only had eyes for Penny the whole weekend."

"That's awesome. I can't wait to hear all about it in detail. Do you want to meet for lunch one day this week?"

"Sure. How about Wednesday? The usual place?"

"Sounds good." Brooke's paper was due Wednesday, but she planned to have it done the night before so she could send it first thing in the a.m. after one last review. By lunchtime, it would be out of her hands.

"Oh, and hey, Brooke?" Olivia said. "Try not to spend the rest of the day thinking about how much you want to ride Dylan's bone roller coaster, okay?"

"Oh my god! You're the worst. I really am hanging up now."

Olivia was still cackling when Brooke disconnected the call.

*

"Something's weird about you today," Tara said as she watched Brooke set up her laptop on one of the desks in their shared office. "Are you all right?"

Brooke reached up to touch her cheek. Was she still blushing from this morning? Quite possibly. Her skin felt feverish under her fingertips. "I think I might be coming down with something," she told Tara. "But it's nothing a little aversion therapy can't cure."

Tara rolled her desk chair closer, peering at Brooke. "Are you wearing makeup?"

"Maybe a little."

Tara's gaze narrowed. "Interesting."

"Is it though? Is it interesting?" Brooke tried to ignore Tara as she opened up the paper she needed to finish revising.

"My life's pretty dull," Tara said, shrugging as she spun her chair. "So I have to take my entertainment where I can get it."

"Glad I could spice things up for you."

Tara stopped spinning and stretched her legs out. She wore battered Doc Martens and loose-fitting men's jeans. "I do think it's intriguing that your boy toy is in town this week and you just happen to show up today wearing makeup, which you almost never do."

"He's not my—" Brooke couldn't even bring herself to say the words *boy toy* in relation to Dylan. "He's just an old friend."

"So you don't deny you're wearing makeup for him."

"Maybe I'm wearing makeup for myself. Who's to say?"

Tara snorted. "You just keep telling yourself that, mate. But enough about your boring lack of a sex life. I have goss."

Brooke glanced over as she tapped the arrow key to scroll through her paper. "Do tell." She was always up for some juicy departmental gossip, and Tara always seemed to have the scoop.

"It appears that yesterday, our man Professor McNamara caught two undergrads having sex on a lab bench."

Brooke's mouth fell open. "*Ew*. No. Seriously?"

"Seriously unhygienic, is what it is," Tara agreed. "Do you think they were wearing PPE?"

Brooke chuckled at the image of two students in personal protective equipment trying to get their rocks off. "I certainly hope so, for their own protection and for the protection of the lab environment. What'd Dr. McNamara do?"

"Told 'em to put their trousers back on and get the hell out. Apparently they were mid-thrust. He was properly mortified."

"Gross." Brooke gave a little shudder. "Can you imagine?"

"Unfortunately, I can, and I wish I couldn't. I need to scrub my brain with Betadine."

"Undergrads are animals. Who was it, anyway?" If it was any of *her* students behaving like that, she wanted to know so she could treat them with the appropriate amount of disdain and possibly assign an additional lesson on lab hygiene.

"He wouldn't say."

"He's not reporting them?" Brooke couldn't imagine them just being allowed to get away with that sort of behavior without any repercussions.

Tara shrugged as she studied her fingernails. "Dunno. If he is, he's not saying either way. Wonder if they'll show their faces at the picnic this weekend." She looked up at Brooke.

"Hey, do you think we'll be able to guess who it was by watching how McNamara interacts with the undergrads?"

"Oh shit." Brooke smacked her hand against her forehead. The departmental picnic was *this* weekend.

"What's the matter?" Tara asked.

"The picnic. I forgot all about it."

"Oops. Is your man still going to be in town Saturday?"

"Yeah, it's his last full day in town."

"Bring him." Tara was grinning. "That way I can gaze upon his sexiness for myself."

"Don't be weird," Brooke said, fighting a smile.

Tara laid a dramatic hand across her heart as if she was mortally wounded. "Moi? Never."

Brooke leaned back in her chair with a sigh. "I'm already dragging him to a wedding with me that night. I don't want to bore him to tears by forcing him to socialize with a bunch of biologists. Plus I'm already leaving him on his own most of the week while I try to finish up that paper."

"How's that going?" Tara asked, scraping a flake of green polish off her thumbnail. "You going to make the deadline? It's Wednesday, yeah?"

"I should be fine." Brooke only had a few sections left to edit, and then her conclusion to rework. "Thanks for reading it over. Your comments were really helpful."

"Bah." Tara waved her hand like it was nothing. "Of course you'll be fine. You're always perfect at everything, aren't you?"

"Not as perfect as Monica Speight," Brooke replied, only sort of joking.

"Whatevs." Tara rolled her eyes. "You need to let the Monica thing go. It's not healthy."

"I'll let the Monica thing go when you let your weird feud with Mathias go," Brooke fired back.

Tara affected an expression of mock offense. "How dare you? Mathias is my sworn enemy and I will not rest until he has met his demise by my hand." She hopped up from her chair. "Right. I'm off to run some samples. Good luck with your revisions."

After Tara went next door to the lab, Brooke threw herself into work. She had a little over an hour until class, which was enough time to incorporate the last of the comments she'd gotten. Once that was done, it was just a matter of cleaning up a few troublesome sections, rewriting the conclusion, and doing some final polishing on the whole manuscript.

The rest of the day passed uneventfully. Brooke gave the exam to her intro class, went to lunch with Tara, and made good progress on her edits in the afternoon. She made so much progress, in fact, that she decided to take a break from her paper and get a head start on grading exams.

Although technically she could have just gone home, she found herself reluctant to face Dylan again after the penis incident that morning.

Yes, fine, she was a coward.

When Dylan texted her at six o'clock, Brooke was cross-eyed from grading and nearly a third of the way through the stack.

> **Dylan:** I'm done!
> **Brooke:** How'd it go?
> **Dylan:** Fine, but I'm starving. Wanna help me eat 100 pizzas?

Brooke looked at the clock, and then at the stack of ungraded exams sitting next to her. She still felt a tug of dread at the thought of facing Dylan, but he was her guest, not to mention a friend she didn't get to see very often. She couldn't just leave him to eat his weight in pizza alone at her apartment. Time to nut up and get this over with.

Brooke: *Order the pizzas and I'll be home as soon as I can. Menu's on the fridge.*

Chapter Six

Brooke stayed on campus working for another half hour, figuring she might as well wait until rush-hour traffic died down a little. No sense leaving right away only to spend an extra twenty minutes in her car at a dead standstill.

It was a perfectly good excuse for dawdling that had nothing whatsoever to do with her nervousness at facing Dylan again.

When she finally let herself into the apartment a little after seven, she found him kicked back on her couch with a pair of pizza boxes and a six-pack of beer on the coffee table in front of him. He'd changed into his sweatpants and glasses already, and it struck her as profoundly unfair that it somehow made him even more attractive.

"Hey!" He got up to greet her, wiping his hands on a napkin. She could tell he was tired from the boneless way he moved and the fact that his smile beamed with only seventy-five percent of its usual wattage.

Brooke hung her bag on the hook by the door. "Sorry I'm so late."

"No worries. I already set out a plate for you, and there's more beer in the fridge so don't worry about running out."

When she turned around, he threw his arms open and hugged her so hard he lifted her off the ground a little. "Wow, you sure give a lot of hugs." Not that she was complaining. Dylan's hugs were amazing. "And I see you've already made a solid start on the beer."

She could smell the alcohol on his breath, and there were three empty bottles lined up on the table. Which likely explained the enthusiastic greeting.

Dylan handed her a beer when she followed him over to the couch. "You still like veggie pizza, right? I got you one to go with my meat lover's."

"Veggie's great."

The pizza was just the way she liked it: that sweet spot halfway between hot and cold where the cheese didn't try to slide off and the crust had gained some structural integrity. Brooke filled her plate and collapsed on the couch next to Dylan.

"Long day?" he asked, giving her a sideways look.

"Long enough," she said around a mouthful of pizza. She finished chewing and swallowed. "How about you? How was the shoot?"

Leaning forward, he snagged his beer off the table. "Not too bad. I'm glad to be done and off for the rest of the week though." He took a drink and pushed a box toward her on the coffee table. "There's wings too."

"Extra hot?" Brooke asked.

"Always."

She helped herself to a chicken wing. "There's more hot sauce in the pantry if you want it, 'cause I know you do." They were both addicted to the stuff. Growing up in

Louisiana had given them a taste for it, as well as a long-standing tradition of trying to outdo each other.

"Aw, yes. You know me too well." Dylan hopped up and headed to the kitchen to check out the pantry. "Only three kinds of hot sauce, Brooke? You're falling down on the job in your old age."

"Hey!" she protested. "I'm three months younger than you!"

"Hot damn, you've got Tiger Sauce!" he exclaimed from the pantry.

"Of course."

He returned to the couch with all three bottles and proceeded to slather a chicken wing with Tiger Sauce, which had been their old standby growing up. "Mmmm," he sighed after he'd taken a bite. "Tastes just like home."

"The pizza's delicious," Brooke said around a mouthful of cheesy crust. "Thanks for ordering it."

Dylan acknowledged her gratitude with a wave of his hand as he reached for another chicken wing and drenched it in hot sauce. He'd finished about three-quarters of the meat pizza already and wasn't showing any signs of slowing down. He seemed determined to make up his calorie deficit with a vengeance.

"Do you always eat like this after a water cut?" Brooke asked.

"God, no," he said as he licked hot sauce off his fingers in a way that made her feel like she was watching a porno. It was hard not to notice how long his fingers were, and what a great mouth he had. Or imagine how he'd look licking something other than his fingers. "My agent would freak if he could see me right now," Dylan went on, shaking his head as he reached for another chicken wing. "He's always on my case about everything I'm eating and drinking because he's afraid I'll get fat."

"You? Fat? Never."

Dylan had always been a skinny kid. No matter how much he ate, the calories had burned away. Especially back when he was running track.

He gestured at himself. "You think all this happens by itself? I have to work 24/7 to maintain this bod."

"Well, you're doing an excellent job. Congrats."

He laughed like he was flattered, but she saw his cheeks pink just before he ducked his head. "Thanks?" He said it like someone who wasn't used to receiving compliments. Which seemed weird, given how attractive he was and what he did for a living, but maybe that was the problem. Maybe all he ever heard were critiques of his appearance. Maybe that was what happened when you turned your looks into your job.

"Feel free to help me with this veggie pizza too," she offered.

"I just might take you up on that."

"Are you still a runner?" she asked as she watched him reach for a slice of veggie pizza.

"Yeah, but mostly on the treadmill these days. It's part of my cardio. Thirty minutes on the treadmill four days a week, boxing intervals the other three, and bodybuilding five days a week."

"Wow. That's a lot of time in the gym." Brooke had been to the gym on campus exactly two times, a year apart, during the first week of January. So much for New Year's resolutions. Now she didn't bother lying to herself and just embraced her sessile bivalve lifestyle.

"Like I said, it's a 24/7 job looking like this."

"You're not overdoing it, are you? Are you sure you're getting enough calories to maintain that activity level? I mean, not tonight, but in general?"

"I've got a nutritionist and a trainer working together to plan my program. Every calorie I consume is calculated to balance the calories I burn."

"Yeah, but are they looking out for your health or just your physique?" she asked, frowning. "Seems like a lot of those celebrity trainers are quacks."

Dylan shook his head, throwing her a sideways smile. "I'm not a celebrity, but thanks. And they're both qualified professionals who are careful with their programming. I vetted them myself, so I can promise you they're not quacks. Although I have encountered more than a few that were."

Brooke realized it might sound like she was questioning his ability to take care of himself. She didn't want to give him a complex with her mother-henning. "I'm sorry. I shouldn't be second-guessing you. You know what you're doing. I just worry about you. You hear so many stories about the modeling industry, and I don't know if any of it's true but it scares me sometimes to think of you mixed up with all of that."

His eyes met hers and held. "You don't have to worry about me, okay? I'm not gonna get an eating disorder or get addicted to speed or anything like that."

"That happens in your business though, right?" She couldn't help fretting. Dylan triggered all her protective instincts.

"It happens some, but it's not going to happen to me," he said, soft and patient like he'd always been with her. He reached across the couch and squeezed her hand. "I promise. But it's nice to know you care."

Goose bumps shimmied up her arm as his calluses scraped over her knuckles. "Still sounds pretty miserable," she said, squeezing his hand back. "I don't know how you stand it."

He let go and reached for another bottle of hot sauce. "It's a living, I guess." He squinted at the label, then shrugged and twisted it open. "I don't know how you deal with whale barf or whatever—"

"Earwax."

"Right. Earwax." He gave a theatrical shudder as he coated another chicken wing in hot sauce. "Nasty. Who even knew whales had ears?"

Brooke smiled as she tipped back the last of her beer. "It's a living, I guess." It didn't pay as well as Dylan's chosen career, but she was doing what she'd always dreamed of doing. She wasn't certain he could say the same thing.

"You know, I still haven't seen this alleged cat of yours." He tasted his hot-sauce-doused chicken wing thoughtfully, like he was judging a Food Network competition show. "I'm starting to doubt you even have a cat. I think you might be making him up."

"He exists," Brooke assured him. "He's just crouched in some secret hidey-hole waiting for you to fall asleep so he can sneak out and rub his face all over your shoes in the middle of the night."

"Freaky," Dylan said around a mouthful of chicken wing.

"That's just how he rolls."

"I'm gonna win him over before I leave here. I'm determined."

"Good luck with that." Brooke leaned forward to trade her

empty beer bottle for another piece of pizza. "Do you have any pets back in New York? You've never mentioned any."

"Naw." Dylan was already fixing himself another chicken wing.

She popped an errant mushroom in her mouth. "Why not? You're such an animal lover, and you always had lots of pets growing up."

He shrugged. "I travel too much. It wouldn't be fair to them."

"You could always get a pet sitter."

He seemed to consider this. "Maybe one day, when things slow down a little."

She helped herself to a second beer from the six-pack to wash down her pizza. "It's going well, then? Seems like you're in a lot of demand." She was dying to know how much money he actually made, but didn't want to ask.

"Yeah, can you believe it?" He took the beer bottle from her and twisted the cap off before handing it back. "Whenever I start to get too stressed I have to remind myself how lucky I am. Things are going better than I ever dreamed they would."

She gave him a meaningful look as she sat back on the couch, juggling her beer and slice of pizza. "You're awesome at everything you've ever done, so I'm not surprised one bit that you're a raging success. It's not luck, it's brains and talent and hard work."

He appeared unconvinced. "Maybe to some extent, but success in this business is mostly about luck. It's all about having the right look at the right time and meeting the right people."

She glared at him over her pizza. "And impressing those

people you meet with your personality and professionalism, and working your ass off to maintain the peak of physical perfection, not to mention keeping the vultures at bay."

"I guess, yeah." It wasn't exactly the resounding agreement she'd hoped her pep talk would inspire.

"Are you not happy?" she asked, cocking her head. "You don't sound super happy for someone who's doing so well."

"I'm fine." He'd been using the word fine a lot, and the more he said it, the less Brooke believed it.

She nudged him with her knee. "Tell the truth. Don't give me any more of that 'I'm fine' crap."

He sighed. "I think I'm just a little burned out. You know how it is when something you enjoy turns into your job and then it starts to feel like work and becomes this source of stress in your life?"

"I think so." She'd never had a full-time job outside academia, but it sounded a little like the transition from undergrad to grad school, which was basically going from "I enjoy studying this subject and would like to spend more time doing it" to "I now eat, sleep, live, and breathe this subject and the work never ends and oh my god what have I done to myself?"

"That's why I wanted to take a few extra days and just hang out here. Get away from the whole scene and recharge. Try to get some perspective."

She watched him thoughtfully as she chewed. "I can understand that."

He gave a little head shake to signal the end of the conversation before changing the subject. "So tell me about this 'sort of' wedding reception thing we're going to. Who's the lucky couple?"

"Penny and Caleb," Brooke said as she nibbled at her pizza. "She's a chemical engineer who works as a patent examiner, and Caleb is finishing up his master's in occupational therapy."

Dylan grinned at her. "So they're both super smart like you. Got it. How'd you meet them?"

"Penny's friends with my college roommate Olivia." Brooke leaned forward and set her empty plate on the coffee table. "She's Penny's maid of honor, so she was at the wedding in Virginia this weekend. She said it was beautiful."

"Is this shindig like a cocktail party or a full-on wedding reception with dinner and music and dancing?" he asked.

"There will be assorted hors d'oeuvres and drinks in addition to a wedding cake." Brooke raised her beer bottle and took a swig. "There will also be a band, apparently, that a friend of Penny's is in, so I assume there will be at least some dancing."

Dylan nodded, smiling as his eyes caught hers. "Cool. I love dancing."

"I remember."

And suddenly Brooke was thinking back to prom night, which was the last time she'd danced with Dylan. How he'd danced every slow dance with her, and how safe and happy she'd felt wrapped up in his arms. The feel of his hands on her waist, the smell of his cologne, the warmth of his body against hers.

And then after, in the limo, when he'd kissed her. How sweet he'd tasted, and how soft and tender his lips had felt.

How would he taste now?

Like hot sauce, dummy. Stop thinking about kissing him or you're gonna get burned.

"Sounds like it's going to be a fun night," Dylan said, getting up to clear away their empty beer bottles.

"I hope so," Brooke agreed, pressing the cool glass of her beer bottle against her over-warm cheek.

"You want another beer?" he asked from the kitchen.

"No thanks. I've got work tomorrow." Two was her limit on a weeknight. Also, it seemed like an extra-bad idea to let herself get drunk around Dylan. The last time they'd been drunk together, he'd kissed her, and she'd enjoyed it a lot more than he had.

She was already having too many feelings about him today. If she let herself go, she might do something insane like climb into his lap and try to kiss him again.

He came back with a fresh beer from the fridge. His fifth, by Brooke's count. The guy could really put them away when he decided to cut loose. Although it sounded like he'd more than earned a little indulgence.

As he walked back to the couch, a hint of movement under his gray sweatpants caught Brooke's attention and reminded her of the eyeful she'd gotten that morning. Embarrassed, she quickly averted her eyes. "It turns out our departmental picnic is also this Saturday, and I totally forgot about it. But I think I'm gonna skip it."

He looked over at her. "Why?"

She gazed at him through her lashes and told the truth. "I'd rather spend the weekend with you."

The corner of his mouth twitched. "Are you allowed to bring a guest to the picnic?"

"Well, yeah. But it'll be super boring, and I'm already dragging you to Penny's reception that night. I figured we'd want to do something more fun during the day."

He bumped his knee against hers. "You should go. I'll go with you and charm all your colleagues."

She smiled at the thought. "I have no doubt you could."

"At least I'm good for one thing." He gave a disdainful head shake. "Gotta keep 'em dazzled so they don't notice I can't hold up my end of the conversation."

"Hey." She hated hearing him talk about himself like that. "You're just as smart as anyone I know, mister."

He snorted. "My SAT scores would beg to differ."

"You had untreated ADHD issues. And who gives a shit about the SAT? Our class valedictorian flunked out of LSU his freshman year because he couldn't handle the stress. High SAT scores are not an accurate predictor of professional success."

Dylan reached for the third bottle of hot sauce, changing the subject again. "What's this one? You haven't even opened it."

"Too afraid." She'd picked it up at a farmers' market because she'd liked the name: El Chupacabra.

"You think it's that bad?" Dylan asked, grinning as he peeled off the plastic seal around the cap.

"I don't know. Try it."

He squinted at the label through his glasses. "It says it's made with seven of the world's hottest peppers."

Brooke couldn't resist goading him. "What are you? Chicken? I've never seen Dylan Price back down from a hot sauce challenge."

He twisted the cap off the bottle and shot her a taunting look. "I'll do it if you do it."

"Fine," she agreed, knowing she was going to regret it.

"There you go." He held up his fist for a pound and

explode, grinning when Brooke supplied it. "Solidarity. That's friendship." He doused a chicken wing with El Chupacabra sauce and passed it to her. "Here you go. Here's your wing."

She examined it warily while he doctored another one for himself. The smell was already burning her nasal passages. This was definitely going to hurt.

"You got yours?" she asked, realizing too late that she didn't have any milk in the fridge that wasn't expired. Probably should have thought of that before she agreed to this.

"I'm ready," Dylan said. "You ready?"

Brooke nodded, steeling herself for the pain. "Let's do this."

"We'll do it together. On three. One, two, three, go!"

They both bit into their wings. It wasn't as bad as Brooke had been expecting. Not at first, anyway. Then it started to get hotter. A lot hotter.

"Okay," Dylan said, nodding as he licked his lips. "All right. There it is."

"Yep. Here it comes," Brooke agreed, wincing as she swallowed. The heat had begun to radiate from her mouth to her whole face, and the pain was creeping up into her sinuses. El Chupacabra didn't disappoint.

"I can feel it." Dylan waved his hand in front of his mouth. "Oh man. That's . . . wow."

"Ugh, I'm snotting!" Brooke reached for a napkin and blew her nose.

Dylan clutched his stomach, laughing and crying at once. "Oh god, it's going into my brain."

His laughter set Brooke off and she let out a painful snort. They always did this to each other—set each other off, ramped each other up, fed off each other's energy.

73

Brooke held her hand out in front of her. "I'm literally shaking."

"I can't stop crying," Dylan wheezed as his whole body shook with laughter.

"Here, take a napkin." She handed him a fresh one from the table. "Don't touch your eyes," she warned him as he blotted his face.

"I think it's too late." Both his eyes were red and streaming. "Either that or I'm going blind from the pain." He took off his glasses and wiped his eyes with the backs of his hands.

"Why do we do this to ourselves?" She hadn't laughed this hard in ages, and it felt cathartic. She needed Dylan around all the time to make sure she belly-laughed regularly.

"Because it's fun. Obviously."

The absurdity set her off again and she doubled over with a fresh bout of laughter, gasping for breath.

Dylan draped his arm around her shoulders. "You okay? You gonna live?" She nodded, and he pulled her against him. "Hang in there."

Brooke curled into him, still laughing and crying, but also enjoying the feeling of being cradled against his chest. "Yep. I'm good. I've got this."

"That's my girl."

Even through the pain haze, she felt a thrill at being called his girl.

Too much of a thrill.

She pushed off him and sat up. "I'm feeling better. Are you feeling better?"

He nodded, still dabbing at his nose with a napkin. "I think it's receding. I might live. I think my taste buds are goners though. They're never coming back from this."

He shouldn't be so attractive with his face bright red and sweaty and his nose running, dammit. Seeing him like this should be the ultimate boner killer, but somehow it just made her want him even more.

She scooted away from him and reached for a fresh napkin from the stack. "Have another napkin."

"Thanks." He used it to wipe his eyes, and reached for his beer.

"No, don't drink beer!" she warned him too late.

He winced in pain. "Ow. Fuck. That was a mistake."

She took the beer away from him and gave him a shove with her shoulder. "You should know better." They were both laughing again.

"I do know better. I don't know what I was thinking."

"Have some more pizza. The cheese will help."

"Will it?" He gave her a skeptical look.

"I don't know. It's got milk in it."

"If you say so, I'm doing it." He grinned at her as he scooped up a piece of now-cold veggie pizza.

Dylan had always done everything she said. No matter what. Even if he knew it was a prank, he still willingly went along with it, figuring the fun would be worth it. His trust in her had always been complete. He'd probably take a bullet for her if she asked.

It scared her a little to think about it. That was too much responsibility. What if she wasn't worthy of that level of loyalty?

"You know, I think it is helping," he said as he munched on cold pizza. "You're a genius."

Brooke's eyes skated away from him and settled on a small

brown shape peeking out at them from the hall leading to the bedroom.

Her hand shot out and grabbed Dylan's knee. "Oh shit. Don't move."

"What's wrong?" His eyes widened and he froze mid-bite of pizza. "Oh my god, is there a spider? You know how much I hate spiders."

"Calm down," Brooke said in a low, steady monotone. "It's not a spider. Murderface just came into the living room. Don't look!" she hissed when Dylan started to swivel his head. "You'll scare him off. Turn your head really slowly so he doesn't startle."

He did as instructed and frowned. "I can't see shit."

His glasses were still on the coffee table. Brooke handed them to him.

He slipped them on and broke into a grin. "Oh wow, look at that. He really does have a murder face."

"I know, right? That's my angry, fluffy guy." She loved that stupid cat. It had been love at first sight when she'd spotted him at the adoption event. Who could resist a face perpetually that irate?

Dylan leaned forward and carefully extended his hand toward the skittish feline. "Hey there, buddy."

At the movement, Murderface froze, his eyes narrowing in his flat, furious little cat face.

"It's okay," Dylan said softly. "I'm not gonna hurt ya, kitty. Let's be friends."

Murderface crouched down, eying Dylan distrustfully. Then he coughed. Followed by a retching sound.

"Oh great." Sighing, Brooke got to her feet and swooped

up the cat, carrying him to the laminate floor of the kitchen before he could leave a stain on her carpet.

"So does vomiting signal trust or is it a commentary on his feelings about me?" Dylan called out, laughing.

Brooke tore off a sheet of paper towel as Murderface spat up a hairball. "Your guess is as good as mine."

His mission apparently accomplished, the cat ran back toward the bedroom, leaving Brooke to clean up his mess, as per usual.

"I think I've been dissed," Dylan said when she came back into the living room. "I just got served a burn notice by a cat."

Brooke snorted as she flopped onto the couch. "He served something all right."

"This is a good reason not to get a pet. Not a huge fan of cleaning up vomit."

"Is anyone? It's not like anybody thinks, 'Hey, you know what I really love? Vomit. I should get a pet so I can clean up vomit all the time!'"

"Fair point. Although coming from the girl who plays with whale earwax for a living, it loses some of its power." Dylan leaned forward and flipped the lids of the pizza boxes up. "One piece left. It's all you, bro."

Brooke shook her head. "You should take it. You're the guest." She already felt like she was going to burst. Full as a tick, as her grandma used to say. It was a mystery how Dylan had put so much food away.

"No, you should have it because you're more . . ," He paused, like he was searching for the right word. "Wonderful," he finished, looking at her like she was some rare and precious gem.

Her heart squeezed in her chest and she swallowed, flustered by his sweetness, but also a little concerned about his negative self-image. This wasn't the first time tonight he'd seemed to put himself down.

The thing was, this wasn't new behavior for him. Beneath his surface veneer of confidence and ease, Dylan had always been overly modest, bordering on having low self-esteem.

Brooke blamed his mother for it. Mrs. Price was a real piece of work. For years, Brooke had watched her aim passive-aggressive barbs at her son, subtly cutting him down and undermining his self-worth. She'd convinced him he was stupid because he struggled in school, when she could have been getting him the help he needed instead. Once he hit puberty, she started riding him about his appearance too, practically bullying him into putting more effort into his looks by convincing him it was all he was good for.

It's a good thing you're so handsome, Brooke remembered his mom telling him more than once. *You'd be in trouble if you had to rely on your brains to get ahead*. Mrs. Price was always saying stuff like that to him. Was it any wonder he'd internalized the idea that he was dumb and only useful for his looks?

"How's your mom these days?" Brooke asked, trying not to sound too sour. "She must be loving all this success you're having."

It was Dylan's mom who'd pushed him toward modeling and managed the Instagram account that helped him get his first agent. Brooke was convinced she'd only done it for the secondhand attention she derived from his growing popularity. As his social media presence started to take off, his mom had blossomed into a full-fledged stage mother, pursuing product endorsements and partnerships with other online influencers, and taking all the credit for Dylan's success.

Until he caught the attention of one of the big New York agencies. When he was only twenty-one, he was offered a contract that paid well enough for him to quit his job as a line cook and leave Baton Rouge and his mom behind.

Brooke figured it had to smart a little, that he'd grown so successful he didn't need his mother running his life for him anymore. He'd even gotten his own social media manager to take over his Instagram account, leaving his mother with no role to play in his professional life, and no way to bask in his reflected glory except from afar.

Dylan rolled his eyes. "She loves the check I send home every month, that's for sure."

"You're still sending them money?"

"Dad's company laid him off last year. He got a new job selling power washing services, but it pays a lot less than he was making before."

"I'm sorry."

Dylan shrugged. "It happens. That's why I put half of every paycheck into savings. I don't want to be dependent on anyone when I get older. This modeling gig won't last forever, so I've got to plan for the future."

Brooke was impressed. If she put half her paycheck into savings, she wouldn't have enough left to pay her rent. She was lucky her grandmother had set up a college fund for her. Most of her undergrad expenses had been covered by scholarships, so she still had a decent chunk left to subsidize her living expenses while she finished grad school. It was the only reason she could afford to have her own place without having to deal with roommates.

"Do your parents come up to visit you in New York much?" she asked Dylan.

He leaned back and rubbed his stomach, exposing an alluring strip of skin that Brooke quickly looked away from. "My dad did once, about a year after I moved up there. I got my parents tickets to *Wicked*, and my mom dragged him through every store in Times Square. He hated every second of it, and hasn't been back since."

Dylan's father was the prototypical distant dad. Brooke had only interacted with him a handful of times, even though she'd been in and out of his house every day when she was growing up. He was always either at work or holed up in his den with the TV tuned to one of the sports channels. Mr. Price's den had been strictly off-limits to the kids, and on the rare occasions he ventured out, he hardly spoke at all.

"My mom used to come up to visit about once a year," Dylan said, rubbing his palms on his thighs. "But she hasn't been in a while. Which is honestly fine with me. It's stressful having to entertain her." His eyes slid over to Brooke. "You been home to see your folks lately?"

She looked away. "Nope."

Dylan knew things were strained between her and her parents, but he didn't know why. Every time he'd tried to bring up the subject, she'd been vague and evasive, until eventually he'd gotten the message and stopped asking.

"So . . ." he started hesitantly. "I wasn't sure you wanted to talk about it, but I've been wanting to ask how your dad's chemo is going."

Brooke froze. Very slowly, she turned to look at Dylan. "My dad's what?"

"My mom told me he's having chemotherapy for his

prostate cancer. Sorry if it was supposed to be a secret." He paused, frowning at what he must have seen in her expression. "You knew, didn't you?"

Brooke didn't know what to say.

She had no words. None.

Because this was the first she'd heard about her dad having cancer or undergoing chemo.

Chapter Seven

Brooke stood up. She didn't know what to do with herself, but she couldn't sit still so she started pacing across the living room.

"Fuck, Brooke, I'm so sorry." Dylan looked stricken. "I didn't mean to blindside you. I assumed you knew."

She snorted derisively. "Yeah, that would be the logical assumption, wouldn't it? You'd think someone would have told me if my dad was having chemo." She paced over to the coffee table and picked up Dylan's beer. There was only a little left, but she swigged it all down.

This was too much to process. A whole spectrum of emotions battled for dominance, and she didn't know which one should hold dominion. There was a lot of anger—a *lot* of anger—accompanied by a side dish of confusion and a soup-çon of disbelief. *That* was quickly followed by a wave of righteous indignation. Because *of course* they'd kept this from her. Of course they had.

Brooke hadn't talked to her dad in years, but her mom called every few weeks to keep up the appearance of a relationship. Somehow, weirdly, Brooke's dad was never able to come to the phone, although her mom always made up some excuse why not. For eight years now, her mom had been making excuses, trying to pretend everything was fine and there was nothing at all out of the ordinary about the fact that Brooke's dad barely even acknowledged her existence.

The last time she'd talked to her mom must have been about two weeks ago, and Brooke had specifically asked how her dad was. She knew she had, because she always asked—although she had no idea why she bothered.

She couldn't remember her mom's exact words, but they sure as hell hadn't included any mention of cancer. She would have fucking remembered that. She was certain her mom had given her usual vague answer about Dad being fine and his work being fine and everything being fine, because god forbid anyone in this family tell the truth or admit to any shortcomings. The fucking sky might fall if they allowed that to happen.

"Okay, but you knew about the cancer at least," Dylan said, watching her. "Right?"

Brooke didn't say anything.

"Please tell me you knew about that, Brooke. Jesus."

"When did you find out about it?" she demanded.

He ran a hand through his hair. "My mom told me . . . it must have been a month ago? I assume she talked to your mom."

"So Mom's telling the neighbors about my dad's cancer. She's just not telling me. That's great. That's awesome." Brooke had learned a long time ago not to expect anything from her father. But her mother should have told her. She'd thought they at least had that much of a relationship. But apparently even that was an illusion.

"I don't understand how things have gotten so bad

between you and your parents," Dylan said. "Y'all always used to be so close. I remember coming over for dinner and seeing you all together, and being envious because your family seemed so happy and normal compared to mine."

"Looks can be deceiving," Brooke said.

She'd never told Dylan about her "trouble" their senior year. For a whole hot minute, she'd considered asking him to drive her home from the clinic, knowing he'd do anything she asked. But she'd quickly thought better of it. He would have felt obligated to help—and maybe give Kyle a piece of his mind as well—and Brooke hadn't wanted to put Dylan in that position.

Once the problem had been taken care of, she'd just wanted to move on with her life. At the time, Dylan had assumed Brooke was upset about her breakup with Kyle, and she hadn't seen any reason to tell him about the rest of it. The fewer people who knew the truth, the easier it was to move on. That was what she'd told herself, anyway.

But really she'd been embarrassed to admit she'd made such a dumb mistake. Dylan had always treated her like she was so smart and accomplished, and she liked that he thought of her that way. She hadn't wanted to shatter his illusions.

There was also maybe a small part of her that had been afraid to tell Dylan. It was irrational, but her relationship with every other person who knew the truth had been irrevocably damaged. She hadn't wanted to risk losing Dylan too.

"What can I do?" he asked, watching her with concern.

"Nothing."

"I feel terrible. If I'd known you didn't know—"

"It's not your fault."

"Do you want to call home?"

"It's almost midnight in Baton Rouge. I can't call tonight." Brooke didn't know what she'd say, anyway. It was going to take some time to process this before she was ready to confront her mom.

Dylan got up and came over to her. "Come here." His arms wrapped her up and she sagged against him. "I'm sorry," he said as his hands stroked up and down her back. "I'm sorry your dad's sick, and I'm sorry your parents didn't tell you. I'm sorry they haven't been there for you the way you needed them to be. It sucks and you deserve better."

Brooke felt her eyes well with tears and disengaged herself from Dylan's arms. She couldn't afford to give in to her emotions right now or she would lose it all over him. The last thing she intended to do was cry over her father.

She started to pace again, but her legs felt too wobbly, so she dropped down on the couch instead.

Dylan sat down next to her. "I know you don't like to talk about heavy shit, but it might help."

Her shoulders twitched. "It's ancient history."

"Not if it's affecting you right now, it's not."

She hunched forward and rubbed her head. Maybe he was right. There wasn't any reason not to tell him at this point. Keeping a secret only gave it more power. She'd made peace with her choice a long time ago, and she refused to be ashamed of it.

Straightening her spine, she stared straight ahead as she spoke in a detached monotone. "There's not really that much to tell. I got pregnant, and I got an abortion. My dad never forgave me. That's the end."

She refused to look at Dylan. Even though she knew in

her heart he would never judge her for her choice, she couldn't entirely dispel the fear of his disapproval.

He laid his hand on top of hers. "When?"

"Senior year of high school." Against her will, her eyes darted to his face.

The only emotion he showed was surprise—which morphed into anger as he put two and two together. "Who was it? Was it Kyle?"

She nodded and looked away.

His fingers clenched around hers. "When? Was it when you broke up? Was it *why* you broke up?"

She bit her lip and nodded again.

"Jesus. Why didn't you tell me about any of this?" Beneath the outrage, there was an unmistakable tinge of hurt in his tone.

"You had a girlfriend, remember?" It felt like a weak excuse now, but at the time it had seemed to matter a lot. High school was a different world. "She definitely would not have appreciated me dumping my unwanted pregnancy in her boyfriend's lap."

"You have no idea how few shits I would have given about *her* feelings in that situation. I didn't care about her the way—" He stopped abruptly and Brooke turned to look at him. His eyes skated away from hers. "I can barely even remember her name."

Brooke remembered her name. It was Stephanie. She remembered watching them hold hands in the hall and feeling—not jealousy, exactly. More like protectiveness.

She shook her head. "The last thing you needed was to get dragged into my mess. People might have thought it was yours."

"I wouldn't have cared about that."

Her eyes locked on his. "*I* would have. I couldn't do that to you."

"So that dickstain Kyle got you pregnant and then dumped you?" The words came out in a growl that matched Dylan's body language, which resembled a big cat poised to attack.

"I was an equal and willing participant in the first part, but yeah, he couldn't get away from me fast enough once he found out I was pregnant."

She'd expected Kyle to be shocked, upset, scared even—all the same emotions she had about it. But he'd responded with anger. Like it was something *she'd* done to *him* instead of something they'd done together. He'd even accused her of trying to ruin his life before demanding she "get rid of it."

A baby hadn't been in Brooke's plans any more than it was in Kyle's, and she was in no way prepared to be a mother at the age of seventeen. But she'd deeply resented the implication that the whole situation was her fault, when he'd been an equal partner in the decision-making process.

Only after she'd not-so-gently reminded him he was fifty percent responsible had he reluctantly agreed to pay for half the abortion—but only so long as she swore never to tell anyone. He'd absolutely refused to go with her to the clinic, however, which required her to be accompanied by someone who could drive her home after the procedure.

Which was how she'd ended up asking her mother to do it.

"What a raging asshole," Dylan growled. "And then he went and said all that shit about you sleeping around."

"That was a lie," Brooke responded reflexively. Not that it mattered at this point. Ancient history indeed.

She'd been so stupidly in love with Kyle. So naive. So blind to the kind of person he really was. Like any idiot kid in the throes of first love, she'd thought they'd be together forever. They'd both been planning to go to LSU, so they could stay together through college. After that, she'd assumed they'd get married. Her first and only boyfriend.

What a joke.

Somehow, Dylan's eyes managed to be both hard and compassionate at once. "I know it was a lie and I know why he said it. He was covering his tracks in case anyone found out. Laying the groundwork to claim it wasn't his. God." He shook his head as his face twisted in fury. "I mean, I knew he sucked, but I didn't realize how much or I would have punched him harder."

Brooke blinked at him. "I'm sorry, you what? You *punched* him?"

"Yeah." Dylan winced a little, as if he was embarrassed. "I heard him running his mouth off about you at one of Brian Boudreaux's parties, and I may have laid him out on the ground."

"I can't believe you did that." She'd never known Dylan to get into a fight or even lose his temper. He was one of the gentlest people she knew. "Is that why he kept his distance from us at prom?"

"Probably."

She squeezed his hand. "My champion."

The hurt returned to his eyes. "I wish you'd told me. I would have helped you."

"I know." Her eyes lowered to where their fingers were interlocked. "I always knew if worst came to worst I could turn to you." She couldn't remember feeling that certainty with anyone since, but she remembered feeling it at the time.

Her life might have been easier if she had turned to Dylan in her hour of need back then, instead of her family, but it also would have been a lie. She would have been pretending to be part of a happy family that wasn't real, because as soon as she'd needed them they were nowhere to be found. At least this way she knew the truth of who they were.

Dylan's thumb stroked over her knuckles. "So I guess you told your parents, and they didn't take it well?"

"I told my mom and she told my dad. He basically never spoke to me again. It was like—it was like I didn't even exist to him anymore. I was so tainted in his eyes, he wouldn't even look at me."

To say her mother was upset and disappointed would be an understatement. She hadn't yelled, because her mother never yelled, although she'd cried a lot. But she'd gone along with it. Brooke had to give her that much credit.

When it became clear Brooke wasn't going to change her mind, that she'd go through with it on her own if she had to, her mother had driven her to the appointment and sat stoically in the clinic waiting room while the doctor scraped the wayward cells out of Brooke's uterus. Then her mother had driven her home and told Brooke's father what they'd done that night when he got home from work. And things had never been the same between them.

Brooke remembered lying in bed and hearing the sound of her parents fighting through the walls. Her father's voice raised in anger, and her mother's a soft, apologetic murmur. It had gone on for hours, and she'd fallen asleep to the sound of her mother crying.

The next morning when she ventured out of her room, Brooke braced herself for the lecture of her life. But her father didn't say a word—or even look at her. From that day forward, he barely acknowledged her existence unless he had to. He never even yelled at her or told her he was disappointed. Never spoke of what she'd done at all. He simply treated her like someone beneath his notice. Instead of a scarlet letter, she'd been given an invisibility cloak.

Brooke's mother had followed her father's lead, giving her the cold shoulder too—but only at home when Brooke's father was around. When it was just the two of them, or when they were around other people, her mother acted like everything was fine. That was when Brooke realized what an actress her mother was. How she could flip personalities on a dime for the sake of maintaining appearances.

But even when she deigned to talk to Brooke, it was only ever about inconsequential things. Dinner, groceries, the weather. She refused to talk about what Brooke had done, or about Brooke's father, or about anything that mattered. Whenever Brooke tried, her mother would shut the conversation down and walk away. So Brooke stopped trying.

Her mother had made it clear where her loyalties really lay, and it wasn't with her.

Brooke had essentially lost both her parents in one fell swoop. Because of one stupid mistake.

"I'm so sorry you went through that," Dylan said, his voice low and emphatic. "I'm even sorrier you did it alone."

Brooke shrugged like it didn't matter. "Anyway." She straightened her spine. "That's why I don't go home anymore. And why my parents didn't see fit to tell me my dad has cancer, I guess."

A fresh surge of anger wound through her insides. She'd thought she was over being hurt by her parents' disapproval, but apparently they still had the power to make her feel bad about herself.

She got to her feet and brushed her hair off her shoulder. "There's nothing to be done about any of it tonight, so I'm going to go to bed. I'll deal with this tomorrow."

Dylan stood up too. "Are you sure?" He hovered uncertainly, looking like he wanted to hug her again.

Brooke stepped backward, putting distance between them. As much as she'd like to lose herself in his arms, she knew if she did she'd break down completely. And that was the last thing she wanted. "It's fine," she said stiffly. "Don't worry about it."

It wasn't fine.

Her dad had cancer.

Underneath the anger, somewhere deep inside, Brooke was terrified. Because despite everything that had happened between her and her parents—all the resentment and recriminations and cold, unfeeling distance that had built up over the years—regardless of everything else she felt, part of her was still a little girl who loved her dad and was terrified he was going to die.

Chapter Eight

Brooke stared at her phone. She'd been staring at it for five minutes, and she still hadn't worked up the courage to call her mom.

It was one o'clock in the afternoon. She'd been on campus since seven thirty that morning. The paper she was submitting tomorrow was as good as done, although she wanted to let it sit before doing one last read-through and final polish.

She'd left Dylan at home this morning with plans to do some sightseeing on his own. She felt a bit guilty about how much of a hurry she'd been in to get away from him, but she hadn't wanted to rehash any of their conversation last night. One secret-baring heart-to-heart per day was her max, and she knew she'd have to make this call to her mom today.

Brooke had thrown herself into her paper this morning to avoid thinking about it. And then once she'd finished all her revisions, she'd spent a half hour reading about prostate cancer on the internet. Which hadn't really done much to improve her peace of mind.

She stared at her phone some more. Her phone stared back.

Her choices were to get this call out of the way, or work on her grading and let it hang over her head some more.

She dialed her mother's number.

"Brooke?" Her mom sounded surprised. As well she should. Brooke couldn't even remember the last time she'd called. It was always her mother who initiated their periodic, ersatz conversations.

"Hey, Mom."

"What a pleasant surprise. You know, I was just thinking of calling you."

"You were?"

"Yes, you'll never guess who I ran into at the Winn-Dixie. Amanda Coursey. Remember Mrs. Coursey, your Girl Scout troop leader? They moved away when you were in—let's see, it must have been eighth grade. Her husband was transferred to Mobile, but she's in town visiting her parents."

"That's nice, Mom, but—"

"She remembered you, of course. 'How is Brooke?' she asked, and I told her you were living in Los Angeles now studying whales, and she was so impressed. She remembered how much you always loved whales and dolphins as a child. You even did a scout project on them, remember?"

"Yeah, Mom, I do. But I'm actually calling about something else."

Her mother didn't seem to be listening to her. *Quelle surprise*. "She told me one of her sons just graduated from UGA and is living in Atlanta now, interning at TruTV. He wants to be a television producer. The older one went to Ole Miss, and he's living in Birmingham. He's married with two kids and works for an HVAC company."

"*Mom*," Brooke interjected, losing patience.

"Yes?" Her mother sounded perturbed to have her monologue interrupted.

"Does Dad have cancer?"

"Who told you that?"

"Dylan."

"Oh, how is he? I didn't realize you two were still in contact. He was always such a sweet boy. You know, his father got laid off by Exxon."

This was how their conversations always went, and why Brooke dreaded them so much. Her mother would ramble on endlessly about insignificant subjects, and deflect like hell whenever Brooke attempted to talk to her about anything meaningful.

"Answer the question, Mom. Does Dad have prostate cancer?"

"Well, yes," her mother conceded. "Just a touch."

Just a touch. Of cancer. Unbelievable.

"Why didn't you tell me?" It was impossible to keep the hurt out of her voice.

Her mother sounded flustered. "Oh, well, your father didn't want people to know. You know how he is."

Unfortunately, Brooke knew exactly what her father was like. "Other people or just me? Because Dylan's mom knows, which means half of Baton Rouge knows by now."

"Well, we tried to keep it quiet, but you know how these things go. Word spreads."

Brooke squeezed the phone. "So you didn't think to call me once everyone else had found out?"

"I did think about it, but I didn't want to worry you, honey. Dad's going to be fine. The doctor says everything's looking positive and his chances of a full recovery are excellent."

Brooke's mother had practically made a second career out of supporting the status quo as embodied by Brooke's father, so it wasn't surprising that she was working double time now to pretend everything was rosy, even in the face of a cancer diagnosis.

"But he's having chemo?" Brooke's research had told her that course of treatment was mostly used when the cancer had spread outside the prostate, which sounded more serious than her mother was letting on.

"Oh, he's all done with that now. He had a spot of surgery, which went excellently, and then they just did a few chemo treatments to make sure they got all the cancer out of him. It's really nothing to worry about."

Brooke couldn't tell if her mother had actually convinced herself that was true, or if she was maintaining the party line to keep up the appearance that everything was fine. "Okay, but it's cancer, Mom. That's a big deal."

Her mother made a tsking sound. "Sure, but it's prostate cancer, which isn't as bad as some of the others. The remission rates are really quite hopeful. You know, they say all men eventually get prostate cancer if they live long enough."

Brooke had no idea where her mom had gotten this weird factoid, but it sounded fake and was not as comforting as she seemed to think it was. "How are you holding up through all this?" she asked, biting her lip.

"Oh, I'm just dandy. You know me. I started a new quilting project."

As her mother rambled on, Brooke listened for evidence of cracks in her veneer of positivity, but if there were any, she'd hidden them too well to be detectable. "Will you keep me updated on Dad's condition from now on?"

"Of course, honey."

Somehow, Brooke couldn't bring herself to believe her. "I'm serious, Mom. I want to know how he's doing."

"I'll keep you in the loop from now on," her mother promised, sounding slightly more sincere. Maybe even a little contrite.

Brooke realized she was compulsively twisting a strand of hair around her finger and unwound it, tucking it behind her ear. "I don't suppose I could talk to Dad."

"Oh, you know . . . I think he's asleep. He had his last infusion yesterday and it really tires him out. Best let him have his nap."

"How did he do with the chemo? Is it making him feel sick?"

"It's not too bad, really. You know your dad. He's strong as an ox."

More like stubborn as an ox. And her mom was no better. The two of them would try to pretend everything was fine in the middle of a category five hurricane.

"It's been lovely talking to you, but I've got to run, honey." It was so incredibly typical of her mother to bail out of the conversation when it started to get too heavy. "I promised your dad I'd make my chicken and dumplings tonight, and I need to pick up some things at the grocery store. But I'm so glad you called. Take care, Brooke."

"Goodbye, Mom." *A pleasure, as always.*

Brooke didn't feel any better after talking to her mom. In fact, she felt worse, which was how she usually felt after one of their conversations. This time was different though, because this time her dad had cancer.

But there was nothing she could do about that from here.

She'd expressed her concern and been rebuffed. Same as it ever was.

Maybe her mother would actually keep her updated from now on. In the meantime, there was no point in dwelling on it.

The heavenly scent of baking cheese and tomato sauce greeted Brooke when she let herself into her apartment at six o'clock.

Dylan had made dinner for the two of them. Apparently he'd stopped at the grocery store after sightseeing. He greeted her from the kitchen where he was chopping vegetables for a salad. He looked liked a dream: glasses on, shoes off, his jeans slung low on his hips as he made her dinner.

"Perfect timing!" He glanced up without missing a beat in his expert knife strokes. "Dinner will be ready in ten minutes."

"Wow, what's the occasion?" She felt like the dad on an old sitcom. Her long day at work and upsetting conversation with her mom didn't seem so bad when there was a hot underwear model waiting at home to put dinner on the table.

"No occasion," he said, smiling at the cherry tomato he was quartering. "I just like cooking. It's nice to have someone to cook for, for a change."

Brooke went to the oven and tried to peer inside the tinted window. "Is that your lasagna I smell?"

"Yes, and I'm about to take it out, so shoo." He took her by the shoulders and guided her out of the tiny kitchen.

"Fine." She stuck her tongue out at him as she headed for the bedroom. "I'm going to change."

Murderface was sleeping on her bed rather than hiding

underneath it, which was kind of miraculous with a stranger in the apartment. Maybe the cat was finally getting used to having company. He jumped up to greet her and twined around her legs while she changed into a fresh T-shirt and pair of shorts.

When Brooke came back out of her bedroom, Dylan was frowning at his phone. As she approached the kitchen, he jammed it back into his pocket and started getting out silverware to set the table.

"Here, I can do that," she said, taking the utensils from him.

She didn't have fancy napkins or placemats, so he'd set out two folded paper towels beside the plates. A couple of candles he'd brought from the living room flickered in the middle of the table, lending some ambiance to the setting.

"Did you talk to your parents?" Dylan asked.

"I talked to my mom," Brooke answered as she laid out the forks and knives.

Dylan brought a bottle of red wine and a bottle opener to the table. "What'd she say? How's your dad?"

"I guess he's doing okay? As okay as you can be with prostate cancer, anyway. It's always hard to decipher the truth beneath my mom's relentless positivity." Brooke shrugged and went to get two wine glasses.

"Did you smooth things over with her?" Dylan asked as he twisted the corkscrew. "About not telling you what was going on?"

"As far as she's concerned, everything's already smooth. It's no big deal that they didn't tell me anything."

"I'm sorry. That sucks."

"Whatever. It is what it is." She didn't want to talk about

it anymore. She'd spent too much time today thinking about her parents already. For the rest of the night, she just wanted to relax and enjoy hanging out with Dylan.

When Brooke turned around with the wine glasses, Murderface was standing at Dylan's feet. "Hey, look at that!" she exclaimed in surprise.

Dylan grinned as he pulled the cork out of the wine bottle. "Oh yeah, me and this cat are totally buds now."

Brooke set the wine glasses on the table. "How'd you work that miracle?"

"I found your stash of cat toys and bribed him with catnip. Turns out he's a total slut for the nip."

"I'm impressed. You really are the cat whisperer."

"Yeah . . . so, that's not all I found." Dylan's grin got wider as he leaned forward to fill both their wine glasses. "While I was poking around for the cat toys, I may have found your stash of—ahem—adult toys."

All the blood drained from Brooke's face. "Oh. *My god.*"

He smirked at her. "That's quite a collection you've got."

"Excuse me, I need to go throw myself off the balcony now."

He let out a throaty laugh. "We're only on the second floor, so I don't think that's going to accomplish what you're hoping. Anyway, it's no big deal."

"It's a big deal to me," she said, rubbing her temple. "I'm not sure I'll ever be able to look you in the eye again."

On an intellectual level, Brooke knew it wasn't something she should be embarrassed about. She was a grown adult, there was absolutely nothing wrong with engaging in self-pleasure, and quite frankly her vibrators made better partners than a lot of the men she'd dated. Vibrators didn't get you pregnant and then call you a slut. They never tried to neg you or promised to call and then didn't. They never got clingy or accused you of being emotionally unavailable.

You only had to spend five minutes in the "Am I the Asshole" section of Reddit to realize how many people were trapped in toxic relationships with truly ghastly men. Looking at it logically, vibrators were a far saner choice than dating.

Nevertheless, Brooke was embarrassed to be having this conversation with Dylan of all people. It wasn't like they'd never talked about sex before, but . . . well, they hadn't ever really talked about it *much*. Not in detail, anyway. Mostly they'd skirted around the subject.

She'd always assumed that was him being respectful. So many adolescent boys made gross sex jokes all the time, like they'd just invented the concept, and Brooke had always appreciated that Dylan didn't do that around her.

But maybe it had been about more than respect. Maybe they'd both shied away from the subject for other reasons.

Like that it struck too close to feelings neither of them had ever acknowledged.

"I think it's cool," Dylan said, shrugging. "Good for you. And now we're even for you seeing me naked yesterday."

Brooke tilted her head. "Are we though? It's not like I didn't know you had a penis, but you didn't know I had sex toys."

The corner of his mouth twitched. "If you ask me, it's pretty hot."

She couldn't tell if he was teasing her or . . . no, he couldn't possibly be flirting. "Is it? Because I was thinking more sad and pathetic."

100

"There's nothing sad or pathetic about getting yourself off. Also? They can be a lot of fun with a partner."

Her eyebrows lifted. "Are you speaking from experience?" It was so strange to be having this conversation with him. They never talked like this. It felt a little like picking through a field studded with landmines: terrifying, but also kind of exhilarating.

He gave her a sideways smirk. "Don't knock it till you've tried it."

"I'm not knocking anything. I'm just curious." She couldn't help wondering what Dylan would be like in bed. Tender? Rough? Or some delicious combination of the two? An image popped into her head of him pushing her up against a wall and dropping between her legs, her wrists clamped in his hands . . .

"The lasagna's ready," Dylan said, heading into the kitchen without answering her question. "Grab the salad, will you?"

Brooke shook her head to rid it of the image, and took a big drink of wine before following him.

Dylan carried the lasagna to the table and cut it into squares. He served up two generous helpings and they sat down to eat.

The lasagna was delicious. Even better than Brooke remembered. Or maybe Dylan had improved on the recipe since high school.

They reminisced about days past as they ate, and laughed over inside jokes they used to have, some of which Brooke had almost forgotten. It felt so natural to be joking around with Dylan again, it was as if they'd never been apart. And yet they were very different people now than they'd been in high school. They'd both changed, though maybe not in the ways that mattered most.

After they finished the meal, they cleared the table, and Brooke helped Dylan with the dishes.

"This was nice," she said as she got out a dish towel to start drying. "I'm not sure I've ever actually sat down at that table and eaten a meal with anyone. Usually it's just me and the cat eating on the couch. I mean, I eat on the couch. The cat eats on the floor in the kitchen."

Dylan handed her a clean plate to dry. "Sounds kind of lonely."

"It's not so bad. I like being alone."

He frowned at the cutting board he was scrubbing with more elbow grease than was strictly necessary. "I hate being alone."

"Why?" It struck Brooke as sad. Everyone should be able to enjoy their own company.

He looked up, as if the question had surprised him. "I guess I just crave companionship."

"If you mean sex, you don't need to be in a relationship for that."

Her vibrator collection spoke for itself. But even if you craved human touch, there were plenty of ways to get that without tying yourself down to another person. She couldn't imagine Dylan would have any trouble finding hookups if he wanted them.

"No, you don't," he agreed as he passed her the cutting board to dry. "But it's more than that. I like having a partner. Knowing there's someone who'll be there when I need them."

"Have you ever had that with anyone?" As far as she

102

knew, he hadn't been in a relationship since he'd moved to New York. Certainly nothing long-term.

"No. I thought once—but no. I'm still waiting for the right woman to come along."

Brooke's heart ached for him a little as she watched him wipe down the counter around the sink. "I don't know why, but I always assumed you preferred to play the field. I guess I didn't think the model lifestyle would be conducive to finding that kind of committed relationship."

"It's not, really. That's the problem." He shook his head before she could say anything else. "I don't mean to complain. You want more wine?"

"Sure."

He refilled both their wine glasses, and they carried them into the living room where they sank down on the couch.

"So you don't like relationships?" Dylan asked, turning to face her as he settled back into the cushions.

Brooke pulled her legs up under her. "I enjoy the beginning of relationships fine, when everything's all exciting and unknown. I love that feeling you get with someone new, when you're still figuring each other out and it's all nerves and anticipation. But that's just the dopamine rush. It's not real."

Dylan's phone buzzed and he looked at it with a weary expression. As he stared at the screen, his frown deepened into a grimace. It was the third or fourth time she'd seen him frowning at his phone tonight. Someone had been blowing up his texts, but whoever it was, Dylan hadn't chosen to respond.

He shoved his phone back into his pocket. "So what happens?" he asked, looking up at Brooke again. "Where does it start to go wrong?"

She thought about it as she sipped her wine. "After a few weeks, I guess, once the excitement wears off, and you learn everything there is to learn about someone. That's when I start to get bored. And I'd rather be by myself than bored with someone else." She gave him a rueful smile. "I think the real problem is I like most people better before I get to know them."

"That's a gloomy outlook on humanity." His look smacked of pity.

She shrugged. "I'm thinking of turning in my amateur misanthrope card and going pro."

He leaned back and rested his wine glass on his thigh. "You really think you can learn everything there is to know about someone in a few weeks?"

"Everything I need to know, yeah."

"You've known me for eighteen years and I promise you don't know everything about me."

She grinned at him over her wine glass. "Are you hiding some big, dark secret? Did you murder a man in Reno just to watch him die?"

An odd expression crossed his face. "No, no secrets. People are just more complicated than that."

"Everyone's got secrets."

His eyes met hers and held. "Not me. I'm an open book. You just haven't read all the pages yet."

She took up the implied challenge. "If you're such an open book, tell me why you keep frowning at your phone. Who's been texting you and stressing you out?"

He took a drink of wine as his grimace returned. "My agent. He's pissed I'm staying out here for the whole week.

There's this party he wants me at on Friday, and he keeps trying to convince me to come back early."

"Do you need to?" Brooke didn't want Dylan to leave, but she also didn't want him to lose an important professional opportunity just to hang out with her for a few extra days. She wasn't special enough to be worth that kind of sacrifice.

"No." He drank again as he shook his head. "I mean, probably, but no. I'm not doing it. I'm tired of going to fucking parties where I'm leered at and manhandled like a prize hog on the way to the slaughterhouse."

It was hard to imagine Dylan in a situation like that. Sure, if she looked at him objectively as the person he appeared to be on the surface, it was easy to see him in that kind of setting where people were only valued for their looks. But when Brooke looked at him she saw so much more. She saw his kindness and his determination and his ingenuity. She saw her friend, who was so much more than what was visible on the surface. It raised her hackles to think of him being treated like an empty piece of meat.

"That sounds awful," she said.

"It can be." He scraped his thumbnail along the seam of his jeans. "It's a whole industry based on appearances and projecting a certain image, trying to jump on the next big trend. Everybody you meet is fake, which makes it next to impossible to make real friends or have a meaningful relationship. Everyone's got an angle, something they're looking for, some way they're trying to use you for their own gain."

His eyes found hers again, and what she saw in the blue depths made her breath catch in her chest.

"You're the only one in my life who's a hundred percent

real. When you look at me, I know you're seeing the real me, not the person I pretend to be."

Brooke didn't know what to say. She felt a knot form in her throat and swallowed.

Dylan looked down at his lap again. "The truth is, I don't know how much longer I want to keep modeling."

"What would you do instead?"

"I'm not sure." He took a long drink of wine. "I just think it would be nice to do something that's about more than just my face and my body." He sighed. "It's probably a pipe dream."

"No, it's not. If your career isn't making you happy, you should find something else that will. You could do anything you wanted. You've probably got talents you don't even know about. If you have a dream, you should go for it."

He looked torn. "Yeah, but I'm already doing my dream job, which is more than a lot of people ever get. I don't know if I deserve a shot at a second one."

It broke her heart to hear so much unhappiness in his voice. "Of course you do. Don't talk yourself out of it. You deserve to be happy."

His eyes flickered to hers and then away again. "Well, I'm not quitting the business just yet. I've got to get my ducks in a row before I jump ship." He knocked back the last of his wine and leaned forward to snag the bottle off the table.

"It might be hard to give up all that money," Brooke pointed out.

He scooted toward her and topped off her glass before refilling his own. "Money's not that important to me."

Her mouth twisted. "Spoken like someone with plenty of it."

Dylan set the wine bottle back on the table and grinned at her. "Fair enough." He was sitting much closer now. Close enough to reach out and touch.

Brooke felt an overwhelming compulsion to run her fingers down his arm. To feel the silky warmth of his skin and trace the curve of his muscles.

She sipped her wine instead. "You know, you're probably the most successful person in our graduating class."

He propped his arm on the back of the couch and rested his head in his hand. "Even more successful than Brandon Walls, who sells weed out of his car behind the Superette?"

Brooke shifted to mirror his pose, propping her own head on her hand. "Even more successful than Steve Raymond, who sells the *fancy* weed out of his parents' garage."

Dylan laughed. They were facing each other, and his head was only a few inches from hers, which meant his *mouth* was only a few inches from hers. All she'd have to do is lean forward a little, and her lips would be on his.

"You're pretty successful yourself," he said.

Brooke made a face. "Tell that to my bank account."

"Money isn't the only measure of success. How many kids want to be marine biologists when they grow up? And you actually did it. That's amazing."

The wine must be going to her head, because the way he was looking at her was making her feel things. More than that, it was making her wonder if he was feeling something too.

No. That couldn't be.

Except.

Maybe . . .

Dylan's gaze was heavy-lidded and intense. Full of heat. If

it had been anyone else looking at her like that, she'd lay money he was thinking about kissing her.

Brooke drew an unsteady breath and licked her lips.

His eyes went darker, and the room suddenly felt too small, because he wasn't looking into her eyes anymore.

He was looking at her mouth.

His hand came up, and his fingertips stroked over her cheek in the lightest of butterfly touches.

He was going to kiss her.

Chapter Nine

The air between them seemed to crackle with potential energy.

Dylan was going to kiss her, and Brooke was going to kiss him back.

The cat jumped onto the couch between them with a loud "Mur-rowr!" and they startled apart.

"Hey, buddy!" Dylan sat up and shifted away from Brooke to stroke the cat's back as if nothing had happened—or almost happened. "Who's my favorite kitty? You are!"

Goddamn cockblocking cat.

Brooke took a long drink of wine. She ought to be grateful the cat had interrupted, or else who knows what might have happened.

Clearly, the two of them and alcohol were a bad combination.

The worst.

Dylan had just gotten through telling her how important their friendship was to him. Did she really want to throw all that away for a drunken hookup they'd both probably regret tomorrow?

This was classic Brooke. Letting herself get swept away in

the allure of something new and exciting. But how long would it be before she started to feel trapped? How long before she grew tired of Dylan?

He deserved better than that. He deserved a real partner who could love him and support him and *stay with him* for the long haul. They didn't even live in the same city, for crap's sake.

She knocked back the rest of her wine and got up to carry her empty glass into the kitchen. Dylan joined her while she was washing her glass, and put the cork back in the almost-empty wine bottle.

"You're not having any more?" she asked, reaching for his glass.

He shook his head, avoiding her eyes. "I think I've had enough wine tonight."

Brooke had a flashback to high school, after their prom night kiss. How they'd both tried to pretend it hadn't happened, but things had still been stilted and weird between them afterward. It had been days before Dylan had been able to look her in the eye, and weeks before she could look at him without thinking about the way his lips had felt on hers.

She dreaded a repeat of that scenario, especially when he was only here for a few days.

Thank god they hadn't actually kissed this time. Hopefully they'd get past this little blip much faster.

Spending this time with Dylan had reminded Brooke how much she needed his friendship and opened her eyes to how much he needed hers. Which meant they shouldn't—couldn't—be anything more to each other than friends.

"I've got an early day tomorrow," Brooke said as she put the wine glasses away. "I think I'm gonna head to bed."

Things would undoubtedly be more normal in the morning. Safer. In the sober light of a new day, it would be easier to act rationally and listen to her brain instead of her libido.

Dylan's eyes lingered on her for a moment before he nodded. "Sounds good. I'll see you in the morning."

"Thanks for dinner," she said, edging out of the kitchen. "It was great."

"Good night."

When she came out of the bathroom after getting ready for bed, Dylan had already turned out the lights in the living room. All was quiet in the apartment. Brooke crept into her room, pushed the door closed except for a narrow crack to let the cat come and go, and crawled into bed.

Murderface wasn't waiting for her like he usually was when she went to bed. *He must be in the living room with Dylan.*

Traitor. First he cockblocked her, then he abandoned her in favor of someone else.

Not that she could blame him. If she made all her decisions based on animal instincts, she'd be cuddling up to Dylan right now too.

He was too much of a temptation. Too comforting. Too easy to talk to. Too *present*. Traipsing around her apartment looking all effortlessly sexy. Anyone's thoughts would turn to lust in the face of that.

But she couldn't sleep with Dylan just for the sake of sleeping with *someone*. Being horny and turned on—and okay, maybe a little lonely—wasn't a good enough reason to ruin a friendship.

He wasn't just her oldest friend, he was probably her best

friend in the whole world. And it sounded like she might be his best friend too.

Brooke shifted restlessly under the sheets, too keyed up for sleep.

What if Dylan had actually kissed her though? What would it feel like? Her memories of their high school kiss were hazy and awash with embarrassment and regret.

He was probably a much better kisser these days.

The surface of her skin buzzed as she tried to imagine it. The tug of his lips, the heat of his mouth. His hands, sliding up her thighs. Before she knew what she was doing, her hand moved down her stomach.

God! Her face flushed as she realized what she'd been about to do. Dylan was right in the next room. The bedroom door wasn't even closed. She shouldn't be getting off to a fantasy about her best friend, and she definitely shouldn't do it when he was only a few yards away with nothing between them. What if he heard her? There'd be no coming back from that kind of humiliation. She'd have no choice but to fling herself into the sun.

Brooke rolled onto her side and pulled the covers up to her chin, determined not to think about Dylan anymore.

She'd think about something else. Something completely unsexy. Like dirty diapers. Or the professor in her department with the dandruff problem. Or Adam Sandler.

Yeah, that's not happening. She was too turned on. Too worked up by that interrupted almost-kiss. It was like getting to the most exciting part of the movie and losing your internet connection.

It didn't help that Dylan had been a star attraction in her spank bank since she was eighteen. He'd made the perfect fantasy, because she knew him better than she knew anyone else alive, but she also knew better than to hope he could think of her the same way.

Except . . .

What if he did think of her that way?

It blew her mind to acknowledge the possibility.

There was no denying he'd been right there with her in the moment. If the cat hadn't interrupted and broken the spell, how far would he have gone? How far would *they* have gone?

No.

She could never go there with him.

Their friendship was too important to gamble away. She'd never do anything to jeopardize it.

Brooke rushed to finish applying her makeup. She was running late, because she'd snoozed her alarm too many times, because she'd been up half the night obsessing over Dylan and their almost-kiss.

Stop. Don't go there.

She wasn't going to think about it today. It hadn't happened. She'd deleted it from her memory bank. When she walked out of her bedroom in a few minutes, she was going to look Dylan in the eye like nothing had changed.

Desperately, she tried to blend her foundation, which she'd slapped on so haphazardly she looked like an Impressionist painting. She didn't wear a lot of makeup—it was a college campus, after all—but she felt more confident with a little foundation to even out her complexion. And she needed all the confidence she could get today.

113

Once she'd done her best with her appearance, she ventured out of her room. As soon as she stepped into the hallway, the bathroom door opened and Dylan emerged in front of her.

Shirtless.

Wearing only his gray sweatpants, his hair still faintly sleep-mussed, looking as sexy as she'd ever seen him.

Their gazes locked, and a muscle ticked in his jaw.

Brooke dropped her eyes, involuntarily taking in the smooth, hairless expanse of his bare chest and sculpted abs. She felt her face heat and swallowed.

"Morning," Dylan said, and gestured for her to precede him.

"Morning," she muttered as she hurried past him. The apartment smelled of fresh coffee, and she followed the scent to its source like a bloodhound on the trail.

Dylan had brewed a pot already, bless him. The guy was going to make some lucky woman one hell of a househusband one day.

"You sleep okay?" he asked as he trailed Brooke into the kitchen.

She glanced at him and caught what she could swear was a hint of a smirk in his expression. Was he teasing her? Did he know she'd been thinking about him all night?

"Yep, great!" she chirped falsely as she opened the pantry and grabbed a granola bar to eat on the drive to campus. "You?"

"To be honest, I didn't sleep that well."

Brooke refused to look at him as she got out a travel mug, afraid of what she'd see in his expression. "I'm sorry. I hope the cat didn't keep you up."

"No, it wasn't the cat."

This was not going the way she'd hoped. Here she was, working hard to pretend nothing was different between them, and Dylan was not cooperating. She was sure he was implying she was the one who'd kept him up last night, which wasn't something she could allow herself to dwell on.

"I'm running late," she announced as she poured coffee into her travel mug, curtailing further conversation on the subject of how either of them had slept. "I've got another class to TA so I've got to run. You're gonna be okay today, right?"

"Sure."

"Good. I'll be home by six." She put the lid on her travel mug and headed to the door for her laptop bag.

"Brooke, hang on a second."

She spun around and came face-to-face with Dylan's bare chest. He was so close she could smell the toothpaste on his breath. As she peered up at him, his blue eyes locked onto hers. Clear. Steady. *Intense*. Watching her.

He leaned in, just a little. Testing her.

She should lean away. Put a stop to this. But she couldn't seem to make herself do it.

He lifted one hand, and the tips of his fingers skimmed the top of her shoulder. Heat seared her as the pads of his fingers dragged over the thin fabric of her shirt.

This wasn't a casual touch. It was an exploration. A dare. Gentle, but challenging.

He leaned in more, and now she was leaning in too, involuntarily taking him up on his challenge. Straining toward him as if her body had a will of its own. Her heart thudded

115

as her breath hitched painfully, and her gaze dropped to his slightly parted lips.

She needed the cat to jump between them and break the spell again, but Murderface was nowhere to be seen. Typical cat. Never around when you needed him.

She should say something to avert this. Put a stop to it before—

Oh.

Dylan's lips brushed against hers. Both smooth and rough. Soft and firm.

Just a light touch, and then they were gone. Just enough to tantalize.

Just enough to drive her mad.

Brooke sucked in a ragged breath and Dylan's mouth met hers again. Her eyes drifted shut. Her lips parted as she felt his hands encircle her waist.

They were kissing with gusto now. Slow, luxurious, tender caresses that were every bit as wonderful as she'd imagined and then some. His tongue sweeping over hers, his teeth scraping against her lower lip. Her limbs melting into goo.

Then it ended.

Dylan pulled back, and Brooke's eyes flew open in shock. He was watching her again. Studying her reaction. His eyes still clear and intense as they scrutinized her.

"Why—why did you do that?" she gasped, her lungs aching like she'd been deprived of oxygen.

He gazed down at her calmly, as if he hadn't just blown up their whole paradigm. "I've been wanting to do that since I got here."

Her stomach flipped over. "You have?"

"I sort of thought it was obvious after last night."

116

"Well, okay, but—" Brooke shook her head, trying to refocus her thoughts. "I can't talk about this now—I have to go. I have to get to class."

Why did he have to choose to do this *now*? When she was already running late?

Dylan reached behind her to open the door. "I know. Go to class." His hands grasped her shoulders and he spun her around, giving her a gentle push out the door. "Have a good day. I'll see you tonight."

While Brooke was still trying to process exactly what had just happened, the door shut behind her.

Okay.

What?

Chapter Ten

"Can women get blue balls?" Brooke asked when she met Olivia for coffee that afternoon.

Olivia dropped her giant bag into an empty chair and slumped into the seat across from Brooke. "Men don't even get blue balls. It's a myth meant to guilt women into having sex with them."

Brooke cradled her venti Frappuccino in her hands. "Not literal blue balls, but like . . . extreme sexual frustration. Where you feel like you're going to explode if you don't get some. Women should have a word for that too." She sucked down a mouthful of frozen sugary caffeine as she thought about it. "Blue eggs? Blue clams? Blue tacos? Why are so many euphemisms for female body parts food-based?"

Olivia's eyebrows lifted over heavily lined eyes as her red lips puckered in amusement. "Am I correct in assuming your houseguest is the one causing your blue lady parts?"

"Maybe," Brooke said glumly.

Olivia regarded her with narrowed eyes. "Something happened. Spill."

"No." Brooke lowered her eyes and sipped her Frappuccino again. "Nothing."

She wasn't sure she wanted Olivia to know the details. For one thing, as soon as Olivia knew, Penny would know, and Olivia's boyfriend Adam would know, and Penny's husband Caleb would know. Since Brooke was supposed to be bringing Dylan to the reception this weekend, she didn't want any of them acting weird around him and letting on that they knew.

Olivia snorted. "Liar. Look at you, you're all red-faced and hyperkinetic. What happened? You can't open with blue balls and then not tell me what's up."

Brooke sighed and slumped down in her chair. "Dylan kissed me."

"Umm, hello? Isn't that what you've always wanted? Why are you fretting like it's a disaster?"

"Because it is a disaster! I can't date Dylan."

"Back up and tell me how it happened." Olivia sounded amused. "When did he lay it on you? How did you react? How'd you leave things? Most importantly, *how was it?* Tell me everything."

Olivia listened as Brooke gave her the bullet points of her almost-kiss with Dylan last night and the surprise kiss this morning on her way out the door. She was frowning by the time Brooke finished.

"So basically he gave you the kiss of your dreams and you just noped out of there? Am I getting this right?"

"It wasn't like that," Brooke insisted. "I was already late for class. I had to go. And he knew I was running late when he decided to kiss me. I don't know what he was thinking. Did he decide to do it then because he knew I wouldn't be able to stay and deal with it?"

Olivia sipped her iced coffee thoughtfully. "Was it an 'I just wanted to see what it would be like for shits and giggles' kind of deal? Or testing the waters for a full-scale escalation?"

"I don't know! That's the problem." Brooke collapsed forward and banged her head on the table. "Uggggh. I don't know what I'm going to do."

"What's the tragedy here? You're hot for him, he's clearly hot for you. If something happens to happen, so be it."

Brooke sat up again. "I can't sleep with Dylan. It'll ruin our friendship."

Olivia tilted her head. "Will it? Or will it make it more awesome?"

"It'll ruin it," Brooke answered emphatically. "When things don't work out, we'll have nothing left."

"But how do you know it won't work out? Maybe it'll work out amazing."

"Because it never works out. Sure, it'll be fun at first, but after the newness wears off I always get bored and start to feel stifled. I couldn't bear it if I started to feel that way about Dylan."

Olivia leaned back and regarded Brooke. "Listen. When Adam and I first got together, I had the same fears. I kept second-guessing my own feelings and his, convinced we were headed for disaster. I thought I was being rational, but what I was really doing was trying to talk myself out of being happy, because I didn't think I deserved it."

"It's not that I don't think I deserve *someone*. I'm just not convinced Dylan's the right choice. That's the problem. No one ever seems to be the right choice." Brooke hesitated. "If things don't work out with him, I can't just pull the chute and bail out of the relationship like I usually do. I mean, I *can*, but if I do, it will mean the end of our friendship. I can't risk it."

"You have to take a risk on something sometime, or you'll never get anything." Olivia's voice was gentle.

Brooke looked down at her hands, which were knotted together. "You should have heard him last night, talking about how much our friendship meant to him. I don't think he's very happy in New York. It sounds like I'm basically his only real friend. Wouldn't it be selfish to throw away our whole friendship just to get laid a few times?"

"I can't answer that for you."

"Even if I don't do my usual thing where I get bored, I just don't see how we can make it work, practically speaking." Brooke gazed across the coffee shop. "In addition to our lifestyles being *totally* incompatible—I mean, good grief, can you picture *me* dating an underwear model? In addition to *that*, we live on opposite coasts three time zones apart. We'd never see each other. How is that even supposed to work?"

Olivia's shoulders lifted lightly. "So talk to him about it. Find out where his head's at. You're compatible enough to stay friends all these years; you should be able to be honest with each other about what you want. For all you know, he's not looking for anything long-term either. Maybe he just wants a friends-with-benefits situation. A vacation fling."

"Maybe." Brooke was still so thrown by the idea that Dylan thought about her like that at all, she didn't trust herself to accurately read into his intentions anymore.

"It's possible, isn't it? Did he actually say anything about wanting to start up something long-term?"

"No . . ." He hadn't said much of anything. He'd just kissed her and pushed her out the door before she could react.

"Maybe it's the lure of the unknown that's got you both all hot and bothered." Olivia swirled the ice in her drink thoughtfully. "You've been lusting after this guy—what?—your whole life, pretty much? And it sounds like he's been doing some lusting after you too. So maybe you just need to get it out of your systems—with a clear understanding that it's only temporary—and then you can part as friends when he goes back to New York on Sunday."

Brooke stared at her. "You think that would work?"

"Sure. Why not?"

She made it sound so simple. Brooke couldn't deny the appeal of Olivia's suggestion. Despite all the voices in Brooke's head, telling her what a terrible idea it was to get involved with Dylan, she wanted it. She wanted him.

Bad.

Olivia was right that Brooke had basically always wanted him, even if she'd tried to shut down those feelings and shove them deep inside.

They weren't shut down anymore.

If Dylan was on board for something casual like that, it could be a win-win scenario.

Just thinking about it made Brooke's limbs quiver. *Imagine.* Having Dylan for herself for the rest of his stay. Four days. Four *nights.* After all these years, finally getting to satisfy her repressed desires.

How amazing would that be?

But as much as she longed to give in to her pent-up desire, she still wasn't certain it was the right thing to do.

Brooke stood outside the door of her apartment. She bit her lip, squeezing the key in her hand.

Dylan was inside. When she opened the door, she'd have to face him. Talk to him. Tell him *something.*

She still didn't know what she was going to say.

Maybe she shouldn't say anything. Maybe she should make him say something. Explain himself. He was the one who'd kissed her, after all. Didn't that demand some kind of explanation? An accounting of his actions? A clarification of intentions at the very least?

This was ridiculous. It was her apartment. She couldn't stand outside forever.

Brooke reached out to put the key in the lock, but the door swung open before she had the chance.

"Were you ever planning on coming in?" Dylan asked, smirking at her.

Why did he have to look so good in a T-shirt and jeans? The man was just acres of radiant skin and solid musculature. Not to mention his face, which was somehow even hotter when he was acting cocky and taunting her.

And he was definitely taunting her. She could tell by the glint in his eyes. He knew he'd thrown her for a loop this morning, and he was enjoying watching her flounder.

"Yes," she muttered, stepping past him and into the apartment. Her arm brushed against his chest and sent a shower of electroshocks through her body.

He shut the door behind her. "How was your day?"

Weird. Confusing. Disorienting. Complicated.

"It was fine." She pulled her laptop bag over her head and hung it on the hook by the door. "I finished my paper and submitted it."

"That's awesome! Well done!"

"How was your day?" It felt strange to be making small talk only a few feet away from where he'd kissed her this morning.

123

Was he planning to pretend it hadn't happened, like they had after their last kiss? Because that really, *really* was not going to work for her this time.

Dylan went into the kitchen. "We should celebrate. You want a beer or some wine?" She heard him open the fridge.

"Maybe in a little bit." She needed to keep a clear head until they'd hashed things out. "I thought maybe we should talk about . . . you know."

When he reappeared from the kitchen the teasing glint was back in his eyes. "The Green New Deal? The controversial final season of *Game of Thrones*? Whether Lizzo is, in fact, good as hell? You're going to have to narrow it down for me." It was infuriating how sexy he was when he smirked.

"This morning," Brooke said, struggling to suppress a smile. "I believe there was kissing."

His smirk got wider and sexier. "You *believe* there was kissing? I must not be doing it right."

She cleared her throat. "No, you did it very well. Outstanding, even."

"Well, that's a relief." The way he was looking at her made her feel weak-kneed and woozy. And he *still* wasn't actually talking about it, despite all the jokes.

Fine. She'd be the grown-up, then.

Brooke took a breath and opened her mouth to start talking. But before she could get the words out, Dylan closed the distance between them.

He moved so fast it took her by surprise, his hands cupping her face as he tilted her head back. When his lips met hers, the shock hit her like an electric current, sending her pulse into overdrive.

It was like his little kissing experiment this morning had

124

been the sound check, and now she was getting a front-row seat to the headlining act. Heat pooled in her stomach as his mouth covered hers, kissing her with a strong, firm, confidence that was still somehow tender.

She tried to savor every second of it, her lips parting as her tongue sought his with greedy strokes. Her hands knotted in his shirt as she kissed him like she'd always wanted to. The way she'd always fantasized about kissing him.

It was even better than her fantasy. He tasted slightly sweet, with a faint hint of mint, and his hands were warm on her face as he held her, his stubble rough as it scraped over her lips, sending a surge of sensation shivering over the surface of her skin. His fingers slid into her hair as he angled his head to deepen the kiss, and for a moment she lost herself in him, in the intoxicating scent of his skin, the velvet slide of his tongue against hers, and the empty ache in her core.

Fuck.

This was Dylan she was kissing.

She broke free with a gasp. "Wait. We should—" She couldn't think. Her heart was pounding too loudly.

"What's wrong?" Dylan's fingers caressed her temple, which wasn't doing anything for her focus.

Brooke squeezed her eyes shut. "What are we doing?"

"Pretty sure we were kissing. Until you stopped."

"No, I mean—you and me—this is nuts." She blinked up at him, breathing heavily.

He gazed at her levelly. "Is it?" The only hint of his discomposure was a slight rasp in the words.

"Yes!" She lifted a hand to smooth her hair and realized her fingers were shaking.

"Why?" He was still gazing at her through his surprisingly long lashes. Still betraying no emotion whatsoever.

His blankness made it easier to remember herself and what they were risking. It helped her make up her mind. "Because it's us. And we're—this isn't who we are." The words fell into the silence between them, shattering the mood like a sheet of glass.

A muscle ticked in his jaw. "Tell me you haven't thought about it."

She swallowed and looked blindly at the wall beyond him. The hands that had been twisted in his shirt a moment ago curled into empty fists. "Of course I've thought about it. But as tempting as it is to drag you into my bedroom and do unspeakable things to you, I think it would be a bad idea. You're too important to me. I can't risk losing our friendship. It wouldn't be worth it."

He nodded and looked down at the floor. "I can understand that."

"Can you?" She was so afraid she'd hurt him. So afraid they'd already crossed the point of no return and screwed everything up.

But when he looked up his expression was clear-eyed and earnest. "I can. You're probably right." The corner of his mouth curled. "I mean, it'd be fun—"

"*So* fun."

"So fun," he agreed with a heart-stopping smile. "But our friendship is important to me too. I don't want to do anything that might jeopardize it."

"So . . . we're okay?" Brooke held her breath as she waited for his answer.

Dylan nodded. "We're okay."

126

"Whew. That's a relief." She felt like a weight had been lifted from her shoulders, and knew she'd made the right decision.

They stared at each other for what felt like a long moment, neither of them knowing quite where to go from here. How to get back to normal.

"You know what we should do?" Dylan said finally. "Go out to dinner to celebrate you submitting your paper. You up for it?"

"Yeah. That sounds great." Getting out of the apartment was probably a good idea. Brooke wouldn't be so tempted to mash her face against Dylan's in the middle of a restaurant.

So they went to dinner. And they didn't talk about the kiss—kiss*es*—at all. They managed to talk about pretty much everything else while they stuffed their faces with Mexican food.

Which was good. They didn't need to talk about it anymore. They'd dealt with it like adults and both moved on. No need to dwell.

Except Brooke couldn't seem to *stop* dwelling on it. Now that she knew what it was like to kiss Dylan—*really* kiss him—how was she supposed to think about anything else? Especially now that she knew he wanted her as much as she wanted him.

Had wanted her, for who even knew how long.

How in the chocolate-covered fuck was she supposed to not think about *that*?

Chapter Eleven

Dylan insisted on paying for dinner. Brooke tried to protest, but they both knew he made a lot more money than her, so she didn't protest too much.

They were both quiet on the drive home from the restaurant. Although things seemed mostly back to normal on the surface, there was still some detectable awkwardness between them. They were each being a little too careful, a little too deliberate in their choice of conversational topics, as if they were afraid of venturing back into dangerous territory.

Brooke's hands squeezed the steering wheel as she waited at a red light, and her knee jiggled with impatience.

"You okay?" Dylan asked.

Brooke nodded without looking at him. "Yeah, fine."

The light changed and she drove the rest of the way home, growing increasingly nervous as they neared her apartment. She couldn't stop thinking about that kiss he'd given her tonight. About everything she'd said no to. She'd wanted Dylan pretty much since she'd known what it was to be attracted to someone, and when she'd finally had her chance she'd turned him down.

Was she nuts?

Brooke wanted him more than ever now that she'd had a taste, and knowing Dylan wanted her back made it that much harder to repress her urges. Now that their mutual attraction was out in the open, everything felt even more charged between them.

Would they ever get back to normal? And what was she supposed to do when they got back to her apartment? When it was just the two of them, alone, in a small space with a bed conveniently near?

Brooke parked the car in her assigned parking space, and Dylan followed her upstairs. She set her purse down and kicked off her shoes. When she turned around, he was leaning into the fridge for a beer. Her eyes dropped to his backside. How had Penny described it? Like two ripe apples.

"You want a beer?" he asked.

Brooke licked her lips, her eyes drinking in the delicious sight of him. The way those damn jeans hugged him like a glove.

Dylan turned around, and she tore her eyes away from him.

"What?" he said, reaching for the bottle opener.

"Nothing." She walked into the living room and stooped to pick up a cat toy Murderface had left in the middle of the floor.

It was way too tempting to give the finger to common sense and kiss Dylan again. If she wasn't careful, she'd end up ruining this amazing friendship because she liked the way his ass looked in his jeans.

Don't think about it. Don't touch him. Don't even look at him.

"Talk to me." Dylan followed her and set two beers on the coffee table. "I know something's bothering you."

Brooke shook her head. "I think I just have to get used to the sea change. All these years, I assumed you didn't see me like that. And now suddenly you do, and . . . everything feels different."

His brows knitted over his ultramarine eyes. "I'm sorry. I shouldn't have put my feelings on you like that."

"No, it's . . . good. It's not like I wasn't feeling the same way, and it's flattering, you know?" Tension hung over them in a thick, choking cloud. She tried to break it with a joke. "I guess I can get it after all."

His answering smile didn't quite reach his eyes. "You've always been able to get it."

"Yeah, right," she muttered.

His gaze locked on hers and she swallowed, unable to look away. "Brooke, the truth is . . ." He took a step toward her and stopped, frowning.

"What?"

He pressed his lips together and gave a slight shake of his head. "Never mind."

"No, you can't do that. You have to tell me." He couldn't just leave her hanging like this with her heart thumping against the walls of her chest.

Deep creases sprouted across his forehead. "I don't want to freak you out."

"*This* is freaking me out." Something in his expression unsettled her. He'd always been good at hiding his true feelings behind a cheerful mask—they both were—but he wasn't doing it now. The emotions were leaking through, seeping in through the cracks around the edges.

"It's just . . ." He looked at the floor and then back up

again, his eyes uncertain as they found hers once more. "You've always been my fantasy. I thought you knew that."

She blinked as his confession hung in the air between them. "Come on." She couldn't help scoffing. It was too hard to accept. It went against everything she'd told herself.

His gaze was unblinking as he watched her. "It's true."

"No it's not." Her voice rose with disbelief that came out sounding like anger. "I was right there. For *years*. And you never looked twice at me except—" She stopped.

Except prom night.

When he'd accidentally kissed her and pulled away so fast he nearly sprained something.

Dylan's gaze flicked to her mouth, as if they were both reliving the same moment. "I wouldn't let myself go there."

"Why not?" Brooke's lips tingled with the memory of that long-ago kiss—and the one tonight.

His mouth twisted with something that almost looked like bitterness. "Because I was the guy who looked out for you. I wanted to be the one person you could always trust not to hurt you, not the creep who used our friendship to put the moves on you."

Her heart gave a reckless thump. "Oh."

"You used to call me your hero. Remember that? I liked being that guy for you. The one you always turned to. I didn't want to lose that. I didn't want to lose *you*, and I almost did in the back of that fucking limo on prom night when I over-played my hand."

"Overplayed?" She took a step toward him as the blood rushed in her ears. "Did you think I didn't like it when you kissed me?"

Pain flashed across his face, slicing through her gut like a knife. "The way you pulled away, it was pretty clear you didn't."

"I didn't pull away! *You* pulled away!" She remembered the humiliation of that moment with perfect clarity, as if it had happened yesterday. The way it had felt when he'd jerked away from her, stammering an apology. The look of panic on his face as he'd distanced himself.

"Only because of the way you flinched when I kissed you!" His voice had risen to match hers.

"Me? I didn't flinch!" she protested, taking another step toward him.

"You did!" he insisted. "I'll never be able to forget the way you stiffened when I touched you." His angry heat felt like her own. They were close enough she could feel it seeping into her skin.

"If I stiffened, it was only because it was unexpected! You took me by surprise!" They were practically shouting at each other, and she forced herself to speak more softly. "That doesn't mean I didn't like it."

His chest rose and fell as his expression shifted to confusion and then incredulity. "*Did* you like it?"

"Yes." She was close enough now to catch his scent. It caught at her, setting the surface of her skin on fire. "I thought *you* didn't like it. When you said we should pretend it never happened, I thought that meant you regretted it."

His eyes were wide and pained as he blinked at her. "I did regret it, because I thought you didn't want me to kiss you."

She couldn't look away from him. She didn't want to. The heat radiating off him buffeted her in waves. Her skin prickled as tendrils of desire coiled through the air between them.

"Well, fuck." Brooke reached for him, her hands cupping his face to drag his lips down to hers.

Dylan's hands wrapped around her waist as his tongue plunged into her mouth. She closed her eyes, breathing him in. Clean cotton, crisp cologne, and the unmistakable scent of his skin.

With every hitching breath, her breasts swelled against his chest, ratcheting up the heat between them. She pressed against him, needing more, wanting all of him, craving his touch on her body. She felt weak and light-headed, but Dylan held her steady, one of his arms locked around her waist as the other roamed up her back to cradle the nape of her neck.

Brooke dropped her hands to his chest, caressing his rock-hard pecs, and a sigh rumbled through him. His hand slid into her hair, his fingers tightening. She leaned into him, and it felt like her body was melding with his.

His palm skimmed her cheek. Then his fingers pressed into her jaw, tilting her head back as he broke the kiss. He gazed at her, and she watched his expression shift from uncertain to resolute. Single-minded.

That look on his face was her undoing. That look on his face wanted to possess her, and she wanted to be possessed by him like she'd never wanted anything before.

She clutched at the front of his shirt, pushing aside all her doubts. There wasn't room to think about anything but the nearness of him, and the heat in his eyes, and how much she needed to give him whatever he wanted from her.

They didn't speak. Their eyes said everything that needed to be said.

Dylan bent down again. His lips ghosted over Brooke's cheek, and he pressed a line of barely there kisses along her jaw. Soft. Warm. Featherlight. She jolted with pleasure when he reached her earlobe and nipped at the delicate skin, his tickling breath sending shivers down her spine.

She tugged at his shirt, twisting the fabric out of shape in her white-knuckled grip. With one arm still wrapped around her, he reached up to untangle her fingers and bring them to his lips. She dragged her index finger across his lower lip, tracing the succulent shape.

He licked his lips, and his tongue flicked against her finger. She pressed harder, parting his lips a little more, and he sucked the tip of her finger into his mouth.

Brooke moaned as an ache formed deep inside her. Dylan watched her, his mouth curving as he bit down on her finger. Her throat went dry, and she took a shuddering breath.

His lids lowered as his gaze dropped to her chest, moving over her body like a caress. She could almost feel it, like a physical force, as it roamed over her curves. But she needed to *actually* feel it. Feel his hands on her. His touch searing her skin.

"Tell me what you want." His voice was almost a growl.

"You. I want you." Breathing harder, Brooke dropped her hands to his chest. Squeezing, fondling, massaging. Touching him the way she wanted him to touch her.

Dylan's chest rose and fell under her fingers, his breath growing more unsteady with every stroke. When she pinched his deliciously hard nipple, he made a low hum in the back of his throat.

His hands slid down to cup her ass, kneading the soft flesh before he jerked her hips against his. She felt his hardness press against her as he lifted her up and carried her into the bedroom.

Brooke's head was spinning, her thoughts disjointed as Dylan laid her on the bed. Her whole body felt torturously tight. Her skin was so hot, she was afraid she'd burn him when he touched her, but she needed him to touch her. She needed it so much.

But they didn't rush. Not after so many years of pent-up attraction. Rushing this moment would have been a travesty. They took their time, kissing until she couldn't feel her lips anymore, and still they kept on kissing. They kissed as they undressed one another, and as they slowly explored each other's bodies, enjoying every inch.

They didn't speak. Their eyes and their hands and their tongues and their bodies communicated without words. Investigating, teasing, savoring.

It was torture and it was heaven.

Every touch felt blasphemous and wanton. Dangerous. *Thrilling*. Like they were breaking the rules. Crossing boundaries they'd never dared cross before.

They kissed until they couldn't hold back anymore, until pleasure had washed away the last of their inhibitions.

Chapter Twelve

"I can't believe that actually happened." Brooke lay sprawled next to Dylan on her bed with one of her legs thrown over his and their skin flushed and dewy with sweat.

"It definitely happened." He nuzzled against the top of her head and his hand squeezed her shoulder. "You okay?"

"I'm not sure," she admitted. "Tell me we didn't just make a huge mistake." Now that she was coming down off the sex high, her doubts were raising their ugly heads again.

"It doesn't have to be."

Brooke lifted her head to look at him. "I'd really hate to think we screwed up an eighteen-year friendship just to scratch an itch."

The corner of his mouth quirked. "But it feels so good to scratch it."

She couldn't argue with that, so she didn't try. "I'm serious." Her fingers spread over his bare chest. "I don't want to regret this."

"Then don't." His fingertips stroked over her back, drawing indecipherable patterns on her skin.

Brooke wished it was as simple as he made it sound. It would be so nice to lose herself in the present moment, but the worry gremlins were whispering in the back of her mind about all the potential problems that lay ahead. "I don't want to lose you over a hookup."

Dylan's eyebrows lifted slightly. "Is that what we're calling this?"

"It can't be anything more than that. Your life is in New York and mine is here. I don't see that changing anytime soon, and I don't see a way to make anything serious work long-term."

"Brooke." He lifted his hand to push a strand of hair out of her face. "I'm enjoying being with you. Can't we just leave it at that and have a good time together while I'm here?"

"Just so long as we both agree up front that this can't be anything permanent or serious. I'm not interested in being a long-distance girlfriend."

His hand curled around the back of her neck, pulling her in for a kiss. "Noted," he murmured against her lips.

Relief poured through her in a rush. She'd been afraid they wouldn't see eye to eye, but if Dylan was on board with the friends-with-benefits thing, this could actually be great. It was just sex, right? Their friendship was strong enough to survive this.

She kissed him again before pushing herself off the bed. "I'm gonna brush my teeth. I'll be back in a minute." Instinctively, her arms crossed over her chest as the sheet slipped down.

"Why are you trying to cover up?" he teased. "After everything we just did to each other, don't tell me you're suddenly shy."

She yanked a handful of blanket out from under him and pulled it up over her breasts. "I'm not used to being looked at when I'm naked. I don't know how you can stand to have people staring at your body all the time."

Dylan rolled over, trapping the blanket she was trying to steal underneath his legs. "It's just work. You get accustomed to it and realize it's no big deal."

"Don't act like you're above modesty. You definitely did some blushing when I saw you naked the other morning." Brooke gave the blanket a tug, but it wouldn't budge with his weight on top of it.

"Well, yeah, because I didn't want you to see how turned on I was."

She quit trying to wrestle the blanket away from him. "Were you?"

"Yeah. Turned on and embarrassed at the same time."

He was too adorable. Especially now, with his hair all sex-mussed and his lips pink and swollen. She leaned forward and kissed him on the mouth, enjoying the fact that she could do it freely and without guilt. "You have nothing to be embarrassed about. Believe me. Nothing."

He hummed against her lips. "If you want to brush your teeth, you better get out of this bed right now before I roll you over and have my way with you again."

Brooke wriggled out of his grasp. "Hold that thought."

"I'm looking at you naked!" He shouted after her as she ran into the bathroom.

Laughing, she shut the door behind her. After she'd peed and brushed her teeth, she grabbed a robe off the back of the bathroom door and went into the kitchen to give Murderface his dinner. He was waiting beside his food bowl, glaring his disapproval at her for making his dinner late. "Sorry, dude," she said as she measured out his food. "I had pressing business that needed taking care of."

When she got back to the bedroom, Dylan was just getting into bed after brushing his own teeth. She paused in the doorway to admire his naked form as he slid between the sheets.

His mouth quirked in a smile when he noticed her. "Planning on joining me?"

"Just admiring the view."

He cocked a disapproving eyebrow. "You're not naked anymore."

"I had to feed the cat and didn't want to give the neighbors a show."

He crooked a finger at her. "Come here."

Something in her belly tightened in response. "I like it when you're bossy."

"Then take off that robe."

She did as instructed, leaving it in a pile on the floor as she moved toward the bed.

He reached for her as she crawled into his arms. His fingers traced the curve of her hip, raising goose bumps on her skin. "You're so beautiful."

"No need to flatter me." She pressed a kiss into his jaw just below his ear. She loved being in his arms. Somehow it felt both completely new and completely familiar. The best of both worlds. "You've already lured me into bed."

He rolled her onto her back, pinning her hips beneath his. "It's not flattery. It's the truth." His fingertips brushed over her cheek, then her lips, then her forehead, smoothing her hair back from her face. "You are beautiful."

Her hands wandered freely over his body, caressing his chest, skimming his abs, gliding over his hips. His muscles

139

were so hard beneath acres of smooth, warm skin, he should be a national monument protected by the Park Service. She'd like to be the ranger assigned to patrol his historic ridges and valleys.

"You spend your days around people who are professionally beautiful," she said. "I can't even begin to compete."

He cupped her face in his hands, holding her gaze with his own. "You're more beautiful than any of them. You're the most beautiful person I know." His eyes sparked with heat as he lowered his mouth to hers.

They didn't talk for a long time after that.

Brooke had to go in for office hours the next morning, and she was an exhausted, frazzled mess. Hours of late-night sexual euphoria and boning like a pair of horny dolphins had taken their toll, but she didn't regret it one bit.

They'd communicated like functional-ass adults. She'd been honest about what she was able to offer, and Dylan had said he wasn't looking for anything more than that.

It was fucking perfect.

Literally. He was the best lover she'd ever had. Aside from the fact that he was by far the best looking, he was also the most attentive, the most dexterous, and the most creative. He made sure all her needs were satisfied, but he also wasn't bashful about taking his own pleasure.

She appreciated a man who knew what he wanted and made sure to give as good as he got. In her experience, they were almost as rare as unicorns.

So what if she was paying the price with a little exhaustion this morning? Totally worth it.

"What do you think about going to Venice Beach this

afternoon?" she asked Dylan as she dug through her closet, trying to piece together a decent outfit.

"Don't you have to work?" He watched her from the bed, where he was lounging in the nude.

It seemed to be his preferred state of being, and she couldn't say she disapproved. Even if it was a little distracting when she was trying to get ready for work.

"Only for a few hours this morning," she said. "I could come back here at noon and pick you up, and we could go to lunch. Maybe walk along the boardwalk?" She stopped flipping through the hangers and glanced over her shoulder. "Unless you have plans today already?"

He propped his head on his hand and grinned. "No plans except to spend as much time as I can with you."

She liked the sound of that. "We can also do something else if you want," she offered. She didn't care what they did, as long as they were together, but she felt like she ought to at least make an effort to play the good host.

"No, Venice Beach sounds fun."

She smiled at him, letting her eyes drift down his body. "Cool."

"Brooke?"

"Hmm?"

"You know you're staring, right?"

Yep, she was very aware. She was also aware of the drool puddling at the corner of her mouth. "Does it bother you?" she asked, quirking an eyebrow.

"No."

"Good." Her smile got wider. "I like looking at you."

His eyes seemed to glimmer. "I like being looked at by you."

141

She took a step toward the bed, absolutely planning to go over there and kiss the hell out of him, but stopped herself just in time. "Fuck. Stupid work. I can't with all this"—she waved her hand, encompassing all of him and his sexy lounging—"right now."

He laughed. "Would it help if I put some clothes on?"

"Never, ever do that on my account." She bit her lip. "But yes, probably."

He pulled on a shirt and a pair of pants, and she managed to finish getting ready for work without assaulting him.

Although she did kiss him for a solid minute before she left for campus.

Brooke was still suffering from an epic orgasm hangover when she slunk into her office thirty minutes later. She'd hoped to avoid talking to anyone until she'd finished her second cup of coffee and could form coherent thoughts, but no such luck.

"Yo, you look like shit," Tara said by way of greeting.

"Thanks, you big flirt." Brooke made a kissy face as she strode past her to her own desk.

Tara's eyes narrowed as she spun in her chair to follow Brooke's progress across the room. "Hang on. Bags under the eyes. Swollen lips. Walking stiffly." Her face lit up in a grin. "Someone got fucked last night! Was it the underwear model? It's got to be the underwear model. Tell me everything." She leaned forward in her chair and rested her chin in her hands.

"Oh, I wish I could, but I've got so much grading to do." Brooke gestured at the stack of exams on her desk.

"No, no, you don't get to do that." Tara wagged a finger

at her. "You can't get me all invested in the saga of your high school hottie and then go all withholding on me. I require deets."

Brooke made a zipping motion across her lips. "A lady doesn't kiss and tell."

"Aha! I knew it." Tara raised her arms over her head in triumph. "Well done, your ladyship. Was it good?"

"What do you think?" Brooke didn't bother to hide her grin.

"You never know with the pretty ones. Sometimes they don't know their ass from their elbow."

"He knows," Brooke said. "Believe me." She was smiling again just remembering the previous night. Best sex of her life was not an exaggeration.

"You bringing him to the picnic, then?"

Brooke hesitated. "I don't know. I'm thinking of skipping altogether." She wanted to spend that day with Dylan, not socializing with her coworkers at a lame picnic.

"Mmmm. Bad plan," Tara said, shaking her head. "You know how the department chair gets about this fucking picnic. He *will* be there, and he'll be making a list of who shows and who doesn't. But I mean, hey, it's your funeral. You want to ride the wave to Bonertown with your underwear model instead, I can't say I blame you."

Brooke scrunched up her face. "Ugh. You're right. Fine. I'll go."

Tara spun back around to face her computer. "Don't forget, you're signed up to bring a dessert."

"When did I sign up for that?"

"You didn't. I put you down." Tara shot a finger gun at Brooke over her shoulder. "You're welcome."

Great. So now not only would half of Brooke's last day with Dylan be spent in some godforsaken park space schmoozing with department faculty, alumni, and students, but now she was also responsible for laying hands on some kind of dessert. Fabulous.

Her phone buzzed and she pulled it out of her pocket. It was a new text from Dylan. He'd sent her a selfie along with a two-word message.

Missing you.

There was nothing overtly salacious about the photo. He was clothed, visible only from the collarbone up. But his expression managed to convey longing in a way that had Brooke's stomach flip-flopping like crazy.

She couldn't get back to him fast enough.

"I have to get a picture in front of this for my Instagram," Dylan said as he dragged Brooke toward the Venice sign at Windward and Pacific. "Will you take it?"

She was nervous about photographing a professional model, but he stood behind her and guided her hands to frame the shot with the sign in the background before jogging over to position himself in frame, striking an effortlessly cool pose. All she had to do was tap to get the perfect shot of him.

Once he'd approved the photo, he insisted on getting a selfie of them together. Again, Brooke felt nervous about posing with a model, but he made a face that made her laugh, and managed to catch a shot of them both looking attractively carefree and happy.

"Please tell me you're not posting that anywhere." She was pleased with how the photo had turned out, but that didn't mean she wanted it blasted out to all his model friends and followers.

"These are just for me," he promised, and snapped another selfie as he turned his head to kiss her.

They walked on toward the beach, and Dylan reached for her hand as naturally as if it was something they'd always done. Brooke couldn't remember ever holding his hand before, but their fingers fit together like it was an old habit rather than a new one.

To anyone else who saw them, they looked just like a real couple. She tried to imagine what that would be like, being in a real relationship with Dylan. *His girlfriend.* Would she still be happy after the newness had worn off? Or would she start to get her usual relationship claustrophobia?

Thank goodness she wouldn't have to find out.

They ate lunch on the patio of a restaurant near the boardwalk. It was a perfect afternoon to visit the beach: sunny and bright, with just a few lazy clouds moving in the late summer sky. Brooke got the fried chicken sandwich, and Dylan ordered the lobster roll with a side of sweet potato fries, which he pushed toward her to share. Once again, she tried to pay for her share of lunch, and once again he wouldn't let her.

Afterward, they strolled up the boardwalk toward Muscle Beach, occasionally stopping to window-shop or gape at the local wildlife.

"Is that person wearing a loincloth and a boa constrictor?" Dylan asked as they passed a man with a huge snake draped over his bare chest.

"Yes. Yes, he is," Brooke answered with a laugh.

145

It was far from the weirdest thing on display. They saw all sorts of street performers, from a guitarist on roller skates to a magician dressed like a mad scientist who was swallowing balloons. There were tumblers, dancers, musicians, and folks in all sorts of costumes. Between the people watching and the stunning view of the Pacific Ocean, no matter where you looked there was always something to see.

Spending time with Dylan was a million times more fun than spending time with any of the other men Brooke had dated. She could be herself with Dylan, in a way she'd never felt able to do with anyone else. They chatted easily as they walked, and Brooke marveled that they never seemed to run out of things to talk about. They laughed at each other's dumb jokes, finished each other's sentences, and had a surprising amount in common after so many years apart leading such different lives.

It turned out they both loved the TV show *Schitt's Creek*, which wasn't so surprising, but also they both read romance novels, which was.

"What, you don't think men can read romance novels?" Dylan asked off Brooke's expression of astonishment.

"It's not a matter of can, it's a matter of whether they choose to, and I've never known any who did."

Most of the men she knew would sooner be caught dead than reading a romance. She'd grown used to being mocked for her reading habits by men who collected World of Warcraft novelizations and liked to pretend they understood Kerouac. It was a novelty to discover one who not only read romance, but liked it.

"I'll admit, I was skeptical at first," Dylan said. "The only reason I picked one up is I was thinking about taking a cover

146

modeling gig, and I wanted to see what kind of books my face would be on."

"Your face or your abs?" Brooke asked as they paused to watch a pair of acrobats who'd attracted a small crowd. "They don't always show the guy's face."

Dylan chuckled. "That's true."

"Wait? Did you end up doing it? Does that mean there's a romance novel out there with you on the cover?" If so, she needed to track it down and purchase a copy immediately. What if it was one she'd already read without realizing the man-chest on the cover belonged to a man she actually knew?

"Not yet," he told her, shaking his head. "It didn't end up working out with my schedule, but I'm totally open to it. Once I started reading romance, I was hooked. I mostly listen to audiobooks now. They're great for getting me out of my head during a shoot, although I have to be careful with the steamy scenes if I want to avoid inopportune wood on the job."

"Oh my god." Brooke hadn't considered that, but now it was all she could think about. "Is the sex what you like about them?" After last night, she could testify to exactly how in touch he was with his sensual side. Based on the single data point of Dylan, she was ready to declare that romance novels should be required reading for all men.

His eyebrows waggled as he turned a grin on her. "I definitely enjoy the sexy parts, but that's not the only reason I read them. What I really like is how optimistic romances are. People always get what they deserve—good or bad."

Brooke hadn't really thought about it, but she supposed it was true. It was funny, really, that she liked to read romances when she was such a pessimist where her own romantic life was concerned. Although perhaps that was exactly *why* she enjoyed them. They provided an escape from her own mundane experiences, in the same way science fiction and fantasy did.

Dylan let go of her hand in order to dig his wallet out of his pocket. "I used to only read books I thought smart people read, because I wanted to prove I was as good as they were. But god, those books were all so depressing. It felt like a chore." He dropped a few bills into the acrobats' tip pail before he and Brooke moved on down the boardwalk. "I finally realized, no matter what books I read, no one was ever going to look at me and think I was smart, so I might as well read what makes me happy."

"Hey, you *are* smart." Brooke tucked her arm through his and gave him a reprimanding shake.

He smiled at her and covered her hand with his. "I know that and you know that, but people are always going to look at me and assume I'm just a hot dum-dum." He shrugged. "It is what it is. I'm not going to be an asshole who complains about being too good-looking. If people underestimate me, that's something I can use to my advantage."

"Good for you." She squeezed his arm, glad to hear him sounding so confident about his own capabilities. Maybe his mother hadn't completely broken his self-esteem after all. "So what's your favorite romance trope?"

His eyebrows pulled together. "Trope?"

"It's like a premise or setup," she explained. "A popular story device that gets written over and over again. Like enemies to lovers."

"Ah." He smiled a dazzling smile. "That'd be best friends to lovers. Obviously."

148

Chapter Thirteen

Brooke dragged Dylan over to a sunglasses kiosk, and they took turns picking out the goofiest-looking frames for each other to try on. He let her buy him a pair of tacky purple frames that somehow managed to look both totally hot and totally ridiculous on him.

They continued down the boardwalk chatting easily as they took in the sights, until they got tired of walking and found a relatively clean patch of sand to sit and look out at the waves.

"This is nice," Dylan said. "I like it better than the East Coast beaches. It's more like the Gulf Coast."

"I love the ocean." Brooke closed her eyes and tipped her head back, letting the sound of the crashing waves sink into her. "It doesn't matter which one."

"I'd sure as hell hope so, with your job."

She smiled up at the sky. "I guess that's true. I'd be in the wrong program if I didn't like the ocean."

Dylan shifted beside her and laid his head in her lap. "How did you know this was what you wanted to do? It feels like something you've always wanted."

She tilted her head forward to look at him, squinting as

her eyes adjusted to the sunlight again. "Not always. I wanted to be a princess when I was four."

"Didn't we all?" He smiled and reached for her hand, resting it on his stomach and covering it with his.

Brooke gazed out at the waves as she searched back through her memories for the one that had set her on her career path. "It was when my parents took us to Gulfport for the first time. It must have been the summer after second grade, not long after we moved to Baton Rouge from Missouri. I'd never been to the beach before. We took a boat ride to Ship Island, and I remember watching the dolphins swim behind the boat and thinking it was the most amazing thing I'd ever seen. It was like I'd achieved nirvana."

"And you've had a nerd boner for the sea ever since."

She laughed. "Pretty much."

"You think you'll stay here in Los Angeles after you finish your degree?"

His hair was tickling her leg and she reached up to smooth it down. "I don't know. I like it here. It just depends where I can get a job." Her fingers lingered in his hair, playing with the thick strands.

His expression relaxed into a beatific smile that reminded her of a golden retriever. "Would you work for a university? Or are there other options?"

"There are museum jobs that would be pretty great—working on stored specimens and doing science outreach, which I love. But there aren't very many of those jobs, and there's a lot of competition for them." She sighed, thinking about the big black hole of uncertainty that lay ahead. Jobs in her field were hard to get, and she wasn't sure if she wanted to stay in academia, even if she had the option. There was always a chance you'd end up as an adjunct teaching Bio 101 in some landlocked state earning less than the average bartender made. "Honestly, I try not to think about the future too much. It's too easy to get freaked out over it. I've got another year before I have to start looking for a postdoc position."

Dylan's fingers flexed on hers, pressing her palm into his stomach. "I like it here. I think I could be an LA person."

"Really? I thought you loved New York." She knew he was suffering from burnout, but the way he'd raved about New York when he first moved there, she figured he'd never want to live anywhere else.

"Love's a strong word. New York's great, but I wouldn't mind living somewhere else for a while."

She gazed at him and smiled at the thought of him living in California. He certainly looked the part right now, with his smooth bronze skin and the sunlight burnishing his hair with gold against the backdrop of the ocean.

Dylan was uncannily, improbably attractive, but what Brooke felt when she looked at him didn't have anything to do with his outward appearance. Her chest wasn't aching over the perfect symmetry of his face, and her stomach didn't clench because of his biceps—nice as they were. The fondness she felt for him went deeper than what lay on the surface.

He lifted up his tacky purple sunglasses and narrowed his eyes at her. "You're staring again."

"There's a lot to look at, and it's all very . . . pleasant."

He gave her a look of mock offense. "Pleasant? That's the best you can do?"

"Fishing for compliments, are we?" She gave his hair a gentle tug. "As if you're not constantly being told how attractive you are."

Something raw and a little too real glimmered in the depths of his blue eyes. "It's different when it comes from you."

And just like that, her chest went painfully tight as her stomach did a series of somersaults. She looked away quickly.

"Brooke?" His fingers clenched around her hand. "What's the matter?"

She shook her head and forced herself to look at him again. "Is this as weird for you as it is for me?" Normally she was impervious to motion sickness, but whenever she looked into Dylan's eyes, the world seemed to swoop and sway around her.

"It's not weird for me at all."

"Really?"

He brought her hand to his lips and kissed it before pushing himself to his feet. "Come on, let's go home."

She let him pull her upright and lead her back to the boardwalk. As they walked back toward the car, she tucked her arm through his and tipped her head to rest it on his shoulder. It fit there perfectly, like his shoulder had been designed explicitly for her to rest her head on.

"What do you want to do for dinner?" she asked. The shadows were growing longer as the sun slipped toward the horizon. By the time they fought the traffic home, it would be evening.

"You," he answered automatically.

"That's a given." She lifted her head to smile at him. "I

152

meant in addition to that. Do you want to go out tonight? Or stay in?"

"Stay in. Definitely."

She liked that answer. All she could think about was getting him home and tearing his clothes off. Going out to a restaurant would only delay her gratification.

Dylan stopped and spun her around, pointing at a figure disappearing into the crowd. "Hey, I think that was Mark Ruffalo."

"Star light, star bright, first star I see tonight." She nudged him with her shoulder. "Make a wish."

"I don't think it works with celebrities," he said, laughing.

She wrapped her hands around his arm and rested her chin on his shoulder. "It works if you believe it works. Now come on, close your eyes and make a wish."

He did as she told him.

"What'd you wish for?" she asked, trailing her finger down his arm when he opened his eyes.

His eyes were smiling as they looked into hers. "If I tell you, it won't come true."

He kissed her as the salty breeze whipped Brooke's hair across her face, getting in both their eyes. Kissing him was sunshine and rainbows and puppies and chocolate cake, but it also made her hot all over. The kind of heat that built low in her center and spread out through her whole body and up into her brain, making her feel giddy and intoxicated.

When he stopped kissing her, she opened her eyes and found him staring at her with surprising intensity.

"What?" she said, reaching up to touch his cheek.

SUSANNAH NIX

He shook his head. "Nothing. Just admiring the view."

She grinned. "Let's go back to my place so you can put your love dolphin in my blow hole."

He tugged her body flush against his, pressed a finger to her lips, and gazed deeply into her eyes. "Don't ever, *ever* say that again. My *god*."

Friday morning, Brooke woke to the caress of Dylan's lips on her mouth.

It was still dark, which meant it was definitely too early to be awake. Especially after their many and varied exertions last night, which had kept them occupied well into the wee hours.

"Go back to sleep," he whispered. "I'm going for a run."

Evidently he was a lunatic. Just because he needed to keep his bod in tip-top shape for his job was no excuse to go dragging himself out of bed for a run at ohmygodwhat-timeisit o'clock when he was supposed to be on vacation. Not when there was a nice, warm bed available for snuggling in.

She reached out sleepily, intending to pull him back into the bed with her, but he was already gone. Sighing, she settled for snuggling into the pillow he'd abandoned and fell right back to sleep.

The next time Brooke awakened, it was to the smell of coffee and bacon, and the sight of sunlight peeking through the blinds. Yawning, she dragged herself out of bed and helped herself to the shirt Dylan had discarded on her bedroom floor last night. Or maybe she'd been the one to do the discarding. The undressing had happened pretty fast and was a bit of a blur. Either way, she saw no reason to wear one of her own shirts when she could wear one of Dylan's.

She found him in the kitchen, making pancakes. A pan of bacon sizzled in the oven, scenting the apartment with deliciousness. As she approached, he glanced over his shoulder at her and smiled. "I like you in my shirt."

"Good, because I like me in your shirt too."

He wore athletic shorts and a sweaty T-shirt, his hair still damp and disordered from his run. It was ridiculous how sexy he looked like that, so she went straight over to him and kissed him.

"Hi," he said, running his fingers through her hair. "Did you get enough sleep?"

"No," she replied. "Someone kept me up half the night."

"That's too bad." He brought her hand to his lips. "Whoever it was should be ashamed of himself."

"I'm not complaining. In fact I'm hoping he does it again tonight. And this afternoon. And this morning." She kissed him again. It ought to be gross with him all sweaty from his run, but it wasn't. It was the exact opposite of gross.

His arms wrapped around her, bending her back a little. When the oven timer beeped, he let go of her. "Hang on."

She waited until he'd taken the bacon out of the oven before kissing him again. This time she let her hand wander down inside his shorts.

"I'm in the middle of making pancakes," he protested, but he didn't pull away.

"I'm not hungry for pancakes right now." Her stomach growled noisily, making her a liar.

He laughed. "Pancakes first. After that, you can have anything you want."

"Anything?" she asked.

He kissed her again and smiled. "Anything."

By eleven o'clock they still hadn't gotten dressed. Technically, Dylan had been dressed for a while when he'd gone for his run, but then Brooke had gotten him undressed again after breakfast, and he had been undressed ever since. She was taking it as a personal victory.

They were curled up together on her couch, because they'd never made it back to the bedroom after breakfast.

"What do you want to do today?" he asked, glancing at his phone.

"You," she answered automatically. His skin smelled lovely. She wanted to huff it like the scented markers her parents would never let her have when she was a kid.

He set his phone down and nuzzled against her throat. He hadn't shaved since Monday, and his face was wonderfully bristly. "Anything else?" His stubble tickled her neck, but she liked it so she didn't move.

"We could do more sightseeing if you want. Is there anything else you want to see while you're here?"

This was their only full day together where they didn't have anywhere else to be. Brooke was torn between wanting to make the most of it and wanting to stay home and snuggle with Dylan all day. Which was another extremely valid way of making the most of it.

"I've always wanted to see the Getty," he offered. "I've heard it's nice."

She could sense him growing increasingly antsy the longer they lay around doing nothing. He was probably itching to

156

get out of the house. This was supposed to be his vacation, after all.

"Then we'll go to the Getty." She kissed the tip of his nose. "Your wish is my command."

"Are you sure it's okay you took the whole day off?" Dylan asked as they wandered through an exhibition of Michelangelo's sketches.

Brooke tilted her head as she peered at a partial sketch of a male nude. "It's fine. I don't have class or office hours on Fridays, and I can take one day off from the lab while you're in town."

"He kind of looks like my Uncle George," Dylan commented as he leaned forward to study the drawing.

"Your Uncle George has a nice butt," she said. "But yours is much cuter."

Dylan threw an amused look at her over his shoulder. "That makes me feel weird."

"You're the one who brought up your uncle's butt."

"I was talking about his face." He poked her in the shoulder. "*You're* the one fixated on butts."

Brooke shrugged. "I know what I like."

"Perv."

"You know it."

His smile turned uncertain as he reached for her hand. "You're not bored, are you? Did I drag you to an art museum against your will?"

"Of course not. I'm having a great time." She leaned in to give him a chaste kiss on the cheek, mindful of all the families around them. "Even if there is a disappointing lack of dinosaurs here."

157

She'd always been more of a natural science museum person than an art museum person, but she was enjoying the Michelangelo exhibit. She'd already learned that Michelangelo was one of the few Renaissance artists to examine corpses and participate in dissections to further his understanding of the muscles and bones of the human body. It was fascinating to see his grasp of human anatomy reflected in his practice sketches for what would eventually become his masterpieces.

Although truthfully, she'd probably be having a good time with Dylan even if they were changing the oil in her car. Brooke felt so happy, it made her wish he didn't have to go back so she could have more of him.

As soon as the thought drifted through her mind, she warned herself not to go there. That was the sex-high talking. Those feelings wouldn't last once the endorphins wore off. On Sunday Dylan would leave, and Brooke's brain chemistry would return to normal again. She'd miss him for sure, but ultimately she'd be glad to have her normal life back.

After the Michelangelo exhibit, they strolled through a gallery of black and white photographs, and Dylan impressed Brooke by pointing out things she wouldn't have noticed on her own, like the use of positive and negative space, the rule of thirds, and the golden ratio.

"When did you turn into an art connoisseur?" she asked him.

He shrugged, looking faintly embarrassed. "I took a couple continuing ed art classes."

"I didn't know that." She regretted not keeping up with him more after she'd left for school, and vowed to do a better job from now on. No more letting months go by in between texts or phone calls.

"It was after you left for college. I thought it would help with my Instagram photography."

"I'd say it worked."

"Yeah, I guess." He pulled his phone out of his pocket and checked the screen. She'd noticed him checking it repeatedly throughout the day with what seemed like an increasing sense of impatience.

Ever nosy, she leaned in for a peep, but there was nothing to see on the screen. "Is your agent bothering you again?"

He slipped his phone into his pocket and returned his attention to Brooke. "No, he gave up, finally."

"Then why do you keep checking your phone?"

"It's nothing. I'm just expecting a call."

"About what?"

Dylan kissed the tip of her nose as he brushed a wisp of hair off her face. "Just boring work stuff. It's not important."

She didn't believe him. *Something* was important enough to preoccupy him, and the fact that he didn't want to tell her what it was bugged her a little.

See? This was exactly what happened when you were in a relationship. Reality poked its ugly head into the fantasy, throwing little frictions and annoyances into the works that built up over time, until eventually you couldn't stand the sight of each other anymore.

It was a *good thing* she and Dylan wouldn't have to go through that. Missing him was far preferable to watching her feelings for him twist into something ugly and unpleasant.

Whatever had him distracted was *his* business. If he didn't feel like sharing it with her for whatever reason, that was his business too.

Brooke rose up on her toes to run her fingers through his hair as she brushed a kiss across his lips. "As long as everything's okay."

He smiled as he rubbed his nose against hers. "Everything's perfect."

After another hour of walking through the museum, they found a patch of grass on the lawn outside and lay on their backs, holding hands and gazing up at the clouds.

"That one looks like a koala," Dylan said, lifting up both their hands to point.

"How is that a koala?" Brooke asked.

"You have to turn your head and kind of squint."

She turned her head and squinted. "Looks more like a blob to me."

"You're not playing right. You have to use your imagination."

"Okay, fine," she said, pointing. "That one looks like a nudibranch."

"A what?"

"A marine gastropod also known as a sea slug."

"So a blob, basically." Dylan laughed. "You're terrible at this."

"Maybe *you're* terrible at this, you ever think of that?"

He turned his head to look at her, his expression soft. "I'm so glad I'm here. I'm having the best time with you."

Brooke rolled onto her side so she was facing him. "Me too."

His hand cupped the back of her head as he shifted closer to kiss her. She'd never been the kind of person who wanted to be seen making out with a guy in public, but when it was Dylan doing the making out, she couldn't bring herself to mind.

She'd had her doubts about the friends-with-benefits arrangement, but it had worked out like a dream. Better than a dream.

Adding sex to the equation hadn't caused any weirdness or tension between them like she'd feared. If anything, it had relieved the tension that had been simmering beneath the surface for so many years. Scratching that itch seemed to have brought them even closer together. Their friendship was stronger than ever, but now with bonus fantastic sex thrown into the mix.

Best of all, they were on the exact same page. No expectations, no commitment, no promises. Just the two of them having a great time for as long as they happened to be around each other. Like a vacation fling, but better.

Dylan rolled away from her and dug his phone out of his pocket. "Sorry, I need to take this call." He got to his feet and wandered far enough away that she couldn't hear what he was saying as he held the phone to his ear.

Shielding her eyes from the sun, Brooke sat up and watched his shoulders move as he talked. His back was to her, so she couldn't read his expression for clues to how the call was going—or what it was about. But she'd be perfectly content to sit there watching this gorgeous man pace back and forth forever. Especially when he lifted an arm to rub the back of his head, making the muscles in his back ripple and flex. *Yum*.

After a few minutes, he turned around to look at her. She

161

lifted her eyebrows in query, and he gave her a thumbs-up. So . . . good news, it seemed.

Shortly thereafter, he ended the call and came back over to her, pressing his lips together like he was trying to contain a smile. The news must have been *very* good.

"Well?" she asked, leaning back on her hands as she gazed up at him. The sunlight glinted in his hair, casting a honeyed glow around his already golden features. "Did you get the news you wanted?"

"I did. Everything's set." Color tinged his cheekbones, and his teeth bit into his bottom lip, but he didn't elaborate any further.

C'est la vie.

When he extended a hand, Brooke let him pull her to her feet and straight into his arms. The softness had returned to his eyes, and it filled her with a warm buzzing sensation.

His hands stroked up her back as he bent his head to press his lips to her neck, just below her ear. The buzzing sensation increased, and suddenly she wished very much that they weren't in a public place.

"Are you ready to go home?" she asked as goose bumps shivered over her skin.

Home.

She kept using that word, as if it was his home too. It was a habit she needed to break before it was broken for her.

He's going to leave, she reminded herself.

But before he did, she planned to have as much of him as she could squeeze into the time they had left.

Chapter Fourteen

They stopped at the grocery store on the way back to her apartment so Brooke could pick up a dessert to take to the departmental picnic tomorrow. She'd planned to grab a tray of cookies from the Ralphs bakery department like the lazy non-baking person she was, but Dylan insisted on making something from scratch for them to take.

"It's really not necessary," Brooke protested as he dragged her through the store.

"Grocery store cookies are for losers," Dylan said as he surveyed the baking aisle.

"That's perfect, because I barely even like most of these people," she snarked in response, only halfway meaning it.

"Don't you want to be the hero who brings the delicious homemade treat everyone's talking about instead of the cheap crap no one wants to eat?" He dropped a tin of cocoa powder into his shopping basket. "I've got the perfect recipe. You're not gonna believe how good these brownies are. They're like an orgasm in your mouth."

"As enticing as that sounds, I'm not really looking to give all my colleagues orgasms at a picnic," Brooke said.

"Don't worry," Dylan murmured, leaning close to her ear.

163

"I'll make sure you get your dessert tonight." He punctuated this tantalizing promise by nipping her earlobe with his teeth.

A tingle traveled up her spine, and she took the basket out of his hand. "Let's hurry and get this done, then. What else do we need?" It had been hours since she'd last felt the motion of his ocean, and she was greedy for an encore.

They grabbed the rest of the ingredients he'd need to make the brownies, and Brooke drove them back to her place. Dylan carried the groceries up the stairs to her apartment and unpacked the bags while Murderface twined around his legs.

Somehow, in just a few days, he'd managed to become her famously standoffish cat's favorite person. Brooke could relate. After tomorrow, both she and the cat would be suffering from Dylan withdrawal.

Pushing aside the melancholy thought before it could ruin her mood, she threw herself into the task of helping Dylan make the brownies by fetching ingredients and kitchen implements for him. She didn't own a mixer, so he was forced to whisk the ingredients by hand. A circumstance she highly appreciated once she noticed how delectable his biceps looked as he was mixing the batter.

The sight of him in her kitchen making brownies triggered all sorts of domestic fantasies she hadn't even realized she had. A man this gorgeous and kind and thoughtful who could bake too? It defied reality. Dylan was like some rare and endangered species of bird that had only been spotted once or twice in the last century, somewhere deep in the rainforest, and whose continued existence was perpetually debated by experts.

Just watching him measure ingredients had Brooke's body

humming. Or maybe it was the chocolate. Didn't they say it was an aphrodisiac? Could the scent of melted chocolate be enough to send her libido into overdrive?

Her mouth watered as she watched him stir in the chocolate chips, his arm and shoulder muscles flexing as he worked. She'd never given a lot of thought to cooking before, but watching his deft, artful movements was like discovering a new kink.

Yeah, it was definitely Dylan that was sending her libido into overdrive. The chocolate was just a bonus.

He glanced her way, and his mouth twisted into a half-grin as he surveyed her over his shoulder.

"Yes, I was staring," Brooke confessed before he could point it out. "Sue me."

"I could take off my shirt if it would improve the experience," he offered casually.

"Would you? That'd be great."

She was kidding, but apparently he wasn't, because he let go of the spatula, reached behind his head, and pulled his T-shirt off.

Whoa.

"Better?" he asked as he tossed his shirt onto the floor of the dining room and resumed stirring the batter.

Brooke licked her lips. "Mmmm. Yeah. Excellent. Thanks." What could be better than a sexy, shirtless man baking brownies in her kitchen? It was like the ultimate lady porn.

"Baking pan?" he asked.

She passed him the metal baking pan she'd prepped with cooking spray, and he poured the brownie batter into it. Once the pan was full, she watched in horror as he scraped his finger along the inside of the bowl for a taste test.

"No, don't do that!" Brooke caught his wrist before he could pop his finger in his mouth. "You could get sick."

Arching his eyebrows in defiance, he stuck his finger in his mouth despite her grip on his wrist, and proceeded to lick every last speck of chocolate batter off in the most pornographic way possible.

Brooke let go of him, barely managing to suppress a laugh as she shook her head in disapproval. "It's your funeral."

"Has anyone ever actually gotten salmonella from eating raw eggs or are haters just trying to stop me from living my life to the fullest?"

"You stole that from Twitter." She'd read that exact same sentiment in a tweet just a few months ago.

He crossed his arms, which did truly amazing things for his pecs and biceps. "I'll have you know I got it from Facebook."

"Which means it originally came from Tumblr, as all the best content does."

"I don't understand Twitter." An adorable little line sprouted between his eyebrows. "It's like five hundred people standing in a room yelling at each other all day."

"That pretty well sums it up," Brooke agreed. "Anyway, it's not just eggs you have to worry about these days. Now it's the risk of *E. coli* in the raw flour."

He screwed up his face and wiped his mouth with the back of his hand. "The world really is going straight into the shitter. Literally."

"You're talking to someone who studies marine life. I could tell you things about the state of the ocean that would keep you up at night."

"I'm sure you could, but let's save that for another day. I've already got enough existential anxiety."

At the mention of the future, Brooke felt another stab of unease. There wouldn't be enough other days to have this or any other conversation. Not in person, anyway. Tomorrow was Dylan's last day here. Their last day together.

After he left on Sunday, things would go back to the way they used to be. The two of them would go back to being friends who talked on the phone occasionally but rarely saw each other. Even if Brooke made a point of keeping in touch better, they'd never have this moment again. They'd never have each other like this again.

When Dylan went back to his regular life, he'd be free to date if he wanted. And it sounded like he did. The way he'd talked when he first arrived, he was looking for a real, meaningful, permanent relationship. Exactly the sort of thing Brooke could never give him.

He deserved to have that, and she wanted it for him, but her stomach felt hollow at the thought of Dylan finding it with someone else.

If he started dating someone seriously, he wouldn't have as much room in his life for Brooke. She wouldn't be his best friend anymore. Not if he found the life partner he wanted. *She* would be his best friend instead, and Brooke would become a distant third wheel.

"Hey." Dylan snapped his fingers in front of Brooke's face. "Did you hear me?"

"Sorry, what?" She hadn't been listening to him at all.

He pointed two fingers at his face. "Eyes up here, sailor."

She belatedly realized she'd been staring into space—and the space she'd been staring into was occupied by Dylan's six-pack.

His mouth twisted into a cocky smirk. "Listen, I know my

bod's, like, hella distracting, but if you're just going to treat me like a piece of meat—"

Brooke grabbed him and kissed him. Full-on, urgent, devouring, tongue-down-his-throat kissed him.

"Okay, I take back what I said about treating me like a piece of meat," he murmured against her lips when he came up for air. "Go ahead and treat me like meat all you want, if it means you're going to keep kissing me like that."

She kissed him again, and his hands roamed under her shirt, skimming the curve of her waist, stroking up her rib cage, and unclasping her bra. Straining against him, she pressed her softness into his hardness. She was so consumed with need it left her shaky and desperate. Her hands explored his torso as their mouths slid together, and she heard herself moan in the back of her throat.

His hands grasped her face, and as his thumbs stroked down her cheeks, he pressed his forehead against hers. "Hold that thought."

Turning, he shoved the brownie pan in the oven and set a timer on his phone before returning his attention to her. He gripped her waist with both hands and shoved her back against the counter, pinning her with his hips as he bent his mouth to hers.

When he kissed her, all she could think about was how much she wanted more. More kissing, more Dylan, more everything . . .

If she didn't know better, she'd think she was falling in love. But of course she wasn't. It was too easy to get mixed up about what she was feeling, because she *did* love Dylan. He was one of her best friends. She'd walk through fire for him.

But that didn't mean she was *in* love with him.

Her sex organs were currently infatuated with his sex organs, but that was all this was. Lust. Craving. Excitement. A shallow, temporary physical infatuation layered over a foundation of long-standing platonic love.

This feeling wouldn't last. It didn't make them soul mates. It wasn't *real* love.

But that didn't mean it would be easy to give him up.

She dragged him into the bedroom while the brownies were baking, and Dylan made good on his promise of dessert—and then some. Brooke was certain she would forever associate the smell of baking brownies with the things he did to her, and she wasn't the least bit mad about it.

The rest of the evening was spent eating takeout Chinese and watching one of their favorite martial arts movies from childhood. Well . . . not so much *watching* the movie as lazily making out on the couch while the movie played in the background.

Eventually, after a languid slow burn, things heated up enough that they turned the movie off and retired to the bedroom again. This time their lovemaking was as slow and indulgent as their fooling around on the couch had been. They took their time, luxuriating in every touch and sensation. Baring their bodies and their souls. Neither of them in a hurry to reach their release, but instead seeking to draw it out, prolonging their shared pleasure. Dissolving into each other.

Much later that night, Brooke lay on her side watching the slow, steady rise and fall of Dylan's bare chest. He slept like the dead, serene and boneless, with one hand thrown over his head. Like a child without a care in the world. Enviously, she reached out and trailed her finger down his chest.

It had been a perfect day. If she could *Groundhog Day* herself, she'd pick today to live inside forever.

Alas, time marched ever onward. As the minutes ticked away toward the morning of their last day together, Brooke snuggled against Dylan and lay her head on his chest. He murmured her name in his sleep without waking and curled his body around hers.

She lay there listening to their hearts beat together in a dreamy state of half-sleep, unable to pinpoint just where he ended and she began.

Chapter Fifteen

It was her last full day with Dylan, and Brooke couldn't believe she was wasting half of it at this godforsaken departmental picnic, pretending to enjoy talking to the same people she was forced to interact with during the week.

She'd woken this morning with dread clawing at her belly. In less than twenty-four hours, Dylan would be headed back home, and their little sexcation would be over. No more kissing, no more orgasms, no more Dylan.

This was what you wanted, remember? Short and sweet. No commitment. No time for complications to develop.

So why did she feel like she was mourning a loss?

Because she wanted more time with him. Not infinite time, just more. A few more days would be good. A few more days and she'd have that itch well and truly scratched. She'd have Dylan out of her system and she could go back to her regular life, satiated and content.

Annoyingly, Dylan seemed to be in an extra-great mood today. Was he just settling into the vacation vibe? Or was he looking forward to leaving?

Brooke felt a fresh stab of irritation as she watched him holding court at the center of a group of female undergrads from her animal physiology lab. They were completely entranced by him, peppering him with questions about the modeling industry. You'd think they'd never seen an attractive man in their whole lives.

This must be what it was like to walk into a room with Henry Cavill on your arm.

They were blatantly trying to flirt with him. Smiling a little too much, laughing a little too loud at his jokes. Touching his arm or his shoulder whenever they could get close enough. Treating him like a show pony because of his job and his good looks. He was a novelty to them, rather than a real person.

While everyone fawned over Dylan, Brooke might as well be invisible. She could probably take off her clothes and dance a jig, and no one would even notice, they were so busy gazing into his eyes and drooling.

It was a taste of what life would be like as his girlfriend. Overlooked, overshadowed, ignored in favor of the shiny, pretty model. You might as well be a piece of used furniture. Brooke guessed it would get old really fast. They'd only been at this picnic an hour and she was already sick of it.

At least Dylan seemed to be enjoying himself. After answering the students' questions about modeling and New York City, he'd proceeded to start arguing with one of them about Bigfoot, of all things.

"If there's no such thing," Dylan was saying, "then y'all tell me what I saw outside Grosse Tête when I was twelve." Usually his accent was barely detectable, but today he sounded like he'd sauntered straight out of the bayou.

The student, who was pre-med and consistently at the top

of the curve, shook her head. "A bear? A person? Literally anything other than Bigfoot."

Dylan gifted her with a dazzling smile. "Come on, you think I can't tell some dude in a bear suit from a Bigfoot?"

"Clearly you can't," the future doctor said, grinning back at Dylan.

"This guy I know back home says he once saw a whole family of Bigfoots deep in the Atchafalaya near Bayou Chene."

"It's not a species," one of the other students insisted. "You can't pluralize Bigfoot."

"Sure you can," Dylan said. "One's a Bigfoot. More than one, you got Bigfoots. Everyone knows that."

He was having fun with them, leaning into both the dumb pretty boy act and the dumb country yokel act. Brooke couldn't tell if the students knew they were being trolled or not. Not that they would care, probably. They were just happy to be gazing into Dylan's beautiful face.

It irked her that they were underestimating him because of his appearance—exactly like he'd told her people did all the time. None of them saw him the way Brooke did: as a self-made success who'd built a million-dollar career, a generous friend who would do anything for the people he cared about, and the goofy guy who made jokes as lame as her own. To them he really was just a piece of meat. A collection of body parts and a nice face.

Although he didn't seem to mind so much at the moment. In fact, he was actively encouraging it with his charming Southern boy act.

Disgusted, Brooke wandered off to check out the selection at the potluck table. The brownies she and Dylan had made last night were almost gone already, and she snagged the last corner piece for herself.

"On behalf of all womankind, allow me to say, well done," Tara said, coming up behind her and clapping her on the back.

Brooke nearly choked on her brownie. "What?"

"Your underwear model toy boy over there."

"I told you, we're just friends," Brooke said irritably.

Anything else that was going on between them was no one's business. It wasn't like they were in a relationship where Dylan would be involved in Brooke's life on an ongoing basis. None of these people were ever going to see him again.

Tara made a scoffing noise. "Sure you are, and I'm Meghan Markle's twin sister. Can't you see the resemblance?"

Brooke shoved the rest of her brownie in her mouth rather than dignify that with a response.

"I love that you're playing it cool," Tara said with an approving nod. "No one would ever guess you two are an item from the way you were glaring daggers at all those undergrads flirting with your man."

Brooke scowled. She hadn't meant for her displeasure to be so obvious. Hopefully her students were too busy being mesmerized by Dylan to have noticed.

"He's not my man," she said. That much, at least, was true. Tomorrow Dylan would go back to his life in New York and back to being only a long-distance friend. "He's free to flirt with whoever he likes. I just think it's ridiculous how obvious they're all being."

"Don't be such a grampus," Tara said, taking the opportunity to work in one of her favorite sea mammal puns. "Let the kids have their fun. It's not often they get attention from a hot older man."

Brooke glanced over at Dylan, who was now posing for selfies with the students. She supposed Tara was right. There was no harm in it. She would have been just as enraptured by him at their age if Dylan had been a stranger to her.

"Did you see Mathias brought potato salad?" Tara said. "I signed up for potato salad. That Nordic bastard stole my dish."

"You need to chill," Brooke told her.

Tara's lips pursed as she stared daggers in Mathias's direction. "Don't worry, I'm not going to fight him here. I'm just going to suck my teeth and move on. But I won't forget this. I nurture my grudges as if they were my children. I keep them healthy and well-fed, and make sure they take their vitamins every day. My grudges will outlive me."

"Sometimes you scare me a little."

"Heads-up," Tara murmured. "Professor Lassman incoming." She grabbed the last brownie out of the pan and moved off, most likely to torture poor Mathias somehow.

Brooke looked up and saw her advisor approaching. Dr. Lassman was one of the younger professors in the department, only about ten years older than Brooke. She had a round, friendly face with a perpetually distracted look these days, thanks to her brutal teaching load this semester.

Dr. Lassman greeted Brooke with a smile. "I hear you brought brownies that aren't to be missed." The professor's eyes landed on the empty brownie pan and her face fell. "Ah. I see I was too slow. That'll teach me to get into a conversation with the dean."

"You can have the rest of mine," Brooke offered, holding out her half-eaten brownie.

Dr. Lassman's nose wrinkled. "Thanks, but I'll pass. I

actually wanted to talk to you about something." She glanced at a group of cell biology students grazing at the other end of the potluck table and cocked her head toward a nearby picnic table. "Let's go over there."

Her curiosity piqued, Brooke followed her advisor to the picnic table. They didn't sit down, which felt a bit ominous.

"It's about the NAMMC award." Dr. Lassman smoothed the hem of her T-shirt. "I happen to know one of the committee members, so I gave them a call yesterday. Just to, you know, put in a good word for you."

"Wow, thank you so much!" Brooke didn't really expect there to be any news yet, because the deadline had only just passed and academics typically took forever to do anything, but she appreciated that her advisor had gone the extra mile for her.

Dr. Lassman rubbed the back of her neck. "So here's the thing: you're not going to get it this year."

"Oh." Brooke felt like someone had dumped a bucket of ice water over her head. "Okay." She swallowed, trying not to let her disappointment show. "I'm just—I'm surprised to hear that, since the deadline was only Wednesday. I wouldn't have thought they'd have had time to read all the papers yet."

"They haven't." Dr. Lassman pressed her lips together in an apologetic grimace. "But she said they prefer to give the award to someone who's at the end of their doctoral program, and since you're only in your fourth year . . ."

"It didn't say anything about that in the awards call." Brooke had read all the requirements carefully. She was positive there'd been no mention of how far into their program candidates needed to be.

"No, it didn't. It's a soft norm—if no one currently on the

job market applies, they'll give it to someone earlier in their program. But preference is given to more advanced candidates." She paused, looking pointedly at Brooke. "And since Monica also applied—"

"She's going to get it," Brooke finished for her, not bothering to keep the bitterness out of her voice.

"Not necessarily. It may go to someone else entirely. But she'll have an automatic edge on you, I'm afraid, by virtue of being a year ahead."

Brooke nodded, looking down at the ground as a dark flush heated her cheeks. Although she'd tried not to let herself think she had a real shot, she'd still harbored a measure of hope. Utterly false hope, as it turned out.

Dr. Lassman's voice grew softer. "I know you worked really hard on this submission, and I know you're disappointed. But it happens. Next year when you apply again you'll be a year deeper into your dissertation and closer to being on the job market, which means you'll have an even better chance."

Brooke tried to keep the disappointment out of her expression. "Thank you for letting me know—and for putting in the call."

She bit back angry tears as Dr. Lassman walked off. The award had always been a long shot, but Brooke was still crushed. It'd be one thing if she'd been given due consideration and lost fair and square because someone else was better. But they hadn't even had time to read her paper. All that work, pushing herself to make the deadline, and it had all been for nothing. She wasn't even in the running.

Suddenly, all the doubts and fears she tried to keep at bay began to whisper in her ear.

You can't finish this degree.

You'll never find a postdoc.

You're going to fail.

Everyone pities you, because they know you're not good enough.

That was what she got for taking a risk and putting herself out there. She should have known better. She never should have let herself think she had a shot at something special.

"Hey." Dylan came up behind her and draped his arm around her shoulders. Brooke stiffened, and he let go, frowning. "What's wrong?"

"Nothing. Sorry." She felt bad for flinching away from him.

"Did you not want me to touch you in front of your colleagues?"

"No, it's fine."

"Are you sure? It doesn't seem fine. Or is something else bothering you?"

"No, nothing's wrong." She reached for his hand and gave it a reassuring squeeze as she shoved her disappointment down deep. "I'm just annoyed that I had to come to this lame picnic today and drag you along with me."

She didn't want to tell Dylan about the award. She was too upset and embarrassed to have put herself forward and wasted all that time she could have been spending with him instead. She'd made it sound like she actually had a shot, when it had all been a fantasy.

"It's not that bad," he told her. "I'm having a perfectly fine time."

"Yeah, you seemed to be enjoying all the attention."

Dylan frowned. "You know I don't give two shits about those girls, right? I was just fucking around."

"I know, I'm sorry. I'm just in a crappy mood for some reason."

His expression softened. "Is it because I'm leaving tomorrow?"

"Maybe a little," Brooke admitted.

"Hey." He reached up to tuck her hair behind her ear. "I'm dreading it too."

She searched his face. "Really? Because you haven't seemed like it."

"I was putting on a brave front. I just want to enjoy our last day together."

"Me too."

It occurred to Brooke that she hadn't kissed him in at least three hours, which was a genuine tragedy. She pulled him toward her and rectified the oversight.

He tasted like apple pie, which almost made everything better.

Chapter Sixteen

Penny and Caleb had never looked happier.

You know that look someone gets when their smile is trying to explode out of their face because even their widest smile isn't enough to contain it? That was both Penny and Caleb as they greeted the guests at their reception.

They'd chosen a venue in Santa Monica surrounded by beautiful gardens and shady trees strung with lanterns. Inside the house, fairy lights hung from the rafters, and bunches of purple flowers surrounded by tea light candles adorned every surface. The air smelled like lavender and vanilla.

Soft music played in the background as the guests mingled over drinks and canapés. Brooke recognized Tessa and Lacey from the bachelorette, and Melody with a handsome date who must be her fiancé. As she made her way over to the newlyweds, Brooke plastered a bright smile on her face, determined not to let her bad mood spill over onto Penny and Caleb's celebration.

"Congratulations!" she exclaimed as she squeezed Penny. "Look at you, you look amazing! I can tell married life agrees with you."

Penny was glowing, not just with happiness, but also from

the tan she'd acquired on her honeymoon. Her blush lace sheath dress perfectly complemented her golden complexion and long red hair.

"It definitely does," Penny agreed as Brooke gave Caleb a congratulatory hug.

He looked devastatingly handsome in his suit and tie, although he tugged at the collar uncomfortably as soon as Brooke let go of him. Caleb was sweet as pecan pie, but the very definition of the strong, silent type. Which made him well-suited for Penny, whose sunny personality was outgoing enough for the both of them.

Brooke introduced Dylan, and they chatted about the wedding and their honeymoon in Cabo San Lucas for a few minutes, before the next guests arrived and the newlyweds excused themselves to welcome them.

"They seem really great," Dylan said as he and Brooke made their way toward the bar.

"They are."

Brooke had known Penny for nearly seven years now, although they really only saw each other when they were with Olivia. Speaking of Olivia, she'd spotted Brooke from across the room and was making a beeline their way with Adam in tow.

"Hey, hot stuff!" Brooke greeted her. "Told you that dress would look killer on you."

"Not bad, right?" Olivia lifted Adam's hand over her head to twirl under his arm in the lavender chiffon bridesmaid's dress she'd worn as Penny's maid of honor at the wedding in Virginia. She'd fretted that it would be too pale against her nearly translucent complexion, but it was just the right amount of color alongside her fair skin and hair.

Brooke tugged Dylan away from the bar to make the introductions. "Olivia and Adam, this is my friend Dylan Price from back home."

Dylan shook Adam's hand and then Olivia's. "Good to meet you both."

Olivia gave him a friendly smile. "I've been hearing Brooke talk about you for years. It's nice to finally put a face to the name."

"Uh oh," Dylan said as he collected their drinks from the bartender and passed Brooke her white wine. "I hope she hasn't been sharing embarrassing stories from our youth."

"No, she has not, and now I'm mad she's been holding out on me." Olivia leveled a challenging glare at Brooke as they all wandered away from the bar. "If there are embarrassing stories, I have to hear them."

"There are no embarrassing stories," Brooke said, cringing inwardly. Dylan had way too much dirt on her. The last thing she wanted was to open up that can of worms. "Nothing embarrassing ever happened to either of us, so I guess we better change the subject."

Dylan's eyes glinted with mischief. "What about the watermelon slushy?"

"Yes, Brooke, what about the watermelon slushy?" Olivia echoed, bouncing on the toes of her champagne pumps. "Do tell."

Brooke rolled her eyes. "It was nothing. I accidentally punched through the bottom of my slushy cup with my straw, and it got all over me."

Dylan bumped his shoulder against hers. "The part of the story she's leaving out is that it happened in the middle of the mall when she was talking to this guy she had a huge crush on."

Brooke shot a warning look at him. "Listen, buster, you better check yourself before you wreck yourself. Or would you like me to tell them about your first kiss?"

Dylan's expression went from smug to panicked. "There's no need for that, now."

"No, there's a need," Olivia said. "I have a mighty need."

"Okay, so we're in sixth grade," Brooke said, dodging as Dylan tried to cover her mouth with his hand. She raised a warning finger at him. "Stop that, or you'll make me spill my wine."

"Oh my god, please don't tell this story." Dylan dropped his forehead to her shoulder, hiding his face in exaggerated shame.

"Well now you've piqued my interest too," Adam said, smiling as he sipped his wine.

"It's not that bad," Brooke said, knowing Dylan didn't actually mind. She'd seen him tell this story himself plenty of times. He was just playing up his embarrassment for entertainment value. "So . . . sixth grade. We're at a party at Jenny Guidry's house, and like the idiots we were, we decided to play spin the bottle."

"As you do," Olivia commented, nodding encouragement.

"Sure," Adam agreed, nodding alongside her in unison.

"So Jenny Guidry starts us off, it being her house and all. She spins the bottle, and it lands on our boy Dylan here." Brooke laid a hand on Dylan's head and gave his hair a playful ruffle.

"In my defense," Dylan said, lifting his head, "I was very naive and had no idea what I was doing. I'd just seen *Dumb and Dumber* and thought that was literally what kissing was supposed to look like."

"Oh my god," Olivia said as Adam snorted into his wine glass.

"Which is to say that when he went to kiss poor Jenny," Brooke went on, "he threw his mouth open and basically unhinged his jaw like a python as he came at her."

"Oh god," Dylan moaned, tipping his face into his hand.

"Poor Jenny took one look at him coming for her like that, screamed, and ran right out of the room."

"I'm not sure she's ever kissed anyone to this day, she was so scarred," Dylan said, hanging his head.

"I think you need to demonstrate," Olivia declared. "I'm really having a hard time picturing it."

"It was basically something like this . . ." Dylan opened his mouth and started to come at Brooke, who ducked and shoved him away.

"I called my teacher 'Mom' once," Adam offered genially.

Olivia kissed him on the cheek. "Oh, sweetie, everyone's done that."

"Yes, but I did it *in front of* my mom," Adam said. "She was so upset, she gave me the silent treatment for a week. And my poor teacher got the stink-eye from her for the rest of the school year."

"What's your most embarrassing childhood moment?" Dylan asked Olivia.

"I know this one," Adam volunteered, slipping an arm around Olivia. "She laughed so hard once she peed her pants at school."

"That's right." Olivia gazed up at him adoringly. "I did that."

"Okay, that's enough embarrassing stories," Brooke said before Dylan decided to play another round and start airing out the *really* dirty laundry. "I want to hear Adam Bomb wow us with one of his amazing facts."

Brooke had given Olivia's boyfriend the nickname Adam Bomb because he was always dropping unbelievable, strange-but-true facts that totally messed with your worldview. Like that there were more fake flamingos in the world than real flamingos—which was totally true, Brooke had looked it up—or that Oxford University was older than the Aztec Empire—which, again, true.

Everyone turned to Adam expectantly, and his brow wrinkled as he thought about it.

"Well, I did see an interesting article recently. Apparently some people have an internal narrative running through their head all the time and others don't. My thoughts always take the form of sentences in my head, like a one-sided conversation, but I guess a lot of people don't think in words so much as abstract images and ideas—more like a concept map."

Olivia nodded. "We were talking about this the other night. My internal monologue won't ever shut the fuck up, so I can't even imagine what it's like not to have one."

"I've always heard voices in my head," Brooke said with a shrug.

"I don't," Dylan offered, and they all turned their heads to stare at him.

"Really?" Brooke said.

"How does that even work?" Olivia asked.

"I don't know. I never gave it much thought." Dylan looked around at them in bemusement. "Y'all really have

185

voices talking in your head all the time?" His questioning gaze landed on Brooke.

"Yes," she said, staring back at him in surprise. "You don't?" She couldn't believe she didn't know that about him. All these years, as close as they'd been, and she never knew his brain worked in a way that was completely different from hers.

He shook his head and brushed his fingers against her temple. "Doesn't that get exhausting? All that chatter?"

"So exhausting," Olivia muttered, downing a mouthful of wine.

"What's it like?" Adam asked Dylan. "What about reading? Do you say the words in your head as you're reading them?"

"Not really," Dylan answered, frowning thoughtfully. "I can if I focus on a particular word, but in general I don't really."

Adam continued to pepper Dylan with questions, clearly delighted to have found someone who supported the article's hypothesis. Dylan answered all his questions gamely, and fired back with some of his own as he tried to understand how the other side lived their interior lives.

While the two men were absorbed in their conversation, Olivia took Brooke by the arm and pulled her away. "I need another drink. Come on."

Brooke allowed Olivia to lead her over to the line that had developed at the bar. She'd only finished half her wine, but if she dedicated herself to the task, she could probably be ready for a refill by the time they got to the front.

"So I'm just gonna take a wild guess that you two are sleeping together," Olivia said as they stood in line.

Brooke took a large drink of wine and gazed across the room to avoid meeting Olivia's eyes. "Maybe."

"Well? How is it? Things seem pretty great between you."

"It's . . . nice," Brooke offered noncommittally.

Olivia poked her in the arm. "Nice? That's all? I was hoping for fucking awesome."

The corner of Brooke's mouth tugged in a grin. "It might be that too."

"So when's he going back?" Olivia asked.

Brooke gulped down another mouthful of wine. "Tomorrow." Her throat felt tight as she said the word. It was too soon. They'd barely had a chance to enjoy this new normal, and it was about to end.

"You gonna be okay with that?"

"Of course." She didn't have a choice. It would happen whether she was okay with it or not.

Olivia arched a skeptical eyebrow and Brooke frowned. "What?"

"Nothing," Olivia said, feigning an innocent expression.

"Stop doing that with your face."

Olivia waved a hand around her head. "This? Is just my face being authentically itself."

Brooke rolled her eyes at her friend. "Dylan and I agreed from the start that this was just temporary. The fun ends when he goes back to New York, which was exactly what I wanted."

"But is it what you still want?"

"Yes," Brooke insisted, fighting off a wave of irritation. "Being with Dylan is great, but it's like Penny's triple chocolate cake. It's amazing while you're eating it and you wish it could last forever, but you know if you eat the whole cake it will make you feel sick, so you stick to just one slice. It's the perfect serving size for satisfaction without unwanted complications."

Olivia shook her head. "You've got more willpower than me. Last time she made that cake for my birthday, I ate three slices and spent the rest of the night curled up in the fetal position."

"See? That's exactly what I mean. You overindulged and regretted it after, didn't you?"

"Nope. Totally worth it," Olivia insisted. "Also? Dylan's not chocolate cake."

"It's a metaphor," Brooke said sourly.

Olivia shot her an annoyed look. "Okay, but you do realize you two make a perfect couple, right? It's kind of ridiculous that you've never gotten together before now."

"We're still not together now." Brooke downed the rest of her wine. "We're just friends having some fun."

"You say that, and yet you two are so cute together, you're actually making me queasy."

They reached the front of the bar line finally and placed their drink orders: two glasses of white wine for Brooke and Olivia, and two glasses of red for Dylan and Adam.

The two men were still deep in conversation when they got back to them. They were joined before long by Esther and Jinny, dragging their dates in tow.

Once again, Brooke found herself growing irked as Dylan charmed everyone. But unlike at the picnic, he wasn't putting on a show this time. It was just him being his genuine, outgoing, and likable self. He talked to Jinny about fashion and to her husband Yemi about Nigerian cooking. He let Esther rant at him for five minutes about the space junk problem caused by zombie satellites and other debris cluttering Low Earth Orbit, then got into an enthusiastic discussion of Coen brothers movies with Esther's screenwriter boyfriend, Jonathan.

Brooke ought to be delighted by how well he got along with everyone, but instead she found herself rankled by it. He'd known these people for all of a minute and already got on with them better than she did after several years of acquaintance.

It didn't help her mood any that everyone kept telling her how great they were together as soon as Dylan's back was turned.

"Oh my god, you two are the cutest!" Jinny squealed after Dylan went off with Yemi to fetch them fresh drinks.

"Thanks," Brooke replied and knocked back a mouthful of wine.

Dylan had grown increasingly handsy as the evening wore on. No more than he had been over the last couple days—which previously she had enjoyed quite a lot—but now he was doing it in front of people she knew. He'd been mostly hands-off at the picnic, in deference to the fact that it was a professional event for her, but now that they were socializing with her friends he was being openly affectionate.

Brooke hadn't done anything to discourage him the first time he'd rested his hand in the small of her back, and he'd since escalated to brushing her hair off her shoulder and stroking her arm, sending a clear signal to everyone that they were a couple.

Which they weren't.

It had been fine to pretend when they were surrounded by strangers at Venice Beach or the Getty, or alone in her apartment, but letting her friends think they were together made her uncomfortable. Tomorrow Dylan would be gone without a backward glance, and Brooke would be the one left to face the prying questions and pitying looks.

Once all the guests had arrived and the waiters had supplied everyone with flutes of champagne, a band named Savage Oxide took the stage. The bass player was a friend of Caleb's from the coffee shop where he used to work, and he led a toast to the newlyweds before launching into a very respectable cover of Alabama Shakes's "I Found You." Penny dragged Caleb onto the dance floor, and one by one the other couples began to follow their lead.

Dylan held his hand out to Brooke. "Shall we?"

"Sure." Conflicting emotions warred within her as she let Dylan lead her away. Dancing with him was one of the things she'd been most looking forward to tonight. But now that they were here, it wasn't playing out the way she'd imagined. She couldn't shake this nagging feeling that everything was going wrong.

Dylan's arms wrapped around her, and she tried to relax in the comfort of his embrace. By all accounts, she should be happy. This was exactly what she'd wanted. As she clung to him, she cast her mind back over the last several days, trying to recapture that contented feeling. But no matter how hard she tried, it continued to elude her.

Brooke watched Penny and Caleb across the room, clenched together on the dance floor, and wondered what was wrong with her that she didn't want what they had.

No, that wasn't right. It wasn't that she didn't *want* what they had, so much as she didn't believe she could ever properly enjoy it. She'd love to be able to give herself up to

190

another person like that, but she just couldn't see that ever happening. It wasn't in her nature.

There was no sense fantasizing about something she wasn't capable of. Better not to let yourself want it in the first place, so you wouldn't be disappointed when you didn't get it.

Dylan ran a hand down her back and pressed a kiss against her temple. As they swayed together under the fairy lights, striking a romantic pose, Brooke was acutely, uncomfortably aware of how many people were watching them and silently making plans for their future wedding, because that was what people did at these things. It was ridiculous.

When the song ended, the band launched into a rousing version of Bruno Mars's "Marry You," and Brooke excused herself to go to the bathroom.

As she freshened up her makeup, she tried to talk herself out of her sour mood. This was all just because of that stupid award. It had thrown her into a funk that she needed to shake herself out of. Dylan was just being his normal, lovely self, and it was unfair to take her bad mood out on him when he was being a perfect date.

Yes, the news about the award had been a disappointment, but it was dumb to let it ruin her last night with Dylan. Life was full of disappointments. If you put yourself out there, chances were good you'd be let down. She shouldn't have been surprised to learn the game was rigged. Most games that mattered were.

Now that the initial shock had passed, Brooke wasn't even upset about all the hard work that had been wasted. She was mostly mad at herself for getting her hopes up in the first place. She knew better than to let herself believe she had a chance at something like that.

Never wager on the long shot. Your money and your hopes were better spent on the safe bet, even if the payout was smaller.

Once she was done with her lipstick and her pep talk, Brooke took a deep breath and headed out to the party again. On her way back from the restroom, she bumped into Penny.

"Dylan is adorable!" she squealed, giving Brooke an impromptu hug outside the ladies' room. "I love him, and I love you together."

"We're not really together," Brooke tried to explain, but Penny ignored her protest.

"He's so sweet! And cute! I didn't expect a model to be so down-to-earth, but he totally is. That one's definitely a keeper."

But he wasn't a keeper, and Brooke wished everyone would stop acting like he was. Tomorrow morning he'd turn back into a pumpkin, and that would be that. Brooke's stint as Cinderella to Dylan's Prince Charming would be over.

When she got back to the party, she spotted Dylan on the dance floor, cutting loose to an Earth, Wind and Fire cover with Jinny and Yemi. Brooke watched him, marveling at how carefree he seemed and envious of his ability to fit in anywhere with such ease. He'd always been like that, and she'd always struggled to keep up with him.

He spotted her standing off to the side by herself and beckoned for her to join him. Unable to think of an excuse not to, but not feeling especially moved to boogie down, she dragged her feet as she made her way over to him.

Her grudging steps brought her to Dylan just as the song

was ending. He grasped her hand and twirled her as the last lively notes played, pulling her into his arms when the band transitioned into a Ray LaMontagne song. His hands settled on her hips as he held her close, and Brooke wound her arms around his neck. The scent of his cologne filled her senses as she rested her cheek against his chest. Closing her eyes, she breathed in a lungful of him and tried to enjoy the moment and the warmth of his body pressed against hers as they swayed to the music.

It was no use. The sense of impending catastrophe she'd been fighting all day refused to let go. It intruded on her thoughts, mingling with the slow, sad song. Her throat burned as she struggled to contain her emotions.

Dylan must have felt the change in her demeanor, because he tilted her chin up to give her a questioning look. Brooke tried to offer him a reassuring smile, but his frown only deepened.

"Let's get some air," he said and led her away from the dancing.

Chapter Seventeen

They went outside to the garden and stopped on the gravel path beneath the limbs of a spreading ficus tree. The night air raised goose bumps on Brooke's bare arms, and she hugged herself as she stood in front of Dylan. If he'd had a jacket he undoubtedly would have offered it to her—that was the sort of man he was, had always been—but all he had was his dress shirt. Maybe he'd offer her that.

He didn't. Instead, he pulled her closer and ran his big hands up and down her arms, trying to transfer some of his warmth to her. It didn't help, although she appreciated the effort.

"Talk to me," he said, gazing down at her with a concerned fondness that was so achingly familiar it made her stomach clench.

She tried to joke it away. "About what? How about pay disparities in women's professional sports? Or I can give a lecture on mammalian endocrine systems if you prefer."

He wasn't amused. "Brooke, I can tell something's wrong. I've known something was bothering you all day. I just kept hoping you'd tell me what it was."

"It's nothing." She pulled away from him and started pacing so she wouldn't have to look him in the eye.

He watched her wordlessly. Patiently. Waiting for her to decide she was ready.

She'd forgotten what it felt like to be under the microscope of Dylan's perceptive gaze. There was no hiding or dissembling with him. He knew her too well. Knew when she was lying, when she was upset, when she was scared.

He probably knew why, as well. He could read her that easily and was so much smarter than he gave himself credit for. He thought because he'd never been able to memorize the steps of the Krebs cycle in high school biology that he was dumb. But even as an adolescent, Dylan had possessed an emotional intelligence most adults never achieved.

It was intimidating when he focused the full force of it on her.

He couldn't just read her. He knew how to get her to give up the goods. He knew where all her buttons were and just how hard to push them to get her to do what he wanted.

Look at how he'd first kissed her. He'd known exactly what he was doing. That hadn't been a spontaneous kiss; it had been calculated. He'd understood precisely how much he needed to warm her up before sending her out the door to stew on it all day, and how that would improve his chances of getting what he wanted.

A flare of resentment spiked through her. Had this whole trip been a booty call? A planned sexcation? Was she the cruise director on the Dylan Price Love Boat?

"This is one of those times when there's an interior

monologue going on in your head, isn't it?" Dylan asked. "I can practically read your lips."

She rounded on him. "Then why don't you? If you know me so well, you tell me what's wrong."

Her sudden sharpness took him by surprise, and he hesitated.

She watched him, wondering if he'd really guessed about the award. Was he truly that perceptive?

He cleared his throat and found his voice again. "Fine. I think what's bothering you is the same thing that's bothering me."

"Something's bothering you?" She hadn't even noticed. Had there even been anything to notice?

A flicker of exasperation passed across his face, and she swallowed a pang of guilt. He was so much better at this than she was. No wonder she'd never been able to sustain a relationship.

"I've been sad about leaving tomorrow." His eyes locked on hers, gauging her reaction.

"Oh." She hadn't picked up on that at all. But now that she thought about it, it could explain all the arm stroking and fussing over her he'd been doing all night. He was feeling possessive.

He shuffled his feet and plunged his hands into his pockets. "I thought maybe you might be too." Suddenly, he looked like a boy again. Vulnerable, shy, a little bit embarrassed.

Brooke's heart gave a twinge, and she reached out to reassure him. "Of course I am." She slid her hands around his waist and rested her cheek on his chest.

The long breath he let out made her feel even more protective, and she squeezed him tighter. He was always so easygoing and carefree, she'd forgotten how insecure he could be underneath the sunny exterior.

His hand cupped the back of her head. Music drifted outside from the party as they clung to each other. Another slow song. They could almost be dancing, the way they were posed. They were even swaying a little.

She felt him take a breath before he spoke. "What if I could come back here?"

"Of course you can. You can come visit whenever you want. I'm always happy to see you. You know that." She gave him a punishing squeeze for thinking otherwise.

The breath rushed out of him in a *whuff* and his arms tightened around her. His heart beat tiny pitter-pats in her ear. She would miss the hell out of this.

"We're good together, aren't we?"

"Yeah, we are. I've had a great time with you." The best. He'd probably ruined her for all future sex partners. In fact, the idea of a standing rendezvous once or twice a year held a lot of appeal—if he'd be open to something like that. It seemed almost too much to ask, but maybe . . .

"What if we could be more than just friends with benefits? What if we could be together for real?"

Brooke's neck and chest started to prickle. "What do you mean?" She pushed out of his arms and rubbed at her itchy skin.

"Don't you think it means something that we can be apart for years and fit right back into each other's lives like no time has passed?" He took one of her hands in both of his, holding it tenderly. "What we've got is special. I've never had a friend or a girlfriend who meant half as much to me as you do. What if we're meant to be together? Maybe we've always been meant to be together. I don't want to lose you because we were too scared to take a risk."

"Be serious." She needed him to be joking. *Please be joking*.

"I've never been more serious in my life."

She backed away from him like a skittish horse. "This isn't supposed to be serious. We agreed on that. You don't even live here."

"What if I did?"

"There's no point torturing ourselves over hypotheticals."

"I could move to LA."

Her stomach dropped.

"What?" Her voice sounded faint. "You can't do that. Your job is in New York. Your whole life is there."

He shook his head. "It doesn't have to be. I told you I wanted to do something different. There's a guy I know, he's starting a clothing line here, and he wants to partner with me. I met with him and his investors this week."

"What? You did? When? *What*?" She felt like she was losing her mind. Had she not just spent the whole week with him? Why was now the first she was hearing about this?

"That was him on the phone yesterday, making me a formal offer."

"So you'd just give up modeling and move here? Just like that?"

"I wouldn't give it up completely." He was starting to sound exasperated with her. "I'd be the public face of the company, but I'd also be helping to run it. An equal partner. It's a chance to help build a business from the ground up."

"Did you give them an answer already?" This whole clothing line thing sounded risky as hell. How well did he even know these people? And how much money were they asking him to invest?

"I told him I needed to think about it, but I don't. I want this. And I want to be with you."

"Whoa." Brooke started pacing again, unable to keep still. Dylan couldn't just *give up his career*—his successful, million-dollar career, no less—and move across the country to be with her. That was a recipe for disaster if she ever heard one.

His head swiveled from side to side as he followed her movements. "Okay, this isn't exactly how I'd hoped this would go over."

She forced herself to stand in one place. "I'm sorry, but you've thrown me for a loop here. I thought we were on the same page."

"What page is that exactly?" He was way beyond exasperated now, verging into actively hurt.

"We're having a good time, remember? That's all this is supposed to be." He'd *agreed* to those conditions. He'd let her believe he could stick to the terms and everything would be okay.

Things were most definitely not okay.

"I want more," he said. "And I'm willing to make sacrifices to make it happen."

Brooke swallowed. Her throat felt like it was lined with nails. "What if I'm not?"

Silence clanged in the air around them.

Dylan looked down at his shoes, like he was gathering himself together. When he looked up again his face was devoid of expression. Cold and empty and beautiful, like one of his photo spreads for some super-luxury brand where the models all looked like they'd been molded out of clay.

"Are you saying you don't want me to move here?" His voice was as remote as his expression. "Because that's sure how it seems."

Brooke started to pace again, this time with added hand-wringing. "Where did moving here even come from? How did I not know you were thinking about this? You've been making plans and having meetings and taking calls all week and keeping it from me why?"

"I didn't want to tell you until I was sure."

"Sure of what?"

"Sure I wanted to get involved in this business venture . . . and sure that there was something real between us, and it wasn't just wishful thinking on my part."

So he *was* doing this to be with her. An alarm klaxon sounded in her head. *Danger. Relationship catastrophe imminent.*

"Oh god," she moaned, rubbing her forehead with the heels of her hands to try and make the noise stop.

"*Can you just be still for one goddamn second?*" Dylan snapped.

She stopped and spun around to face him. He never raised his voice at her. Ever.

"You didn't answer my question," he said more quietly.

"What question?" There was a hollow pit growing where her stomach should be. Pretty soon it would swallow her up.

"Do you not want me to move here?"

"I can't make that decision for you."

His temper flared again. "Goddammit, I'm not asking you to." She watched him take himself in hand, packing all the emotion away as that hollow blankness took over his face again. "I'm asking if you want to see if this could work."

200

"What is *this*? What are you envisioning for us?" She couldn't envision anything right now but misery, heartbreak, and the utter destruction of the most important friendship in her life.

"A relationship. A *real* relationship."

"I don't want to be anyone's girlfriend. I told you that."

"No, you said you didn't want to be anyone's long-distance girlfriend."

"I don't want to be either."

He closed his eyes and drew a long breath. "I see."

He really didn't. If he was seeing clearly, he'd know how insane this idea of his was. He'd never have suggested it. His brain was fogged by vacation sex and nostalgia for a past that could never be recaptured.

The lines of risk were so clear. Someone like Dylan could never be content with someone like her—and Brooke could never be content with anyone. It was just a matter of time before they grew to resent each other, and that resentment would poison everything between them.

"If you lived here, how long do you actually think we would last as a couple?" she asked him.

"I don't know." He threw his hands up. "I was sort of hoping for forever." He looked more sad than angry now, and she hadn't missed his use of the past tense.

"I'm just trying to be realistic." She said it in the same soothing tone you'd use with a toddler who'd skinned his knee. *This is just a little boo boo*, her tone said. *It will stop hurting in a minute.*

He laughed without any humor whatsoever. "That's rich. You know you can't predict the future, right, Brooke? Maybe things will work out, or maybe they won't. But being scared of failure isn't a reason not to try."

It was, actually. It was the best reason there was.

"I can predict *this* future," she shot back, "and I'm telling you, this thing?" She waved her hand to encompass the empty space between them. "Would most definitely *not* work out."

"So that's a no, then. You don't want to be with me." His voice was so devoid of feeling it sent a shiver through her body.

"That's not what I'm saying."

"That's exactly what you're saying." He looked through her as he spoke, like she was a blank spot on the wall he just happened to be staring at.

Her heart twisted. "Just let me explain."

"You don't need to." He could have been carved out of marble, his expression was so cold. "Honestly, I'd rather not listen to your reasons, if that's okay with you. It doesn't really matter why."

It mattered to her. It mattered that he understood, so he didn't hate her. She needed him not to hate her.

She reached a hand toward him, but he backed out of reach, kicking up a gout of gravel in his haste to get away from her. "I'm gonna take an Uber back to your place. I've still got my key."

"Please don't—" she started, but he held up a finger and she closed her mouth.

"I can't be here anymore. Tell your friends—" His lips pressed together in a tortured grimace. "Tell them whatever you want."

He spun on the ball of his foot and walked away. Out the garden gate to the street beyond.

Brooke almost ran after him. She even took a few jerky steps, her high heels kicking up the stones of the gravel path.

But she decided it was better to give him some space. He needed a cooling-off period. They both did. Once he got over his initial hurt feelings, he'd be more reasonable. They'd be able to talk calmly, and he'd see she was right.

They could still salvage this.

They had to.

She couldn't lose him.

Chapter Eighteen

The whole drive home from the reception, Brooke's mind played out different versions of the conversation she'd have with Dylan when she got home. She practiced making her case, tried to anticipate his responses, and rehearsed different ways to counter any arguments he might make.

She'd been afraid this would happen. They never should have let their libidos run away with them. Now look what they'd done. They'd gone and fucked up a perfectly good friendship by getting sex all over it.

This was all fixable though. Dylan's feelings had been hurt, and he'd need time to recover, but she still believed they could come back from this. They'd had fights before, and they'd always found their way back to each other.

Brooke hadn't told her friends anything before she left the wedding reception. She'd sat on a bench in an out-of-the-way corner of the garden, letting the cold air sober her up. She wasn't drunk—her last glass of wine had been over an hour ago—but she felt light-headed. This wasn't the pleasant buzz of alcohol, but the sickening nausea of vertigo.

As soon as she'd felt calm enough to drive, she'd walked straight out of the reception and to her car.

She didn't trust herself on the freeway when she was this distracted, so she took surface streets instead, which gave her more time to go over what she'd say to Dylan. Figure out how she'd make this better.

When she opened the door to her apartment, Brooke was met by a frightening silence.

Her insides started to slide.

"Dylan?" Even as she said his name, she knew he wasn't there. The pit in her stomach widened into a crevasse.

His backpack wasn't propped against the end of the couch anymore. His suitcase no longer lay open in the corner of the room. But there was a note on the coffee table.

She walked toward it, feeling like she was going to throw up.

He'd scrawled it on the back of a pizza receipt. There was only one sentence.

Your key is under the mat.

Just that. Just those six words. No *Dear Brooke*, or *Love, Dylan*. He'd left her no best wishes or warmest regards. The only thing he'd left her was her key, on his way out the door.

He hadn't even said goodbye.

The world tilted around her, and she crumpled to the couch.

Murderface wandered over to her and let out one of his angry-sounding meows, like he was berating her for driving Dylan away. She deserved it.

Fumbling for her phone, Brooke scrolled to Dylan's name in her contacts and hit the call button.

It went to voicemail on the second ring.

Really starting to panic now, she typed out a text with

shaking fingers while Murderface tried to headbutt the phone.

Please come back. We need to talk.

Murderface forced his way into her lap. Brooke scratched his head absently while she stared at her phone's screen like she could will Dylan's reply into existence with the power of her mind.

He was probably driving. He'd answer her at the next red light. Or when he got to wherever he was going.

Where was he going? He didn't know anyone else in town.

Except this mystery business partner he'd been keeping a secret from her. But Dylan wouldn't go to him, would he? More likely he was headed to a hotel.

Brooke swiped over to the map app on her phone to see what hotels showed up as closest to her apartment. While Murderface continued to headbutt her, vying for her attention, she tried to predict which one Dylan would pick.

Five minutes now and still no reply. The closest hotel was less than five minutes away, but it wasn't very nice. He'd probably want to stay somewhere a little more comfortable, since money wasn't an issue for him.

She waited another five minutes, and then she texted again.

Please don't leave like this.

She got to her feet and paced into the bathroom. Dylan's toothbrush and deodorant were gone. She flung aside the shower curtain. In his haste to get away from her, he'd forgotten his shampoo. Stooping, she retrieved the black plastic mini-bottle from the rim of the tub and flipped the lid open. Her eyes watered as she breathed in a lungful of the spicy aroma.

Was this all she had left of him? A travel-size bottle of men's shampoo?

Brooke wandered back into the living room and sank onto the couch again. She sent Dylan another text.

I'm sorry. Please can we talk?

And another, five minutes later.

Tell me where you are. I'll come to you if you want.

And finally:

Please can we fix this? I can't lose you.

Eventually, she fell asleep on the couch clutching her *Everything Whale Be Okay* pillow, waiting for a reply that never came.

A week later, Dylan was still giving Brooke the silent treatment.

"He'll get over it eventually," Olivia said, putting a glass of wine in Brooke's hand. "Drink this."

Brooke did as she was told. The wine had no discernable flavor, but it was probably her fault and not the fault of the perfectly respectable sauvignon blanc Olivia had brought. Everything tasted flavorless this week.

She sighed. "Pretty sure he won't, or he would have answered one of my texts by now." She'd been texting him every day since he'd left, with no response. Chances were high at this point that he'd blocked her number completely and wasn't even seeing them anymore.

Olivia sank down at the opposite end of the couch, cradling her own glass of wine. "He just needs time to lick his wounds."

"He's had time. I'm forced to conclude his wounds were terminal." It was time to face facts and stop hoping for a reply that wasn't coming. Dylan had cut her out of his life. Her worst fears had come true.

"You don't just throw away an eighteen-year friendship that easily."

"Sure you do. People do it all the time." Brooke swallowed another mouthful of wine and shook her head. "I broke us. I didn't mean to break us, but that's what I did."

"Broken things can be fixed."

"Not if he doesn't want to fix it."

Twisting a piece of her blonde hair around her fingers, Olivia seemed to debate something. She looked up. "Let me ask you this: What do you actually want? What's your best-case scenario from here?"

That was easy to answer. "I want him to be my friend again."

"Is that all? Just your friend?"

"Yes," Brooke answered too fast.

Olivia's gray eyes were skeptical. "You don't want anything more than that? Really?"

Brooke shifted on the couch, moving her wine glass from one hand to the other. "Life isn't like a romance novel. Just because we were friends when we were kids, before our brains had finished developing or we'd had any actual life experience, doesn't mean we're supposed to be soul mates." It was a very good speech. She almost believed it, even.

Olivia clearly didn't. "Counterpoint: sometimes life *is* like a romance novel. Look at me and Adam. I never in a million years would have imagined the two of us would find a way to make a relationship work. And yet, we did."

"Just because you happened to win the love lottery doesn't mean I should run out and blow all my money on scratch-offs."

"No, but maybe you should scratch off the ticket that's *already right there in your hand* instead of throwing it away."

Brooke stared at her friend. "Are you trying to say I'm the asshole in this situation?"

One side of Olivia's face scrunched up. "Welllllllll . . ."

"Oh my god. You think I'm the asshole."

"It's not about being an asshole."

"It kind of is." Brooke swallowed another mouthful of tasteless wine.

Olivia shook her head. "Let's put a pin in that for a minute. You've been moping around like your heart's broken ever since he left." She fixed Brooke with a penetrating look. "If you could have Dylan, would you want him?"

Brooke sat forward and reached for the wine bottle on the coffee table to top up her nearly empty glass. "It's more complicated than that."

"Ignore the complications. Pretend they don't exist for a second, and you've got a wish-granting genie on your side so anything you want is possible. Would you want to be with Dylan if you knew you could be happy?"

209

Sinking back into the couch, Brooke gazed at her wine glass as she thought about it. "Yes," she answered finally, feeling the truth of it resonate as she spoke the word. If he wasn't him, and she wasn't her, and there weren't any obstacles between them? Hell yes she'd want him. In a heartbeat. She'd be crazy not to.

"That's all that matters," Olivia said with much more confidence than Brooke felt. "The rest is just logistics, and logistics can be negotiated."

"Not always."

"For sure not if you don't even try." There was a hint of reproach in Olivia's tone that stung.

"It's too difficult," Brooke said, shaking her head stubbornly.

"It's always difficult. But it's worth the effort, even if you fail. And you know me well enough to know I don't say that lightly. Rejection is *literally* my greatest fear. But if I was you? I would not let that man go. Not if there was any way at all to hold on to him." When Brooke didn't say anything, Olivia shrugged. "But hey, I'm not you. I don't keep people at a distance the way you do."

"I don't do that," Brooke shot back, bristling.

"You do. And look, I think I have some idea why—although not really, because you've never actually told me the details—but you're not doing yourself any favors with this island-unto-yourself stuff. How many close friends do you even have other than me?"

"I have friends."

"*Close* friends. Not just people you sometimes talk to when you happen to be around them. People you go out of your way for."

Brooke had to concede Olivia might have a point about that. The two of them had basically imprinted on each other like baby chicks when they were assigned to be roommates Brooke's freshman year of college because they'd both been scared and alone in a new city, but she hadn't developed many close friends since. Or any, really.

But that was by choice. Brooke was an introvert who treasured her alone time. She didn't need to be out socializing every night or baring her soul to whomever would listen. There were plenty of human interactions to be had, between her students, the faculty she dealt with, and her fellow grad students. Sometimes too many, in fact.

She liked coming home to an empty apartment at the end of most days. And if, on occasion, she wanted to go out after hours, she had people she could call on for that too.

She was fine.

"You're acting like it's some kind of involuntary defense mechanism," Brooke told Olivia. "It's simply a preference. I'm not as outgoing as you or Penny. This is how I like it."

"You keep telling yourself that," Olivia said, giving her a wry look. "I just think, if there's anyone worth opening your heart for, it might be this guy."

Maybe. But maybe that was exactly the reason why Brooke shouldn't do it.

She took a drink of her wine. And then she admitted what she was really afraid of. "What if he moves here, and then two months later I get sick of him like I do everyone else?"

"What if you don't?" Olivia said.

"What if I do? I don't want to be sick of Dylan. That's not

going to hurt him any less. In fact, it will hurt him a lot more if he uproots his whole life for me and *then* I dump him."

Brooke's phone rang in her bag and she scrambled for it, in case it was Dylan finally calling her back. But it was only her mom. She let it go to voicemail.

"Who was that?" Olivia asked.

"Just my mom." Brooke could call her back later—or not. She really wasn't up to dealing with her mother tonight.

She sipped her wine, thinking about what Olivia had said. *Was* she the asshole?

She'd certainly broken Dylan's heart. There was no denying that. She hadn't meant to, for whatever that was worth. She'd tried really hard not to hurt him, in fact. From the outset, she'd been very clear with him about what she was and wasn't capable of. They'd had an arrangement. He'd agreed to the terms—quite enthusiastically, as she recalled. And he was the one who'd pushed to make their relationship physical in the first place. Brooke had actively tried to avoid it for fear of *this exact situation*, but he'd persisted until he convinced her.

And somehow now she was the bad guy? Because he'd tried to change the terms of the arrangement on her? That didn't seem fair.

Except Dylan had been hurt. And Brooke couldn't help feeling guilty about that. She was haunted by the look on his face when he'd thought she didn't want him. But it was so much more complicated than just wanting him. Wanting him wasn't enough.

Her phone rang a second time, and she sighed as she checked the screen. Her mother again. Couldn't the woman have left a voicemail the first time she called?

"Should you answer that?" Olivia asked as Brooke declined the second call.

"No, it's fine." She probably just wanted to try and smooth things over after their last conversation. Brooke wasn't in the mood to be smoothed right now.

But when the phone started ringing again, just a few seconds later, she felt a trickle of unease. "Mom?" Brooke said, accepting the third call.

"Oh honey, it's your father," her mother said in a voice that sounded very small and very scared. "He's had a stroke."

Chapter Nineteen

At 8:35 the next morning, Brooke stepped off the plane in Baton Rouge.

Her eldest brother, Teddy, picked her up at the airport. She hadn't seen him in years, and she was shocked at how much his hairline had receded—and how much he looked like their father.

She'd never been super close to her brothers. Teddy was six years older than her, and Justin was four years older. They'd both left for college by the time she entered high school, and they hadn't come home a whole lot after that. Brooke's mother kept her informed about their lives, but the siblings had never bothered to keep in touch with each other. Without their mom to connect them, they'd basically be strangers. They basically *were* strangers.

Brooke didn't even know if her brothers knew why she'd fallen out of her father's good graces. Probably not. Her parents probably wouldn't have wanted to pollute them with the knowledge of her shame.

It was entirely possible Teddy and Justin hadn't even noticed the change in her relationship with Dad. They had their own issues with him, truth be told. He'd been strict and judgmental with all his children, but he'd been especially hard on his sons. Even as a young child, when she was still Daddy's best girl, Brooke had been aware of the tensions. It had taken her a little longer to recognize the inequity in the way they were treated and understand the gender dynamics behind it.

She probably should have been more sympathetic. But she'd been young, and it had been easier to stay out of the fray and enjoy her father's praise when she could earn it. Easier to tell herself that her brothers deserved the punishments they got for being less perfect than she was.

It was a coping strategy that had backfired on her when she got knocked off her pedestal by one positive pregnancy test. All those years of sucking up meant she'd had farther to fall, and so the crash had been more spectacular and less recoverable than the persistent, low-grade disappointment her brothers had always lived with.

Brooke exchanged a stiff hug with Teddy at passenger pickup when he got out of the car to put her suitcase in the back of his Ford Explorer. It was a nice car, nearly new. He worked in information security for a company she couldn't remember the name of, but it seemed like he was doing well for himself.

"Is there any news about Dad?" Brooke asked as Teddy pulled away from the airport. Her flight had left LAX at one in the morning, so she hadn't talked to their mom since last night.

Teddy shook his head, his knuckles whitening as his fingers gripped the steering wheel. "The doctor's supposed to come by this morning and give us an update."

They made a few minutes of strained small talk on the way

to the hospital. She'd never had to make small talk with her brother before, and *good grief* were they both terrible at it. After they'd run through all the standard conversational bases, they fell into an uncomfortable silence for the duration of the drive.

Brooke had never been so happy to arrive at a hospital, although she had no idea what awaited her inside. Her father was in the intensive care unit after suffering a stroke, and they didn't know how bad it was yet. Whether he'd recover, or if there'd be lasting damage if he did.

She mostly felt numb when she thought about it. She'd been operating on autopilot since she got the news last night. But the decision to come home had been a no-brainer. Brooke wasn't here for her father, who probably wouldn't want her here if he was able to speak for himself.

She was here for her mother, who was scared of losing her husband and shouldn't have to go through this alone.

Debbie Hilliard looked small and pale and fragile. But her relief when she saw her daughter walk into the ICU waiting room was so palpable that Brooke knew it had been the right decision to come here.

It was the first time she'd hugged her mother in almost six years, and she had to blink back tears as they clung to one another.

Brooke's brother Justin was there too, looking quite a lot more grown-up at thirty than the twenty-four-year-old stoner she remembered. He gave her a slightly more exuberant hug than the restrained one Teddy had given her, and they all sat down to wait together.

The mood in the ICU waiting room was oppressively

216

solemn, despite the bright paintings of wildflowers that attempted to lend some cheer. Brooke was keenly aware that every family sitting around them was there because of some personal catastrophe.

Usually Debbie could be relied upon to fill the silences at family gatherings with banal chatter, but today their mother was uncharacteristically silent. That scared Brooke more than anything else.

The neurosurgeon came to talk to them an hour later. He explained that Brooke's father had suffered an acute ischemic stroke. They'd been treating him with intravenous thrombolytics, and he'd regained a lot of the feeling he'd lost in his arm and leg, but was still unable to talk. They'd done a CTA scan to pinpoint the remaining blockage and found a clot in the cerebral artery that the neurosurgeon believed could be accessed with endovascular surgical treatment.

After going over all the risks, he requested the family's permission to perform the procedure, which they gave.

They spent the next several hours drinking shitty hospital coffee and trying to keep Debbie's spirits up. Brooke assigned herself the task of bringing everyone food from the hospital cafeteria. Justin was more extroverted than Teddy, and attempted to keep the conversation going and focused on neutral topics. Teddy mostly sat and stared at the floor.

By noon, Ed Hilliard was reported to be awake and in recovery. At two o'clock, they moved him into his own room on a different floor.

The procedure had worked to clear the remaining clot, and Ed was doing as well as could be hoped. He was out of danger, and expected to regain some if not all of the abilities that had been affected, although recovery would be slow

217

and entail months of rehabilitation. It was fortunate he'd finished his last course of chemo, which had left him physically weak. Hopefully he'd get stronger much faster as he recovered from the chemo treatments.

Only two visitors were allowed in the room with him at a time. By unspoken agreement, Brooke and her brother Teddy stayed in the waiting room by the elevators while Justin and her mother went to sit with Ed.

Justin came out a while later and told them Dad's vitals were good, but he still couldn't talk. He was sleeping now, and Mom wanted Justin to go to the house and pick up some things for her and Dad. One of the chairs in Dad's hospital room reclined into a bed, and Mom would be sleeping here tonight—and probably for the next several nights.

Brooke volunteered to go get the stuff instead. She didn't plan on seeing her dad, on the assumption her presence would cause him more stress than comfort. So she might as well make herself useful some other way.

Justin was happy to hand off the errand, and went over the list of requested items with Brooke, passing on their mother's car keys and detailed instructions on where everything could be found in the house.

That was how, a half hour later, Brooke found herself alone in her childhood home.

The house hadn't changed a bit in the last six years. Brooke would have thought some small details, at least, would be different, but it was like a TV show set that had been freeze-framed, or a museum exhibit trapped behind glass. Same textured rug in the entryway, same framed elementary school

218

photos of her and her brothers on the living room wall, same floral wallpaper in the kitchen.

Same smell, even.

It all hit her like a freight train full of memories, and she had to stop and grab onto the doorframe for support while she got her bearings again.

So many years spent in this house. So many emotions connected to the experiences she'd had here. All of it churning up out of the place where she'd buried it and hoped to keep it buried down deep.

It didn't help that she was dead tired. She'd barely slept on the plane, and a long, tense day spent sitting around a hospital with her family had her yearning to crawl into her old bed and take a nap.

Not a possibility, unfortunately. Mom wouldn't be comfortable until she had all the stuff she wanted. After she'd brought everything back to the hospital and made sure Debbie ate some dinner, then maybe Brooke could come back here and get some sleep.

She pulled out her mother's list and got a reusable grocery bag out of the cupboard next to the fridge to carry everything she'd need to take back to the hospital. There was medication on the kitchen counter, for both her father and her mother: a collection of tiny bottles to stave off the assorted ailments of aging. Some of them were new. The meds for her father's high blood pressure and acid reflux were familiar, but now there were also anti-inflammatories and estrogen for her mother, and—

Lexapro. Which was used to treat anxiety and depression. Prescribed to her father.

Brooke stared at her father's name on the prescription

label. She didn't know how to feel about that any more than she knew how to feel about everything else that was happening.

She dropped the antidepressants into the sack and swept the rest of the bottles in with them. Moving on, she grabbed a few pieces of fruit out of the bowl on the counter. In the pantry, she found a Costco-sized box of granola bars that she snagged as well.

The last thing her mother wanted from the kitchen was the small magnetic whiteboard and marker that hung on the side of the fridge. For her father, who was currently unable to speak.

Refusing to think about that too much, Brooke moved on to her parents' bedroom.

Even though everything was exactly the same, as she moved through the house it all felt much smaller than she remembered. It was like her memories had gotten muddled up, and the ones from when she was small had wound up superimposed over the later memories. Or maybe she'd just done such a good job blocking out her last few years in this house, she'd accidentally reset her memories of it to an earlier time.

As much time as she'd spent ruing this place and the childhood she'd spent here, it hadn't all been painful. There had been plenty of good times among the bad. For better or worse, the experiences she'd lived here had made her into the person she was now.

In her parents' room she found the bed neatly made as always, covered by the same handmade quilt they'd had for at least twenty years. Brooke gritted her teeth at the lingering scent of her dad's drugstore aftershave as she went into their bathroom to collect toothbrushes, toothpaste, deodorant, and other sundries her mother had requested for the two of them. From the bureau, Brooke gathered an assortment of socks, underwear, and pajamas, before moving on to the closet, where she selected clean clothes for her mother and a robe and slippers for her father. The shopping bag was getting too full, so she got her mother's overnight bag down from the shelf in the closet and repacked all the clothes and toiletries into it.

When everything on her list had been collected, Brooke paused and looked around her parents' room. For some reason it felt odd to think of them continuing to live their lives here the same as they always had. All their kids grown and gone now. Just the two of them shuffling around this empty house.

She shook her head as she turned to go. On her way down the hall, she paused at the closed door of her own bedroom. Her fingers wrapped around the doorknob, and she pushed it open.

To her surprise, nothing had changed in there either. It hadn't been turned into a sewing room or a home office. Her old polka-dotted comforter still covered the bed, presided over by the stuffed bulldog she'd gotten for her thirteenth birthday. Her Ian Somerhalder and Robert Pattinson posters still adorned the walls. Pep squad ribbons and Academic Decathlon medals decorated the corkboard over her desk.

Everything she'd left behind was still here. Waiting for her.

Funnily, the sense of nostalgia was lessened in her own room. The things in here were the things that didn't mean anything to her anymore. The things she hadn't deemed important enough to take with her when she left.

Brooke pulled the door shut and made her way down the hall, past her brothers' old room, through the living room, and to the front door. She cast one last look around before turning off the entry light and stepping out onto the porch. It took her a second to fumble the house key out of her purse and remember the trick for wiggling the old sticky deadbolt into place.

When she finally turned around, Dylan was standing on the front walk.

Chapter Twenty

Brooke's heart stopped at the sight of him. Then it started up again beating double time. She put a hand to her chest and felt it thumping wildly against her ribs.

Dylan's smile was weary and hesitant. Behind him, she could see the outline of his house with its red shutters and white trim, and the yard where she'd first laid eyes on him eighteen years ago.

"You're here," she said, still a little in shock.

He wore loose black jeans with a tight gray T-shirt, and he was the absolute last person she'd expected to find standing on the cracked front walk of her parents' house.

But maybe he shouldn't have been, because Dylan Price always showed up exactly when she needed him most.

Brooke sucked in a hitching breath that turned into a sob. Her eyes blurred as he came toward her.

Dylan's arms closed around her, strong, comforting, supportive, and for one beautiful moment her whole world became the smell of his skin and the warmth of his chest. Squeezing her eyes shut, she choked back another sob, fighting the urge to let herself fall apart all over him. She wanted to—so badly—but if she let herself start crying now she wouldn't be able to stop, and she needed to know what he was doing here and what he was thinking. Before she took advantage of his comfort, she needed to know where they stood.

She knew it would hurt when he let her go, and it did. Her body immediately went cold at the loss of contact, even though it was a sweltering eighty-degree night, still brutally hot this late in the year.

He stepped back, shuffling his feet uncertainly. She could see the struggle in his eyes as he gazed at her.

"What—what are you doing here?" she asked, her voice ragged and a little choked.

"My mom told me about your dad." He gave a small shrug, as if that explained everything. The air around them smelled like pine needles and fresh-cut grass, with a faint whiff of sulfur from the nearby refineries, and Brooke was seized by a powerful sense of childhood nostalgia.

"And so you just jumped on a plane?"

"Well, yeah." He shrugged again. "I thought you might need a friend."

She couldn't stop the small sob that escaped her then, and Dylan's brow furrowed as he came closer again, his hands reaching out for her upper arms and squeezing.

"I thought—" Brooke swallowed around the lump in her throat. The bags she was holding cut into her palms as if they weighed a hundred pounds. "I thought you were done being my friend. I thought I'd screwed up and lost you."

Dylan's expression softened as he gave her an affectionate shake. "I thought you knew me better than that."

Brooke tried for a smile and failed miserably. "I thought I did, but—"

224

"I'm sorry I shut you out." His hands slid up her arms, settling onto her shoulders with his thumbs nestled against her collarbone. "I needed some time to sulk. But you and me, we're a team. That's how it's been since the day your family moved into this house, and that's how it will always be. Even when we're a team who's mad at each other, or lives three thousand miles apart. When something bad happens, I'm gonna be there for you. You can't shake me that easy."

She nodded, too choked up to speak, and he pulled her into another hug. This time there was an almost tangible click as the world settled back into its rightful place, and she let herself sag against him, her arms winding awkwardly around his waist as she juggled the bags in her hands.

Brooke had lived too many years without the security of an emotional safety net. She'd forgotten what it was like to have someone there to catch you when you fell. To know you could count on it.

Dylan kissed her temple before letting go and taking the bags from her. "So what's the plan? Is this stuff going to the hospital?"

Brooke nodded, and he put a hand on her back to guide her toward her mom's Toyota in the driveway.

"Give me the car keys," he said. "I'll drive."

She started to hand them over and then hesitated, turning to face him. "Dylan . . ." Her hand squeezed the keys hard enough to hurt. "I just want to say—"

"Don't." He touched her cheek, his thumb stroking just below her lower lip. "We don't need to talk about it. You've got more important things to worry about right now."

Relief coursed through her as he took the keys out of her hand. They *did* need to talk about it, but she wasn't in the right headspace to put her best effort into it at the present moment.

For now, she was content to let him take the driver's seat.

"Dylan Price, is that really you?" Brooke's mom said, breaking into a weary smile as she came into the waiting room.

Dylan stooped to give her a hug. "How you doing, Mrs. Hilliard?"

"Oh honey, I've been better." Debbie gave him a squeeze before reaching up to pat his cheek. "But aren't you sweet for showing up here?"

"My mom says to give you her love," Dylan said.

"We brought dinner," Brooke said, holding up a big plastic bag full of fast food. Dylan had insisted on pulling into Sonic and picking up dinner for everyone on the way to the hospital.

"Hot damn," Justin said, taking the bag off her hands and peeking inside. "I'm hungry enough to eat an elephant."

The waiting room on their dad's floor was empty except for Brooke's family, who'd taken over the back corner of it after camping out there in shifts half the day. Which was good, because the smell of the hot food was strong.

"There's burgers and tots for everyone." Brooke handed Teddy one of the soft drink carriers she was holding and set the other one down on an empty chair. "And cherry limeades."

"Here, Mom. Eat this." Justin held a paper bag containing a burger and tater tots out to their mother.

Debbie shook her head, waving him off. "Oh, I'm not hungry. You can have mine."

"You gotta eat, Mom." Teddy took the bag from Justin

226

and thrust it into their mother's hands. "You need to keep your strength up."

"Did you find everything at the house?" Debbie asked fretfully, popping a conciliatory tater tot into her mouth as she turned to Brooke.

"Sure did." Brooke nodded at the two bags she'd packed. "It's all right there."

Her mother looked relieved. "Oh, good."

Brooke wanted to ask about her dad's antidepressants. How long had he been on them? What symptoms had precipitated the prescription? Was he seeing a therapist? But she knew her mother wouldn't want to talk about it in front of Dylan. Or at all.

"Eat," Teddy ordered, frowning at his mother.

Debbie rolled her eyes and unwrapped her burger. "I'm eating, I'm eating."

They sat around chatting while they ate their food. With Dylan there to share the extrovert load with Justin, and Debbie trying her best to put on a falsely cheerful face in front of him, it was actually almost pleasant. They hadn't felt this much like a real family in years. Not since Brooke and her brothers were young, before they'd started to rebel against their father's strict expectations. Brooke found herself relaxing a little, for the first time all day.

It struck her as profoundly sad that they were only able to enjoy each other's company like this because her father wasn't here. He'd taken this from her, from all of them.

Ever since she'd left home, she'd told herself she didn't have any need for family. But the truth was it would have been nice to have this these last few years. There was a special kind of connection you had with people who knew who you used to be and where you came from. It wasn't the only kind of connection you could have, or even the most important, but there was something grounding about it. Something stabilizing.

Brooke had missed having that, even if she'd worked like hell to pretend she hadn't.

It didn't last long. Their mom started to fret about being away from their dad, and only ate half her food before packing up the rest "to nibble on later." Justin shoved the last of his burger down his gullet and accompanied Debbie back to Ed's room with the bags Brooke had brought.

That left Brooke and Dylan alone in the waiting room with Teddy. They continued eating in silence, but this time it was a more companionable silence than earlier.

Brooke studied her brother as he ate. Teddy had inherited their father's looks and stolid gruffness, but the resemblance ended there. There was a gentleness to Teddy, and a hesitancy, that their father had never displayed.

"Do you still go by Teddy?" she asked him. It seemed funny that she didn't even know if her brother still used his childhood nickname.

He shrugged. "It's better than Ed."

She certainly couldn't blame him for not wanting to use their father's name.

Brooke wondered if her brother was happy. There was so much she didn't know about him. About either of them. About her whole family. All she had to go on were her mother's cheerful updates over the years, which undoubtedly left out whole swaths of their lives.

She reached for her cherry limeade. "Did you know Dad was on antidepressants?"

Teddy looked up, surprised. "No."

Dylan pushed himself to his feet. "I'm gonna go find the bathroom." He gave Brooke's shoulder a squeeze as he left her and her brother alone.

Teddy watched him go, frowning as he scratched the back of his head. "I don't really know what to do with that."

"Yeah, me neither," Brooke agreed. It was impossible to reconcile depression with the father she remembered. Was she supposed to have more sympathy for him because of that? Or forgive him even? She wasn't sure she could do that. "Have you seen much of Dad lately?" she asked.

Teddy shook his head. "Not really. I get together with Mom for lunch every month or so, but . . ." His lips pressed together. "You know how it was with Dad."

"Yeah," Brooke said. "I do."

Their eyes met and held for a second before Teddy looked away. "I saw him at Christmas, and right after his surgery when he was first diagnosed. I kept offering to come by when he started chemo, but Mom always said he was too tired."

"I wonder . . ." Brooke murmured, thinking of all the times over the last few years that her mom had made excuses for her dad, saying he was too tired to come to the phone.

Teddy looked at her. "What?"

"Just . . . I wonder how long he's been depressed. If it's a recent thing or something that's been going on for years and Mom's been hiding it for him."

"I don't know," Teddy said. "Could be."

Brooke popped her last tater tot in her mouth and squashed the carton flat. "You know . . . Mom didn't even tell me about his cancer."

Her brother looked surprised, but not shocked. "She didn't?"

"Nope. I had to find out from Dylan, who found out from his mom. She told the neighbors but not me."

"I didn't know that," Teddy said, looking regretful. "I would've . . . I guess I should have called you or something. I didn't even think about it."

Brooke shrugged as she wadded up her trash. "It's not your fault. I haven't been around much."

"Can't really blame you for that."

She looked at her brother, trying to figure out if he was speaking generally, or if he knew the actual reason she'd distanced herself. It was impossible to tell anything from his reticent demeanor.

"Hey, Brooke?" Justin said from the doorway.

She turned and saw Dylan hovering just behind Justin. "Yeah?"

"Dad's asking for you."

Chapter Twenty-One

"Me?" Brooke said, staring at her brother in surprise. "Are you sure?"

Her father couldn't speak. They must be confused about what he was trying to communicate. Either that or this was her mom's way of trying to smooth things over.

Justin nodded and jammed his hands into the front pockets of his jeans. "He wrote your name on the whiteboard."

"He really wants to see me?" Maybe he'd written her name for another reason, although Brooke couldn't think of a single one that made sense. She wondered if they could have misread his handwriting.

"I asked him if he wanted me to get you," Justin said. "He nodded."

Brooke looked over at Teddy, who shrugged.

Dylan sat down next to her and took her hand. "You don't have to do it," he said, squeezing her fingers. "Not if you don't want to."

She nodded as she stared at their clasped hands, although she wasn't convinced that was true. It felt like something you were supposed to do. What kind of heartless monster would refuse to see a father who was asking for her in the hospital?

"He's right," Teddy said. "You don't owe him anything."

She looked up at Justin, who offered a shrug that mirrored the one Teddy had given her. "Do what you want. I'm just passing on the message. I can go back and tell them you've already left."

She didn't want Justin to have to lie for her. And maybe . . . maybe she needed this.

If she didn't do it, she'd always wonder what her father had wanted from her. There were enough unresolved feelings between them. She didn't need to add more. Maybe facing him would give her some closure, at the very least.

Brooke stood up. "I'll go." She looked down at Dylan and tried to give him a brave smile.

"Are you sure?" he asked her.

She nodded. "I'm sure." As she said the words, she knew they were true.

He gave her hand another squeeze before letting go. "I'll be right here."

The man in the hospital bed didn't look anything like her dad. The man lying in the bed was much too small to be the tall, commanding man she remembered.

Her father had always been active and in good shape for his age. The man in the bed looked frail and shrunken. His pale skin hung loosely on his skeleton. Tubes and wires peeked out from under the yellow blanket, hooked up to machines that regulated his IV drip and monitored his blood pressure, pulse ox, and heart rate.

Most shocking of all, though, was the gray stubble that

covered his jaw and throat. Brooke couldn't ever remember seeing her father with more than a half day's worth of stubble before. That, more than anything, drove home how helpless her father was in his present condition.

Her mother sat in a chair beside the bed. She waved Brooke into the room and laid a hand on her husband's arm. "Ed? Honey? Brooke's here."

Ed Hilliard's eyes opened. It took him a moment to focus on his wife's face.

Brooke realized she was holding her breath, and forced herself to exhale, long and slow. Her heart thumped loudly in her ears, and her stomach clenched into knots as she hovered just inside the doorway.

Perhaps this had been a mistake. Now that she was in the room, she wasn't sure she was ready to face her father after all.

Before she could change her mind and flee, his head turned toward Brooke, and his eyes found her. They took her in, widening slightly, though whether in surprise or something else, she couldn't tell. He gazed at her for a long, tense moment, and she gazed back at him. His expression remained impossible to interpret.

She knew she should say something—he couldn't talk, so it had to be her—but she couldn't force even the simple word hello out of her throat.

Her father's mouth twisted, and her stomach sank instinctively, thinking he was scowling at her. It took her another moment to realize he was smiling.

His left side had been weakened by the stroke, so his smile was thin and lopsided, but her father was smiling at her. Not just smiling while she happened to be in the room, but smiling *at her*. For the first time in eight years, he looked glad to see her.

With what was obviously a considerable effort, Ed lifted his left arm—the weak one—a few inches off the bed and wiggled his fingers.

He wanted her to come closer.

Brooke obeyed, moving to stand beside the bed. Ed's fingers twitched, reaching out for her.

She shifted closer and took his hand. It felt cold and feeble in hers, but his fingers grasped at her with surprising strength.

The two of them stayed there like that for a while, just looking at each other and holding hands, before Ed's mouth moved again. This time it opened, and a ragged sound came out. He did scowl then, and she realized he was trying to speak. His right hand reached out toward his wife as he turned his head to look at her, and Debbie set the whiteboard beside him and put the uncapped marker in his hand.

Brooke's stomach roiled as she watched him start to write. *This must be what it feels like to be seasick*, she thought. She'd never been seasick in her life, but she'd spent a summer working on a whale-watching tour boat, which the job description had failed to mention mostly consisted of nursing seasick passengers. This terrible nausea and unsteadiness definitely fit the bill. Even though she was standing still, her legs were all wobbly like she'd just stepped off a boat onto dry land, and her stomach lurched as if she was sailing on choppy seas.

She looked down at the floor, trying to regain her equilibrium.

Her father finished writing and shoved the whiteboard in front of her. His handwriting had always been messy, and it hadn't been improved by the stroke and his current weakness. It took her a second to decipher his scrawl:

I'm sorry. I love you.

She was a little surprised she didn't cry. But there *was* a lump in her throat making it difficult to swallow.

All her life, she'd been grasping for her father's love, only to have it snatched away from her. And now here he was offering it again, after she'd finally accepted she didn't need it.

Maybe she was too tired to cry. Tired of the resentment and silent recriminations. Tired of carrying all this bitterness with her.

Her father was watching her, his eyes watering as they tracked her reaction. He was waiting for her to respond. He'd made his overture of reconciliation and the ball was in her court now.

Brooke squeezed his hand and forced a smile. "I know, Dad," she said. "I love you too."

She wasn't entirely certain that second part was true. It would take some time to parse her own feelings, and she was too numb right now to properly do that.

But it might be true, and more importantly, it seemed like the kind thing to say under the circumstances. For now, that was a good enough reason to say it.

She didn't quite forgive him, not yet. But she did feel sorry for him. She didn't wish him ill. He wasn't a monster; he was just a weak and unhappy person. He didn't deserve to be lying in this bed like this, and if she could offer him a little comfort by saying what he wanted to hear, she was a generous enough person to do it.

Brooke's father was a stubborn asshole who'd refused to

compromise his worldview to accept her for who she was, but she did believe he loved her. If he hadn't, he would have forgiven her more easily. It was stupid, and shitty, but there it was. People were flawed and messy. Even the ones who loved you.

She didn't *need* her father's love, but it was nice to know she had it.

It wasn't everything, but it wasn't nothing either.

Brooke stayed with her father for another ten minutes, holding his hand until he dozed off. Once he started snoring, she slipped her fingers out of his and quietly kissed her mother goodnight.

When she walked back into the waiting room, Dylan and both her brothers looked up. The sight of the three of them together, waiting for her with matching expressions of exhaustion and worry etched into their faces, made her heart feel too big for her chest.

All this time she'd thought she didn't have a family anymore, and yet here they all were. Waiting for her to come back to them.

Dylan's eyes were brimming with questions he didn't ask as he got up to meet her. For a second it looked like he wanted to give her a hug, but instead he stopped just in front of her, plunging his hands into his pockets like he didn't know what to do with them.

"Everything go okay?" Teddy asked.

"Yeah," Brooke answered, never taking her eyes off Dylan. "It was fine." She watched his whole body relax as he exhaled the tension he'd been holding on to.

"I don't know about y'all, but I'm beat," Justin said,

standing up and stretching. "I'm gonna go home and get some sleep. Meet back here in the morning? I'll bring breakfast."

Teddy pushed himself to his feet and looked uncertainly at Brooke. "You can stay at my place," he offered. "If you don't want to go back to the old house."

Brooke looked at Dylan, then back at her oldest brother, who seemed to understand her better than she expected. "I appreciate it, but I'll be okay at Mom and Dad's."

She needed to take Dylan back to his parents' house anyway. He'd probably be happy to get himself home in a cab, but she wasn't ready to say goodnight to him yet. She wanted to have him to herself for a little while longer.

They made their goodbyes in the hospital parking lot. Teddy transferred Brooke's suitcase from his Explorer to their mom's car for her, then Dylan drove Brooke home.

"Was it really fine?" he asked, throwing a worried glance her way as he pulled out onto the highway.

Brooke looked down at the hand her father had fallen asleep holding. "He told me he was sorry. And that he loved me."

Dylan reached across the console and took her hand, his fingers strong and warm as they covered hers.

She wanted to reassure him that she was fine, but she really had no idea if she was. Her exhaustion—both physical and emotional—had wrung her out completely. It was all she could do to keep her eyes open for the rest of the drive home.

Ten minutes later, Dylan parked behind her dad's F-150 in the driveway of her parents' house, carried Brooke's suitcase up the three steps onto the porch, and unlocked the front door before handing over the keys.

"Are you okay?" he asked, studying her with concerned eyes. "I know today was hard for you."

"It's been a lot better with you here," she answered honestly. "I really can't thank you enough for coming." She hoped he hadn't missed anything important to come here. She hadn't even thought to ask, but if he'd missed a job because of her . . .

"You don't have to thank me," he said, and gave her a hug.

She let out a long breath as she rested her cheek against his chest and felt his arms wrap around her. God, his hugs were amazing. The one place she felt like everything was okay was curled up inside his protective warmth. If only she could live inside one of his hugs forever. Or even just for the rest of the night . . .

She'd missed him so much, and now he was here and she still missed him, because everything was different and uncertain between them, and she didn't know how to fix it.

He let go of her and shuffled backward uncertainly, shoving his hands deep in his pockets. "I should . . ." He hooked a thumb over his shoulder at his house.

Brooke nodded, but didn't say anything. She wanted to ask him to stay, she wanted it desperately, but she didn't have the right. She'd hurt him, and they still hadn't talked about that.

Her brain was too scrambled with exhaustion right now to think clearly, but the one thing she did know was that she didn't want to be alone in this house tonight. She didn't want to let Dylan go, even though she knew that wasn't fair to him.

"Unless . . ." He studied her for a long moment, brow furrowed.

A moth flapped around the yellow porch light behind his head as Brooke held her breath and waited for him to finish. She wouldn't say it for him.

"Unless you want me to come in," he offered finally.

"You don't have to." Her voice sounded so small it was almost drowned out by the nighttime chorus of cicadas and humming air conditioners around them.

Dylan's eyes stared into hers. "Do you want me to?"

Brooke nodded even as guilt stabbed at her. She didn't want to be like the kid in *The Giving Tree*, taking and taking without ever giving back, heedless of the damage she was doing. But she wasn't strong enough to turn down his offer. "Only if you don't mind."

"I don't mind." Dylan cocked his head and gestured for her to precede him inside.

Brooke wheeled her suitcase into the living room, flipped on the lights, and kicked her shoes off as he locked the front door behind them.

The house felt eerily empty—even more so than it had earlier—and a shiver traveled down her spine to the pit of her stomach.

Then Dylan stepped up behind her and put his hands on her shoulders, and suddenly the house didn't feel empty at all. It felt full of love and kindness, like a home should. There was comfort in the familiarity of Dylan's presence here, in this house where they'd spent so much time together as kids. Where their friendship had first formed and bloomed.

"Can I do anything?" he asked, and the tenderness of his voice, combined with the gentle pressure of his hands, was too much for Brooke's depleted reserves.

She spun around and hugged him, shoving her face into

his neck as she squeezed his torso, clinging for dear life. The tears that had failed to come earlier showed up in full force, clogging her throat. All the emotion she'd been holding back all day—or for years, really—poured out in an unstoppable torrent that racked her body.

Dylan's arms wrapped around her, one hand coming up to cradle the back of her head as she sobbed against him. "Brooke," he murmured, smoothing his palm over her hair. "Hey, it's okay."

It *was* okay, but only because he was holding her.

He kept holding her until she'd cried herself out, until her gasping breaths had quieted and her tears had slowed, and then he scooped her up and carried her into her bedroom. With loving gentleness, he laid her on the bed and curled his body around hers.

It was exactly what she needed. *He* was exactly what she needed.

Feeling safe and serene for the first time all day, Brooke slipped into a deep and dreamless sleep.

Chapter Twenty-Two

When Brooke woke, it was to a pounding headache. Her cheek was sticky where it rested on her hand, and her eyes felt like they'd been stabbed with hot pokers.

But Dylan's arms were still wrapped around her, and his body was a solid, grounding presence against her back. The sound of his slow, steady breathing imbued her with a feeling of peace. And also a remarkable sense of clarity.

Brooke knew exactly what she wanted.

Him.

She'd been wrong earlier. It hadn't been her father's absence that had made her family feel complete. It was Dylan's presence.

Dylan made everything easier and better, just by being there. *He* was the place where Brooke felt happy and safe and loved. He was home and family and everything she'd convinced herself she didn't need, because she'd thought she couldn't have it.

But he was right here. He'd offered himself to her, and then stuck by her even after she'd rejected him. She'd never believed in unconditional love, but here it was lying next to her.

And she'd tried to throw it away because she was too scared to let herself hope for it.

Brooke wanted to fall asleep in Dylan's arms every night and wake up next to him like this every morning for the rest of her life. And she could have that. *She* was the only thing standing in her way. The only thing standing in both their way. Because this was what Dylan wanted too. He'd made that crystal clear. She could give it to him and to herself both. She wouldn't be like *The Giving Tree* kid then, because she'd be giving him something as important as what she was getting.

Brooke rolled over and pressed herself against Dylan, breathing in the familiar scent of his skin.

She *could* live inside one of his hugs forever. She only had to make the choice to do it. To fight for it. To keep fighting for it, even when it was hard.

His arms instinctively folded around her even before he was fully awake. "Brooke?" he murmured in a sleep-roughened voice. "What's wrong?"

"I screwed up," she said to his chest.

"What? What are you talking about?"

"I'm sorry I hurt you. You deserved better."

"Hey." His arms tightened around her, but his tone was sharp-edged enough to make her gut twist. "I told you we didn't need to talk about that. It's over and done with."

She pushed out of his arms and winced at the pain she saw in his face. The pain that was her fault. "Please, will you just let me say this? I have something I have to tell you. And then if you don't want to talk about it anymore, we won't."

"Okay." He bit down on his lip as he nodded, and she

242

longed to soothe away his pain with a kiss, but first she had to tell him how she really felt.

And then find out if he even still wanted her anymore.

She took a deep breath and looked into his eyes, finding strength in their clear blue depths. "I was scared. I've never had a relationship that worked before, and I was scared to try and make one work with you, because the cost of failure was too high. I couldn't stand the thought of losing you."

"You're not going to lose me."

"I might. I almost did—or I thought I had, and it scared the shit out of me. I still could, if this goes really badly."

"What are you saying?" His expression was shuttered and wary. She'd already hurt him once before.

"I'm saying I want you. I want *this*." She laid her hand on his heart and felt the frenzied beat of it against her palm. "I want to try to have a real relationship with you, and I'll do whatever it takes to make it work, because I want you in my life. I want as much of you as you'll let me have."

She watched Dylan's Adam's apple move as he swallowed, but he didn't say anything. Brooke was afraid he was still mad, so she kept talking in the hopes that if she said enough words, maybe eventually she'd land on the right ones, and he wouldn't be mad at her anymore. Maybe she could earn another chance to make this right.

"I don't know if you gave those clothing guys an answer yet," she said. "But you don't have to move to Los Angeles if you don't want to. I'll be your long-distance girlfriend if that's what it takes. I'll be whatever you need me to be. You don't have to give up your career just for me. There are a lot of great programs on the East Coast, and if I really bust my ass I could be done here in a year, and then maybe I can come to you, or at least closer to you. Maybe Boston, or even Nor-folk would be better."

"Brooke." It wasn't until he spoke her name that she real-ized his eyes were glistening, and my god they were even more beautiful like that, blue and sparkling like the surface of the ocean on a sunny day.

He didn't say anything else, just her name, and she started to be afraid her words hadn't been enough. He was breathing kind of hard though, which might be good or might be bad. It was difficult to read the signs at this point.

But then his beautiful eyes dropped to her lips like he wanted to devour them, and that definitely seemed like a good sign.

Especially when he lurched forward to kiss her.

His whole body was wound tight like a giant spring, but his lips parted as they met hers—just a little—and she felt the lightest brush of his tongue against hers before he pulled away again.

That was—*what was that?* Did it mean he was giving her a chance? Her eyes searched his for answers, hoping that wasn't just some sad goodbye kiss.

"Yes," Dylan said thickly. "I want—"

He kissed her again.

This time his mouth opened for hers with a hoarse little sound at the back of his throat. He licked her tongue once, frantically, before he thrust it all the way into her mouth, hungry and needy and messy.

Her hands tangled in his hair, trying to hold on to him. She was never letting him go again, not if she could help it. She felt him grip her waist and jerk her closer on the bed, and that was when she knew he wasn't letting go of her either.

When he finally pulled back, his breath sounded noisy and harsh, like he was hyperventilating, and he was holding her a little too tightly, his fingers digging into her hard enough to leave bruises.

She loved it.

Brooke kissed the corner of his perfect mouth, then his jaw, then his throat. She licked just below his ear, enjoying the salty and sweet taste of his skin. "God I missed you," she murmured, kissing him all over. "I love you so much."

Dylan went very still. He pulled back to look into her eyes. "You love me?"

She was confused for a second, because she hadn't actually realized that was what she was saying as she'd said it. The words had just tumbled out of her, raw and honest and unrehearsed. She had to go back and rewind what she'd said.

She *had* said it. She'd said she loved him.

And she did. She loved him. More than anything.

The only surprise was that it had taken her so long to acknowledge it.

"Yes," she said, looking into his eyes and trying to imbue the words with everything in her overflowing heart. "I love you."

The corner of his mouth twitched, and she wanted to kiss it, but she thought maybe she should wait in case he wanted to tell her something.

"I said yes to the partnership." He looked almost smug. "I'm moving to Los Angeles."

Brooke felt her heart lift like a hot-air balloon. "You did? You are?"

"I'm doing it for me," Dylan said. "Even if you didn't want me around, this opportunity was too good to pass up. Los

Angeles is a big city, and I figured we'd find a way to patch things up and get back to being friends again eventually." He gave her a reproachful look. "I couldn't let you out of my life completely. You're my best friend."

This time Brooke was the one lurching toward him, pulling him in for a frenzied kiss. It felt like a first kiss, both sweet and sloppy, like she was kissing Dylan for the first time after wanting it her whole life and then finally getting it.

When they stopped for breath, she gave him a little shake. "Why didn't you return any of my calls or texts? Do you have any idea how freaked out I was? I thought I'd lost you."

"I'm sorry." He kissed her forehead and she snuggled against him. "Partly I was pouting because I was hurt—and maybe I was punishing you a little too."

"I deserved it."

"No you didn't. I should have stayed to talk it out, but I reacted emotionally."

"I would have done the same thing if you'd rejected me."

His arms tightened around her and he nuzzled his face into her hair. "As soon as I got back home, I regretted it. But I knew I wanted to accept that partnership in LA, and I was afraid if I let myself talk to you, you might talk me out of it. So I told them yes, and I threw myself into finishing things up in New York and making plans for the move. I was going to reach out to you as soon as everything was set, when it was too late to back out."

"I'm so sorry," Brooke said. "I thought I knew what I wanted, but really I was too scared to let myself take a chance. I was so afraid of screwing up what we had—"

"I know." He held her face in his hands and traced her

cheekbones with his thumbs. "Believe it or not, I know you pretty well. I can tell when you're scared."

"It's a good thing, because I'm definitely going to be bad at this. I'm not sure you're aware, but historically I am a *terrible* girlfriend."

"Listen, this isn't going to be perfect. Relationships are hard, and this is all new for both of us. There are going to be plenty of challenges along the way. Like, I know I'm not brainy enough for you, and I'll never fit in with your academic colleagues."

"Hey, that's not true." She gave his waist a sharp pinch and he wriggled in her grasp.

The thing about Dylan was that he didn't know what he was worth. He had no idea how special he was. Brooke had been trying to tell him their whole lives, but it never seemed to take. Maybe because she'd only been doing the job part time. Loving Dylan should be a full-time career. She could dedicate herself to the task 24/7 and it still wouldn't be as much as he deserved.

But maybe then he'd at least understand how much he mattered.

"One of my brainy colleagues poured liquid nitrogen down the sink in his apartment and shattered the pipes, so I wouldn't go giving them too much credit."

Dylan's spontaneous laugh broke something apart in her chest. "Okay, well maybe not *all* of them."

She reached up to smooth his hair off his forehead as she gazed at him. He was absolutely gorgeous, just stupidly beautiful, but she couldn't see his physical appearance objectively anymore. All she saw was *him*. "You're the smartest man I know, and don't ever let anyone tell you otherwise."

247

Reverently, she kissed his cheek, his jaw, and finally the corner of his mouth.

He turned his head to capture her lips with his. As he kissed her he pushed her onto her back, levering himself above her on the bed. Sighing in pleasure under the sheltering weight of his body, she stroked her hands up and down his back as their tongues tangled together.

At some point they'd need to get up and go back to the hospital, but the prospect didn't seem so daunting anymore. And there wasn't any rush. They still had time to enjoy this.

They had all the time in the world.

"I love you," Dylan said as he pressed open-mouthed kisses along her collarbone.

Brooke smiled as the words sank into her, warming her from within. "Horrible decision on your part. You should probably reconsider."

He caught her earlobe between his teeth. "Nope, you're stuck with me."

"Good." Her eyes drifted closed as that sense of rightness clicked into place again. Whatever they were on the precipice of didn't frighten her anymore, because the foundation under their feet was rock solid. Unbreakable.

She'd never been so happy to be stuck.

Epilogue

Brooke was late. There'd been no parking to be found anywhere near the address Dylan had texted her, so she was forced to speed-walk the four-block hike from her car.

On the bright side, it gave her the opportunity to take the measure of the neighborhood. It was a quiet residential street in Culver City, not too far from her apartment in Palms. A mix of small apartment buildings and duplexes lined the street, with a few single-family homes thrown in here and there. Many of them had actual front yards, which seemed like an unimaginable luxury to Brooke after eight years of dorm and apartment living.

A couple of children played in one of the yards ahead. A little boy and a little girl of seven or eight were having a Super Soaker fight as two women watched them from the shade of the porch. The children's gleeful shrieks and laughter filled the air as they chased each other around the small patch of grass. They paused as Brooke approached, calling a temporary cease-fire to greet her with matching waves. She returned their greeting and smiled at the two mothers on the porch.

The sidewalk in front of their house was covered with

chalk drawings, and Brooke stepped onto the narrow strip of grass along the street so as not to disturb their art. There was a hopscotch grid, a picture of a unicorn, and a race car. Next to that was a drawing of a girl with the name Ava scrawled beneath it, and another drawing of a boy with the name Mason. Between them, the letters BFF had been encircled with a crudely drawn heart.

When Brooke looked up again, she saw Dylan a few houses down. Her breath caught at the sight of him. Tall and handsome, his blond hair shining in the sun, he was talking to a woman in front of a Spanish-style duplex. In contrast with Dylan's jeans and untucked button-down, the woman was dressed up in slacks and high heels, her brunette hair the kind of smooth and wavy you could only get from a curling iron.

Dylan smiled at the woman as he spoke, and she laughed and touched his arm. Brooke didn't bother to hide her grin, not the least bit bothered by the woman's blatant flirting. She'd grown used to it by now. Everywhere Dylan went, women—and quite a few men—went doe-eyed and dreamy around him.

Brooke couldn't bring herself to blame them, since she did the exact same thing herself.

In that moment, Dylan turned, catching sight of Brooke for the first time, and his whole face lit up in a dazzling grin.

The way he was looking at her right now? That was why Brooke never worried when women tried to flirt with him. Because that look on his face was one he reserved just for her.

He walked away from the woman with the pretty hair without a backward glance, opening his arms as he came to meet Brooke. She practically skipped the last few steps and launched herself at him, pressing her lips against his cheek. "I made it."

Dylan squeezed her, lifting her off the ground a little, and kissed her on the mouth. "Hello, you."

"Sorry I'm late," she said as he set her down again. "Parking's a bear around here."

"Fortunately, this unit includes a driveway for off-street parking," the brunette woman said, coming toward them with a broad smile. "Are we ready to take a peek at the inside?"

Dylan introduced Brooke to the leasing agent, whose name was Lauren, and they followed her up the front walk. He put a gentle hand on Brooke's back as they stepped onto the front stoop of the white stucco house with its red tile roof. He'd been leasing a one-bedroom apartment in a nearby high-rise since his relocation to Los Angeles, but now he was in the market for something bigger.

They were in the market for something bigger. After five months of trading off nights at their respective apartments, Brooke and Dylan were moving in together.

It was a big step. Huge.

Shockingly, it had been Brooke's idea. Despite her initial fears that she'd tire of having Dylan around all the time, what she'd actually tired of was shuttling her things back and forth between their separate apartments. Even as weeks turned into months and the shiny newness of their relationship wore off, she'd found herself increasingly reluctant to spend a single night apart from him.

Dylan's apartment was much nicer than Brooke's, but it was small and it didn't allow pets. Brooke's cheap mattress was much less comfortable than Dylan's plush pillow-top and her closet wasn't big enough for all his clothes, but she felt guilty about not spending enough time with Murderface whenever she stayed over at Dylan's place.

The only solution was the obvious one: cohabitation.

Dylan had nearly fainted with shock when she proposed it, but once she'd convinced him it wasn't a prank, he'd eagerly agreed.

"I like the wood floors," Dylan said as they stepped inside the duplex. "And the space."

It was long and narrow, with a decent-sized living room and dining room beyond, separated by a wide arched doorway. Arched windows that matched the Spanish-style detailing on the outside let in plenty of natural light.

"It's a sizable kitchen," Lauren pointed out, leading them through the dining room. "Recently remodeled."

"Are those new appliances?" Brooke asked.

"That's right," Lauren answered. "And new granite countertops."

"It's got more counter space than my current place," Dylan commented. "Plenty of room for cooking."

"It's not quite as stylish as your place," Brooke observed, thinking of the modern light fixtures and tile backsplash in his current kitchen.

"I don't care about that." Dylan took a peek inside the stainless steel oven. "It's more functional." He turned to grin at Brooke. "And a lot homier too."

It did feel much more like a house than an apartment. Lots more windows, only one shared wall, and its own little yard.

Brooke returned his smile as she took his hand and tugged him toward the bedrooms. There was a decent-sized master with its own bathroom and a closet large enough to hold all of their clothes.

"The guest bedroom's a little smaller," Lauren pointed out. "But there's a full guest bath."

"This will be plenty big enough for your parents when they come," Dylan said, trailing his knuckles down Brooke's back.

She nodded, trying to imagine it. Her parents, here in LA, visiting her for the first time.

Her father's recovery was progressing well. He'd regained the ability to talk, although his speech was still a bit slurred, and he was walking with the aid of a cane. Best of all, he'd gotten the all clear from his oncologist. He was officially cancer free. There were still a couple months of occupational therapy ahead of him, but he was talking about coming out to visit Brooke in the summer. He mentioned it almost every time they talked on the phone in fact, which was weekly since he'd been discharged from the hospital.

Things still felt a bit precarious between them. But he was making a real effort, and Brooke was trying to get used to having a father who wanted to be part of her life again. It was a work in progress.

Although she hadn't yet told her father she and Dylan were moving in together. It would be the first real test of their reconciliation, and she was a bit nervous about it.

"Maybe your brothers will even want to come out."

"Maybe," Brooke said. She'd been talking to her brothers more too, the last few months. Catching up on their lives, getting to know them finally. Maybe one day they'd want to come out for a visit.

"There's a small yard and shared laundry facilities out back," Lauren said, glancing at her phone. "I've got to take a call, but feel free to explore on your own."

When she'd left them alone, Dylan turned to Brooke, his

smile fading into a look of concern. "Are you really sure you want to do this?"

She blinked up at him through her lashes. "Do I not look sure?"

"I know you had your doubts about moving in together."

"Had." She reached up to smooth his hair back from his face. "Emphasis on the past tense."

His hands encircled her waist. "I just don't want you to feel pressured to give up your own space."

She cocked an eyebrow at him. "Okay, now it's starting to feel like you're the one having doubts. Are you trying to wriggle out of this? It's okay if you are—you just have to say so."

"Nope. No doubts whatsoever." His blue eyes shone with as much certainty as she'd ever seen in them. "I'm unbelievably excited about moving in with you. I just want to make sure you're happy."

"I can't remember ever being happier," she replied as she rose up on her toes to kiss him.

He returned her kiss much harder and deeper, the passion flaring easily and quickly between them as he pushed his hips into hers.

Before things could get too hot and heavy, Brooke dragged herself away from the kiss and tugged Dylan toward the back door. "Let's look out back. I want to see these shared laundry facilities."

A small, plain patch of grass filled the space between the duplex and the small garage that hosted a washer and dryer. They weren't as new as the appliances in the kitchen, but they were perfectly serviceable, and sharing with only one other household would be a step up for both of them from their current circumstances.

"I really like this place," Dylan said, pulling Brooke into his arms as they stood on the driveway overlooking the backyard.

She grinned at the eagerness in his expression, which reminded her of a child begging his mom for a new toy. "It's the first place we've looked at," she reminded him.

"I know, but . . ." His nose nuzzled against hers. "It feels like us. I can picture us living here."

Winding her hands around his neck, she gazed past him at the house. "It's expensive though." She didn't even know what the rent was, but she could guess. This much space? In this area? It must be unimaginably expensive.

Brooke had another year left of her PhD program. She wasn't in a position to contribute much to their household expenses and wouldn't be for a while. She was on target to defend her dissertation next spring, but everything after that was a big question mark. Hopefully, she'd be able to find a job here, but there was always a chance she wouldn't. They'd talked about it a little, about the possibility she might need to leave Los Angeles. *They* might need to leave. Dylan had said he'd go with her, wherever she ended up. He'd find a way to make it work, he'd said, and she believed him.

She didn't worry about the future as much as she used to. Whatever happened, she knew Dylan would be there with her. They'd figure it out.

"Not that much more expensive than my current place," he pointed out. Which was also unimaginably expensive as far as Brooke was concerned. His lips brushed her temple as his hands stroked up her back. "And I told you, you don't have to worry about that."

Dylan's clothing line was really starting to take off. Their pieces were already available at three prominent Los Angeles boutiques, and they were in negotiations with two more in Manhattan. Justin Theroux and Rami Malek had both worn their designs, and Rami's stylist had hosted an exclusive dinner on the rooftop of a trendy West Hollywood hotel to fete the label, which would be debuting its first full-fledged collection this season.

All of this was extremely weird for Brooke. She wasn't used to being someone who had occasion to use the word "fete" in normal conversation, much less went to parties where Rami Malek was in attendance. But she was learning to fake it.

"It's even walking distance to our favorite bookstore," Dylan pointed out.

Brooke wasn't sure she'd classify two miles as "walking distance," but perhaps she could work her way up to a hike over to The Ripped Bodice. It was easy to picture herself taking walks with Dylan in this neighborhood, the two of them strolling hand in hand down the sidewalk in the evenings, saying hello to their neighbors as they passed.

"Maybe I'll take up gardening," she mused, shielding her eyes from the sun as she turned to survey the small yard. "We could put some containers along there, and maybe some patio furniture."

Dylan's arms wrapped around her from behind. "We could start a kitchen garden. Grow herbs and some vegetables maybe."

"We could compost."

"I could get a barbecue grill." He nuzzled her cheek, his breath raising goose bumps on her arms. "Imagine us, living in our very own house."

"Half a house." She could imagine it so easily. The two of them coming home to each other at the end of every day.

There were a few more places they'd planned to look at today, but she had a feeling they'd end up taking this one. Dylan was right. It did feel like them.

"Can we get it?" The question was a murmur in her ear. "Please?"

Brooke spun in his arms and smacked a kiss on his mouth. "Yes. If it's the one you want. Whatever makes you happy makes me happy."

She didn't really care where they lived. All that mattered was that they were together.

As long as she was with Dylan, she was home.

Acknowledgments

First and foremost, I have to thank my fabulous marine biology consultant for generously sharing her knowledge and experience with me. Without her, this book wouldn't have been possible.

Special thanks, as always, go to my wonderful husband, Dave, for being the best partner anyone could ever want.

Also to my faithful beta reader Jo, for catching so many of my continuity errors.

And extra special thanks to my editor Julia, for always being so reliable, professional, and fantastic at what she does.

A special shoutout to Linda Lassman for placing the winning bid on an opportunity to name a character in this book in the Romance for Puerto Rico Auction organized by author Lucy Eden. Linda actually named two characters: Brooke's lab mate buddy Tara Phillips, and Brooke's advisor Dr. Lassman. Congrats, Linda! And thank you for your generous donation in support of The Hispanic Federation and World Central Kitchen.

You may also enjoy the next book in
the Chemistry Lessons series . . .

The Infatuation Calculation

Mia has had her whole life mapped out since she
was eighteen. She's supposed to follow up her maths
PhD with a research position and become a professor,
but her twenty-year plan takes a surprise deviation
when she's forced to settle for a temporary teaching
job at a small-town university in the
middle of nowhere.

It's not easy adapting to rural life when you're a
city girl, but Mia tries to make the best of it. Things
finally start to look up after a run-in with some
terrifying local wildlife sends her careening into
the arms of a sexy local farmer.

Mia finds herself unexpectedly drawn to Josh's gruff
charms, especially after she learns what lies behind
the thick walls he's built around his heart. But despite
their growing connection, Mia can't afford to stay.
Not unless she's willing to give up on her
dream – or trade it in for a new one.

Read on for an extract now . . .

Chapter One

Mia Ballentine was lost. Metaphorically *and* literally.

She must have missed a turn somewhere. Surely she was not meant to be on this dusty farm road on the outskirts of some backwoods town in the middle of Texas.

And yet, here she was. Trying to find her way to an obscure regional university she'd never heard of before she'd applied for a visiting lecturer position in their mathematics department.

This wasn't how things were supposed to go. She'd earned her PhD from one of the top math programs in the country, for god's sake. Gotten her bachelor's at Princeton, where she'd won the Andrew H. Brown Prize before graduating with high honors. She'd laid out a twenty-year career plan for herself, and the next step was supposed to be a three-year postdoc at a top-tier university.

Not *this*.

Unfortunately, the economy had its own ideas. The country was coming off the biggest recession of the twenty-first century and higher education had taken a major hit. Budgets had been stretched to the breaking point as endowments shrank, grants evaporated, and enrollment dropped with the national employment rate. Postdocs were being cut, and hiring freezes were now the norm at most universities. Even low-paid adjunct contracts had become hard to get. It was the worst possible time to go on the job market with a brand-new PhD.

Most everyone in Mia's cohort was struggling—particularly those, like her, who'd done pure instead of applied mathematics. Some had put off defending their dissertations, some had taken temp jobs to make ends meet, and some had been forced to move back in with their parents when their fellowships ran out.

Mia had been scouring mathjobs.org and *The Chronicle of Higher Education* and everywhere else she could think of, applying for anything and everything she could find in academia. Up to now, she hadn't had a single serious expression of interest.

When Bowman University had invited her to come to Texas for an interview, she'd jumped at the opportunity.

At least it was a step up from an adjunct position, most of which were limited to part-time and only paid a few thousand dollars per semester. The Bowman job was full-time and paid enough that Mia wouldn't have to take a second job just to cover rent. It was only a one-year contract, but she couldn't imagine being stuck here in Podunksville for more than a year, anyway. Twelve months seemed like the absolute limit of what she'd be able to stand in a place like this.

Mia peered out the dusty windshield of her rental car and shuddered at the cow pastures around her. Country living had never held any appeal for her. She was a city girl through and through. A New Yorker by birth who'd found Los

Angeles enough of a culture shock when she'd moved there for grad school.

Could she really survive in small-town Texas? Seventy miles from the nearest airport and who even knew how far away from a decent restaurant or grocery store. You probably couldn't even get food delivered here, except whatever passed for pizza in these parts.

They might not even have reliable internet. Or FedEx deliveries. She'd read the stories in *The Atlantic* and the *New Yorker* about all the ways rural America was being left behind by tech advancements, consumer monopolies, and crumbling infrastructure.

And now she might be living it firsthand.

She'd definitely missed a turn. This couldn't possibly be the road to the university, could it? There was nothing out here but pastureland, farmhouses, trees and—

Are those goats?

They were. There were freaking goats standing in the road up ahead. Three of them. And even more milling around the overgrown ditch that ran alongside the blacktop road.

Did people just let their goats roam freely out here?

Could they be *wild* goats? Did they have wild goats in Texas? Were wild goats even a thing? Mia had no idea. The closest she'd ever gotten to a goat was at a petting zoo.

She honked her horn as she neared the goats in the road, but they didn't seem interested in getting out of the way. They simply stared at her rental car as it rolled to a stop in front of them.

"Seriously?" Mia put the car in park, unclipped her seat belt, and shoved the door open.

The humid heat hit her like a slap from a hot towel. Her

weather app had predicted highs in the low nineties for Central Texas today—which had seemed ludicrously hot for May—but it felt more like a thousand degrees out here.

She took a few steps toward the nearest goat and waved her arms, trying to look menacing. "Shoo! Go on. Get out of here!"

Instead of moving out of the road like a reasonable creature should, the goat stood its ground, regarding her with its unnerving sideways cat-eyes. These goats weren't anything like the cute baby billy goats Mia had encountered at petting zoos. These goats were big and wide, almost half her height, with huge udders hanging between their back legs.

She felt a moment of trepidation as she remembered a video she'd once seen of a man getting knocked over by a rambunctious goat. The video had been hilarious, but it was probably a lot less funny if you were the person being attacked by the goat.

Maybe she should have stayed in the car.

She was dressed for her job interview and didn't fancy being butted into the ditch by an angry goat. Imagine explaining that to the hiring committee. *Sorry I'm covered in dirt and vegetation, gentlemen, but you see I was attacked by a wild goat on my way here.*

These goats didn't look particularly angry, fortunately. Or inclined to rambunctiousness. Mostly they looked bored—and hot.

Mia could relate.

"I don't think you're supposed to be here," she said to the goats in the road. 'And I'm *definitely* not supposed to be here."

The nearest goat tilted its head at her and bleated. Though

it was almost more of a honk than a bleat. It had a big nose for a goat—not that Mia was any great expert on goat noses. But it seemed to have an unusually large, convex nose that gave it a distinctly comical appearance. It also had long, floppy ears that hung down past its chin like a lop-eared bunny.

It was pretty cute, actually.

Based on the bulging udder, she deduced it was female. It also didn't have any horns, which she hoped meant it wasn't the sort of goat who went around butting people into ditches.

It started walking toward her, and Mia stiffened in fear. But all it did when it reached her was nudge her hand with its head—the same way her friend Brooke's cat did when it wanted to be petted.

Mia gave the goat a tentative scratch between its floppy ears, and it closed its eyes in what was clearly an expression of ecstasy.

When it noticed its friend getting attention, one of the other goats wandered over and bumped its head against Mia's leg. She gave it a head scratch too. They seemed friendly and sweet as long as you gave them what they wanted. They reminded her of dogs, and she'd always liked dogs, despite never owning one herself.

A third goat wandered over, and Mia alternated pets between her three new friends. "You like that, huh? Just call me the Goat Whisperer, I guess."

This was certainly not how she'd expected today to go. She was supposed to be meeting with members of the Bowman University math department in fifteen minutes, not standing on a dusty farm road sweating inside her interview clothes while she catered to a herd of affection-starved goats.

"How do you guys stand the heat out here?" she asked her hoofed companions as a trickle of sweat puddled inside her bra.

"They're goats," a man's voice said behind her. "They're used to it."

Mia started and spun around.

A man in a cowboy hat stood in the road a few yards away from her. He seemed to have materialized out of thin air. There was no other car in sight, and no buildings within half a mile. She had no clue where he'd come from or how he'd managed to sneak up on her.

"Sorry." The man raised his palms in a placating gesture. "Didn't mean to scare you."

Mia had never encountered an actual cowboy before, but she assumed that was what he was. In addition to his cowboy hat, which was made of straw and fraying around the brim, he wore scuffed cowboy boots and dusty jeans. His arms were thick and deeply tanned, and his sweat-stained T-shirt pulled tight across broad shoulders. It was exactly the sort of hearty physique she imagined one developed from years of wrestling recalcitrant cows, lassoing horses, and hoeing crops.

Or whatever it was that cowboys did. Honestly, she had no idea.

The man nodded at her car. "You lost?"

"Is it that obvious?" Squinting, she lifted a hand to shield her eyes from the sun and nearly started again when she got a good look at his face.

She'd been so distracted by the whole cowboy thing, she hadn't appreciated how attractive he was. His strong, square jaw featured exactly the right amount of stubble to look manly and slightly rough, while his cleft chin added character to his face. But it was his eyes that struck Mia the most. Dark, deep set, and piercing beneath the brim of his hat, they regarded her with a startling intensity.

He scratched his stubbly jaw as those sharp eyes looked her up and down. "Well, you're not really dressed for a hike in the country. Let me guess: you're looking for Bowman."

"That's right," she said. "Am I close?"

"You're a couple miles off the mark. The GPS is wrong."

"How can the GPS be wrong?"

Pushing his hat back, he wiped the sweat off his forehead. "It just is. Been that way for years. I guess they don't care about getting it right out here, or they'd have fixed it by now." He pointed down the road behind her. "It's trying to direct you to the old Bowman Farm, which is on the far east side of the campus. The main entrance to the college is two more exits up the highway you came in on."

She turned to look in the direction he'd pointed, then back toward the highway she'd come from, resting her hands on her hips. "So you're telling me everyone just gets lost trying to find the university?"

The cowboy shrugged. "Most people going there already know where it is."

"Right," she said. "Of course they do."

He started toward the goats, who were watching him with interest. "I'll just get these fugitives out of your way so you can turn around."

"You mean they're not supposed to be wandering around loose?"

He let out a deep, throaty laugh. "Not so much, no. They're escape artists. Especially Alice. She's the mastermind.

Always leading the others into trouble." He made a kissing sound and the goats clustered around him.

"They're cute." *And so are you,* Mia thought, but fortunately refrained from saying out loud.

"Don't think they don't know it. They'll charm the pants off you and then start chewing on your shoes once your guard's down. Speaking of ... " He nodded at Mia's feet, where one of her new goat friends was nibbling at the hem of her pants leg.

"Ack! Stop that!" She jerked back, out of the goat's reach, and it gave her an indignant look.

"Come on, Bell. Back where you belong." The man made another kissy noise and Bell trotted over to him, joining the others.

"Do they all have names?" Mia asked as she watched him lead the goats to a gap in the wire fence running alongside the road. She hadn't noticed it before, but it must have been where the goats had slipped out.

"Yep." He stooped to widen the hole in the fence and gestured the goats through. "That's Agatha," he pointed to each of the goats as he named them, "Zora, and Charlotte."

"Agatha Christie, Zora Neale Hurston, and Charlotte Brontë are all novelists." Mia read mostly nonfiction these days, but as a child she'd read a lot of classic literature because her father had told her it would make her smart.

The man nodded as he shooed the last goat through the fence. "That's right."

"Some people say *Jane Eyre's* erotic masochism makes it the nineteenth-century *Fifty Shades of Grey.* But I think its complex depiction of female agency was profoundly feminist for its time."

270

The cowboy lifted his head and squinted at her.

"Charlotte Brontë is my second-favorite nineteenth-century author," Mia added, as if that could somehow explain why she'd said the words *erotic masochism* out loud to a total stranger.

"Are you an English professor?" he asked, frowning slightly.

"No, my PhD is in mathematics."

He accepted this information silently. At least he hadn't warily backed away from her. Yet.

Mia shuffled her feet, eager to end the conversation before she blurted out anything else embarrassing. "Thanks for, um . . . moving your goats."

The man's lips twitched in what she suspected was amusement at her expense. "If you head back the way you came and get on the highway heading east, you'll see a sign telling you where to exit for the college."

"Got it. Thank you very much."

Mia got back in her car, turned around, and drove back to the highway as fast as she safely could.

Chapter Two

Once she found the university, Mia's interview went well. So well they called her a few weeks later and offered her the job.

That left her with a difficult decision to make. On the one hand, it was the only decent job offer she'd received. On the other hand, she wasn't thrilled about the location, the school, or the job itself.

On the *other* other hand, she'd probably be so bored and lonely living in a small town that she'd have nothing else to do but spend her free time working on the proof she hoped to publish, which would go a long way to boosting her CV and helping her get a better job next year.

When it came right down to it, she didn't have a choice. It didn't matter how conflicted she was because she had no other options. None.

Mia called her boyfriend and arranged to meet him for dinner at their favorite Mexican restaurant to break the bad news. Paul worked at a tech company as a software programmer. They'd met via a dating app last year and hit it off immediately. They challenged each other, had deep, intellectual conversations, and were both focused on their careers and their mutual goals of financial independence. The two of them were ideally suited.

Except for the small matter of her career requiring her to move away from LA. She'd always known it was a possibility, but they'd never talked about it much. Every time she'd raised the subject, Paul had said they'd figure it out when the time came.

Well, the time was now.

Once they'd gotten their drinks, Mia moved straight to the bad news. "Bowman offered me the job. A one-year contract teaching three courses a semester. Starting in August."

Paul sat across the table from her picking through the bowl of tortilla chips. She watched his face carefully, but his ice-blue eyes betrayed no reaction as he selected a chip and used it to scoop up an implausible amount of salsa before shoving the whole thing in his mouth.

"Tell me again where this place is?" he said when he'd finished chewing.

She tucked her chin-length hair behind her ears. "Crowder, Texas. About seventy miles outside Austin."

"Wow. Okay." Was that a smidge of disappointment she detected in his voice? It was hard to tell. He reached for his michelada and licked some of the salt off the rim. "Are you going to take it?"

She took a long, deliberate sip of her margarita before answering. "I think I have to." She looked at him. "Don't I?"

He shook his head, pushing his drink away. "I can't tell you what to do."

She'd always appreciated that he never tried to exert influence over her life, but right now she'd give anything for someone to tell her what to do. "The way things are going, I

273

might not get another offer this good. I think I have to take it."

Paul nodded and took a sip of his drink. "Then I guess we should probably break up," he said without any trace of emotion.

"What?" Mia jerked her head up. "Just like that? You don't want to—"

"Move to Texas?" His scoffing tone cut deep. "That's not on the table. I thought you knew that."

She hadn't known that. How could she when they hadn't talked about it? Was this what he'd meant all along when he said they'd figure it out? That they'd just break up?

Admittedly, rural Texas was a big ask. Paul's answer might have been different if she'd been offered a job in the Bay Area or New York City. It would be nice to think so, anyway.

Mia swallowed, trying to hide how much his reaction had hurt. "You're always saying how great it is that you can work remote from anywhere."

"Theoretically, yeah. But I've got a good job right now that's here, and they like to see my face in the office. This is where I need to be for networking and career advancement. There's nothing for me in wherever-the-fuck Texas."

"Crowder." Mia wanted to point out that *she* was the something for him there, but he clearly didn't consider that enough of an incentive.

"Whatever," he mumbled, as if the name of the place she'd be living wasn't important enough for him to remember.

"Okay but ..." She struggled to find a solution to the problem. A way through that didn't mean the end of their relationship. "We don't necessarily have to break up. We could try to make it work. It would only be temporary."

He regarded her with a pitying expression. "This job's temporary, but what comes after? You'll have to move somewhere else in a year, right, to take another job? What are the odds it'll be here in LA? Or even on the West Coast? You'll be back in the exact same situation: at the mercy of whatever job you can get." He shook his head as he reached for another tortilla chip. "Even if you knew you were coming back here, a year is a long time."

"If you accept Einsteinian relativity, the passage of time is an illusion," she said. "Past, present, and future exist simultaneously with the three dimensions of space."

Paul rolled his eyes. "Don't go all weird on me now. This isn't a theoretical problem. I'm talking about real life."

The laws of physics *were* real life, but Mia didn't argue the point.

"You can't expect me to live like a monk for a year while you're half a continent away," Paul said.

It didn't seem like that much to ask.

Unfortunately, he didn't seem to agree. "A lot can happen in a year. We could grow apart, we could both become completely different people, I could meet someone . . ." His mouth twisted into a mocking smile. "Hey, maybe you'll fall in love with a cowboy and decide you never want to leave."

Mia would have laughed at the suggestion if she hadn't felt like crying.

Paul reached across the table and took her hand. She squeezed his fingers gratefully, comforted by his touch. But his next words offered only cold comfort. "I know this move isn't what you want, but you can't ask me to put my life on hold for you. We've had a good run. I think it's best if we call time of death now and move on."

Mia took the breakup hard.

She couldn't believe they were done, just like that. Everything had seemed to be perfect between them—right up until the moment it was over. The part that hurt most was how easily Paul had let her go. He hadn't even seemed upset. She'd seen him display more emotion over a Lakers game than he had over the end of their year-long relationship.

If he'd been torn up about it—acted even the least bit regretful—it might have been easier for Mia to accept. Instead, she felt like he'd pulled the rug out from under her. Everything she'd believed to be true—that he loved her, that they were a team, that he'd be there to support her through good times and bad—had turned out to be false.

Had she been deluding herself all this time? Overestimating the depth of his commitment? Or had he actively misrepresented his feelings? She couldn't stop rewinding her memories of every moment they'd spent together, searching for signs she should have picked up on before now.

A month after Paul had unceremoniously dumped her, Mia was still struggling to regain her footing. It didn't help that she was in the midst of uprooting her whole life, preparing for a move she didn't want to make in order to start a job she hadn't wanted to take. But at least it gave her something to focus on besides her broken heart.

She'd thrown herself into lesson planning for the three courses she'd be teaching, all of which were part of the university's core curriculum offerings: Calculus I, Foundations of Mathematics, and something called Math in Society, a math class tailored for humanities majors. Mia was expected to create her own lesson plans around the department's vague framework for the courses. In her previous teaching experience as a graduate student, she had been provided with a lesson plan by the professor she was assisting. This was the first time she'd ever had to come up with one on her own. To prepare for it, she'd been delving into educational resources online and brushing up on pedagogical techniques.

She was deep into a paper on active-learning approaches to post-secondary mathematics education when her phone rang on the table beside her. Seeing her sister's photo on the screen, she smiled.

Holly was basically a younger, cuter version of Mia. The same medium brown hair and eyes that looked so plain on Mia were somehow much prettier on Holly, who was a full four inches shorter than Mia's six feet.

She and Holly had always been close, despite their three-year age difference, but Holly still lived with their mother in New York, and Mia missed her like crazy.

"Heya. How's it going?" Holly said cheerfully when she answered.

Mia leaned back and rubbed her tired eyes, forcing cheer into her voice. "Fine."

"You're not still pining over what's-his-name?"

"No way," Mia lied. "I'm *so* over it."

It was much easier to pretend she was taking it in stride than admit she was struggling. And maybe, if she kept up the act long enough, it wouldn't be an act anymore. She *would* be over it.

"Good," Holly said. "I never liked him anyway."

"You didn't?" This was news to Mia. Holly had only met Paul once, but they'd seemed to get on like gangbusters. Her sister had never voiced any criticism of him. "Why?"

"He never seemed to pay enough attention to you. You know all those little things guys do when they're head over heels in love? Like—I don't know—rubbing your back or checking if your drink needs a refill. Or gazing lovingly at you from across the room when you're talking to someone else. He never did any of that."

"Not all men do those things." What Holly was describing sounded like a fantasy rather than real life. They were the sorts of things Mia had assumed men only did in books and movies.

"They do when they're infatuated," Holly said. "You deserve a boyfriend who hangs on your every word. And that wasn't Paul."

It definitely was not. Maybe Holly was right. Maybe those were exactly the sorts of signs Mia should have picked up.

She squeezed her eyes shut, feeling like a fool. "You never said anything."

"Well, you know . . . you were so into him." Holly sounded regretful. "I didn't want to make waves."

"Promise me that the next time you don't like my boyfriend, you'll tell me. You could have saved me a lot of grief and wasted time."

"I promise," Holly said. "As long as you promise not to hold it against me."

"Deal." Mia reached for her coffee cup, which had long since grown cold. "So did you call just to check up on me?" She swallowed the dregs with a grimace.

"Not exactly. I have a question, although I think I already know the answer."

Uh oh. Mia recognized that tone, and it usually presaged something unpleasant. "What is it?" she asked, pushing her chair back to carry her empty mug into the kitchen.

"Have you told Dad about the job and your move yet?"

Mia hung her head with guilt as she set the mug in the sink. "Ummm . . . well . . ."

"Sis." For a younger sister, Holly was surprisingly good at sounding stern and disappointed.

"I know."

"You have to tell him."

"I will."

It wasn't entirely Mia's fault. She hadn't actually heard from her father in several months, which was par for their relationship. Sure, she could have called him herself to break the news, but it wasn't a conversation she was eager to have. So she hadn't.

Mia knew exactly how her father, a quantitative analyst who'd put his doctorate in statistics to work on Wall Street, would feel about her new job. He'd made his disappointment in her academic and professional choices clear enough already.

If she'd followed in his footsteps like he'd wanted, he could have helped her at every step of her career, smoothing the way for her to jump from the right schools into the right jobs with the right companies. Which might have been fine if she'd had any appetite for finance or the ambition to make ungodly amounts of money the way he had.

Mia preferred the creativity and challenge of pure mathematics—something her father had never been able to understand. Her choice of graduate school had been yet another disappointment. Choosing UCLA over his precious alma mater, Princeton, was madness as far as her father was concerned. A deliberate choice to be mediocre instead of exceptional.

Mia had followed her heart instead of her father's advice, and now she was paying the price for it. She wasn't in a hurry to tell him it wasn't turning out as well as she'd hoped.

Holly let out an annoyed sigh. "I'm seeing Dad on Saturday and I don't want to have to cover for you."

"What are you seeing Dad for?"

Even though Holly only lived a borough away from their father, she didn't see much more of him than Mia did. Generally, his interactions with his daughters were confined to the winter holidays and odd special occasions—when he could be bothered to spare the time. Mia had lost count of all the birthday parties, recitals, and award ceremonies he'd missed over the years. He'd even missed Holly's high school graduation, canceling at the last minute because of a "work trip" they later learned had actually been a tryst in Hawaii with his mistress.

Holly sighed again. "It's his and Mindy's fifth anniversary, don't you know? So of course they're having a big party to show off how blissfully happy they are, and my presence has been commanded."

Mindy was their father's third wife. Not the wife he'd cheated on with the mistress in Hawaii, but the woman he'd cheated on his second wife with in Hawaii.

"Guess my invite must have gotten lost in the mail." Not that Mia would have wanted to go—or even been able to afford it—but she still felt salty about being excluded. No matter how many times she swore she wasn't going to let her father's chronic disregard affect her anymore, it still managed to hurt.

"I'm sure if you lived within commuting distance, you would have been summoned to make an appearance as well." She could practically hear Holly's eye roll over the phone. "But if you want to fly out here and take my place, by all means . . ."

"You don't have to go, you know."

"I know." Holly sounded defensive now. "But it's not worth the fight. I'd rather not deal with the bitching and moaning about how I've let him down—never mind that he's been letting me down my whole life and only ever remembers he has daughters when it suits him."

Mia winced at the familiar bitterness in her sister's voice. They'd had this conversation, or some version of it, hundreds of times before.

"Besides, it's free catered food and an open bar," Holly added. "That's worth putting up with Dad for the five whole minutes he'll spend talking to me."

"You know . . ." Mia chewed her lip. "If you're going to see him anyway, you could tell him about my new job for me."

Holly made a scoffing sound. "No way. I'm not your proxy."

"Fine. Be that way."

"Baby, I was *born* that way. You're going to have to deliver your own news."

Mia blew out a defeated breath. "I'll call him. No promises I'll actually be able to get hold of him by Saturday though."

"As long as you make the effort. Rip the Band-Aid off and get it over with. You'll feel better when it's not hanging over your head anymore."

"Will I?"

"Maybe? Do it anyway. Today."

"Just be ready for him to complain to you about what a disappointment I turned out to be."

"You're not a disappointment. *He's* the disappointment." Holly spat the words like an overprotective yet adorable kitten. "And I'll tell him exactly that if he tries to say any shit about you."

"Don't get into a fight with Dad on my behalf. Please." The last thing Mia wanted was to be a source of even more tension in her family.

"It's on him if he can't behave. Don't start shit, won't be shit." Holly didn't share Mia's devotion to conflict avoidance. "Listen, I've gotta run. My lunch break's almost over. I'll talk to you soon, okay?"

Mia bid her sister goodbye and disconnected the call.

Before she could lose her nerve, she called her dad. Holly was right. Better to get it over with so it wouldn't be something else hanging over Mia's head.

She got his voicemail, of course. He never answered his phone. Not when it was one of his daughters calling, anyway.